Black Wolf

Eileen Merriman

16pt

Read How You Want
LARGE PRINT BOOKS, BRAILLE & DAISY

Copyright Page from the Original Book

Eileen Merriman's three young adult novels, *Pieces of You, Catch Me When You Fall* and *Invisibly Breathing,* were finalists in the New Zealand Book Awards for Children and Young Adults in 2018 and 2019, and all three are Storylines Notable Books. Her fourth young adult novel, *A Trio of Sophies,* was published in 2020 to huge critical praise and was also published in Germany. *Violet Black,* the first volume of the Black Spiral Trilogy, was published in 2021. Her first adult novel, *Moonlight Sonata,* was released in July 2019 and longlisted for the Jann Medlicott Acorn Prize for Fiction 2020. Her second adult novel, *The Silence of Snow,* was published in September 2020.

Eileen's other awards include runner-up in the 2018 *Sunday Star-Times* Short Story Award, third for three consecutive years in the 2014–2016 *Sunday Star-Times* Short Story Awards, second in the 2015 Bath Flash Fiction Award and first place in the 2015 Graeme Lay Short Story Competition. She works full-time as a consultant haematologist at North Shore Hospital in Auckland.

*For my brother Michael,
who knows that there are other worlds
than these.*

THE BLACK SPIRAL TRILOGY

BOOK 1: VIOLET BLACK
BOOK 2: BLACK WOLF
BOOK 3: BLACK SPIRAL

CHARACTER LIST

SPIRAL FOUNDATION SURVEILLANCE FILE
CONFIDENTIALITY RATING: HIGH

BLACK FAMILY
Violet Black: survivor of M-fever; 17 years old
Nicholas Black: Violet's father; prominent research scientist
Ursula Black: Violet's mother; naturopath

WRIGHT FAMILY & ASSOCIATES
Ethan Wright: former survivor of M-fever; Violet's recently deceased boyfriend
June Wright: Ethan's mother; paediatric nurse
Freddie Wright: Ethan's 5-year-old brother
Lyndall Wright: Ethan's 14-year-old sister
Rawiri Sullivan: Ethan Wright's best friend; 18 years old

OTHER SURVIVORS OF M-FEVER/VORTEX MEMBERS (PHASE II)

Phoenix (Jonathan) Fletcher: 19 years old
Audrey Spelling: 18 years old
Harper Mehta: 17 years old
Callum Templeman: 16 years old

PHASE I VIRALLY OPTIMISED

Sarah Schumann: the prototype; 21 years old

PHASE III VIRALLY OPTIMISED

Mila Schmidt: 17 years old
Leon Sachs: 21 years old
Emma Wagner: 20 years old

SPIRAL FOUNDATION STAFF

Noel Marlow: Director of the Spiral Foundation; neurologist
Melody Nenge: general physician
Greta Ziegler: neuropsychologist
Bruno Hoffman: junior doctor
Dash Petrakis: physical and weapons trainer
Jane Griffin: cardiologist
Alice Wang: junior doctor

OTHER

Hans Bauer: Chief of Intelligence, International Terrorism Agency (ITA)
Conrad Abelson: American tourist
Kelly Sherman: American tourist
Scott Murphy: Inspector, Alice Springs Police Department
Harry Wilson: Detective Constable, Alice Springs Police Department

ONE

PHOENIX

I am running through the desert, the red earth firm and unyielding beneath my trainers. It's twenty degrees Celsius, even at midnight. My chest is bare, my singlet knotted around my forehead to stop the sweat running into my eyes.

I could have chosen to leave my earthly body behind, to join the others in their nightly ritual soaring high above the desert, but I haven't done that since we returned from Berlin two months ago. I'm scared that if I leave my body behind, I won't want to return.

So I'm running, relishing the pain in my muscles, the burning in my lungs. For an hour I will forget who I am, what I have done. For an hour, I will be Phoenix again.

But in the morning, I know, I will wake with the heavy knowledge that I am the Black Wolf, never to be trusted, never to be loved—because the only people I've ever loved are either dead or hate my guts.

*

Violet won't even look at me. At breakfast, she sits at the opposite end of the table. During our physical training sessions, she takes care to avoid me, except in martial arts, where we swap partners every few minutes and she has no choice.

That's almost worse, having to touch someone who has the power to burn me with her thoughts alone.

At least, she would if I were allowed access to her thought-stream, but there's a permanent blockade coming from *that* direction.

That's fine, because I'm blocking her too.

This morning, Dash is taking me and the rest of the VORTEX members (aka Virally Optimised Telepaths, aka captives) through drills where we practise turning in for throws but don't actually throw each other. He's got us counting in different languages as we do it. First, Audrey counts in Japanese: *ichi, ni, san, shi.* Next, Callum counts in Māori: *tahi, rua, toru, whā*. Harper counts in Mandarin, and Violet in Russian.

It's my turn, and all I can think is: *eins, zwei, drei, vier*. But I can't count in German, not in front of Violet.

Harper says Violet must have post-traumatic stress disorder, following what happened in Berlin. Who wouldn't, after being stabbed twice in the back and nearly bleeding to death, after collapsing a lung and finding out her boyfriend had died while she was unconscious?

I say, 'Yeah, I guess she must.' And when I have occasional selfish thoughts like *No one asks about whether I get flashbacks too, because shooting a woman in the head and watching her die wasn't a bloody walk in the park, even if she was a terrorist,* I keep them to myself.

'Fletcher,' Dash barks, 'where's your brain?'

I want to tell him I left it in Berlin, but instead, I start counting in French; *un, deux, trois, quatre,* as Violet twists and pulls me up on her shoulder again and again. When I get to *dix,* ten, she bends her knees and sends me flying over her shoulder and—*wham*—I'm blinking up at the ceiling, all the breath knocked out of my lungs.

'Nice,' Dash says.

Violet doesn't say anything, just leaves me there and moves on to her next partner, Callum.

No one says, 'Man, burnt.' No one even thinks it. If they did, I'd be sure to hear them.

No one dares, because it's no laughing matter that Violet hates me because I killed her boyfriend, Ethan.

If I were her, I'd hate me too.

TWO

VIOLET

I still can't believe you're gone, Ethan. I can't help thinking that if I keep talking to you, the way I used to, that one day you might reach out from wherever you are—the way you reached out to me the first time, when we were both in hospital, recovering from M-fever. But this morning, for the first morning in two months, I woke up and that split second of unknowing before I realised you were dead wasn't there. Of all the terrible things that have happened to me over the past several months, your leaving me is the worst.

It's time for my debriefing. Melody says I need to stop delaying, that it will be *good for me.* The last time they tried to debrief me, four weeks ago, I started crying and couldn't stop.

I haven't cried since then. Maybe today will be better.

DEBRIEFING
COMMENCED: 2.01PM

PRESENT: VIOLET BLACK (VORTEX MEMBER),
DR NOEL MARLOW (NEUROLOGIST),
MR HANS BAUER (CHIEF OF INTELLIGENCE,

INTERNATIONAL TERRORIST AGENCY, ITA), DR MELODY NENGE (GENERAL PHYSICIAN).

Bauer: I would like to welcome everyone to the meeting. For the record, it is 2.01pm Australian Central Standard Time.

Marlow: Thank you.

Nenge: Would you like a glass of water, Violet?

Black: (shakes head)

Bauer: Thank you for agreeing to meet with us again, Violet. I appreciate the last attempt at debriefing may have been a little too soon for you.

Black: Can we just get this over with as soon as possible?

Bauer: Certainly. Violet, I'd like to go over the events that happened in Berlin from the time you arrived on 24 December.

Black: Right from the start?

Marlow: Yes, right from the start. As much as you can remember.

Black: We arrived on the plane.

Bauer: By we, you mean you and Phoenix?

Black: Phoenix, Wolf Schwarz, whatever else you want to call him.

Marlow: Yes, well for the sake of this debriefing you can use your real names rather than your aliases. Which, for the record, were Wolf Schwarz and Liesl Meyer.

Black: I travelled with Phoenix and Bruno. Bruno left us at the airport in Berlin, and then Phoenix and I took a Zuber to our apartment. We were really tired, so we had a sleep before sightseeing. Then we went to the Christmas markets, had an early dinner and went back to our apartment.

Bauer: Can we please note for the record that Doctor Bruno Hoffman is a medical officer employed by the Foundation. Violet, did you make contact with the suspects, Thomas and Klara, at any time?

Black: Not on Christmas Eve, no. Thomas and Klara weren't due to arrive back from Munich until late that evening. We were really tired.

Marlow: Did you make contact with anyone else on Christmas Eve?

Black: Just the people we bought our food and groceries from. We didn't have any long conversations, if that's what you mean.

Marlow: Did you attempt to contact anyone from your former life? Parents, friends, that sort of thing?

Black: No.

Nenge: How about your friends back here, did you communicate with them?

Black: I talked to Ethan. Is that a crime?

Marlow: The point of this conversation is just to gather facts, Violet. You're not going to get into trouble.

Black: (laughs) Yeah, well, what are you going to do? Lock me up? Oops, already done that. You could torture me, I suppose.

Nenge: That was unnecessary, Violet.

Black: Look, what do you want to know? We—Phoenix and I—went to Thomas Neumann and Klara Becker's apartment on Christmas morning. We got a fix on them.

Bauer: A fix?

Black: We connected with their thought-streams, which made it easier to track them. We didn't get much at first, but we intercepted a conversation Thomas had with his friend, Dieter, at lunch time. That's when we realised they were planning to use explosives to attack the research facility in four days' time. The following morning, we waited until the family had left the apartment before we went to try and locate the explosives.

Marlow: Did you try to contact the ITA with this information prior to that?

Black: No, we didn't.

Bauer: Why not?

Black: We didn't know if we had enough information for the ITA to make an arrest. We wanted to get as much evidence as possible.

Marlow: And yet, you put yourselves at significant risk.

Black (faintly): Clearly.

Bauer: Tell me what happened from the time you entered the apartment.

Black: I went straight for the wardrobe in the main bedroom.

Bauer: Why was that?

Black: Because ... that was the image I'd received from Thomas the day before, of explosives in a wardrobe.

Marlow: And yet, the explosives were in Dieter Fischer's wardrobe, in his apartment on the other side of Berlin.

Black: I guess we got it wrong.

Bauer: Did you find anything at all in their wardrobe?

Black: Nothing interesting. Just clothes.

Bauer: Where was Phoenix while you were searching the wardrobe?

Black: Outside, in the stairwell. Keeping watch.

Bauer: Were you aware of the presence of anyone else in the apartment?

Black: Not until she stuck a knife in me, no.

Marlow: So you didn't sense— what do you call it?— her thought-stream?

Black: No. Just like I can't hear you now. Funny, that.

Nenge: Perhaps we should take a break.

Black: No, I'm fine. Do you know why I couldn't hear her? Because she had a blocking device in her ear, just like the ones you're all wearing. Do you know where she got that from?

Marlow: We're trying very hard to find out, Violet. But I can assure you that your attacker had nothing to do with the Foundation or the ITA.

Black: But she knew who we were. She knew what we were.

Bauer: Yes, somehow she did. But we want to thank you and

Phoenix for a successful mission. With the information Phoenix was able to give us, you averted an attack not only on Präzision, but probably future, even more worrisome attacks. We just have one more question for you.

Black: Let me guess, you want to send me somewhere else?

Bauer: In time. But that wasn't the question. Tell me, did you intercept any information from Klara, Thomas or Dieter about the Javier virus?

Black: Javier what?

Marlow: It's a deadly virus.

Black: Like M-fever?

Bauer: Much worse. A metal cylinder went missing from the lab, just like the one in this photo.

Black: I've never seen anything like that before.

Nenge: I think we should give Violet a break. Can we resume this tomorrow?

Bauer: It's all right. I think we have all the information we need. And, Violet...

Black: Yes?

Bauer: We're sorry for your loss.

Black: It wasn't my loss. Can I go now?

Marlow: Yes, you may be excused. Thank you, Violet.

CONCLUDED: 2.23PM.

(RECORDING ENDS)

My loss. It's not a *loss*, like misplacing your PA down the side of the couch. Death is final, irretrievable.

As for Javier, it's fortunate for me that the Foundation staff can't read *my* thoughts. If they did, then perhaps they wouldn't be treating me quite so well.

If they could read my thoughts, they'd never let me go. I'd be a liability, and I know what happens to liabilities.

They die.

THREE

PHOENIX

Today is Callum's sixteenth birthday. He's happy because the staff have given him a new toy, an electric snowboard, which was delivered to his room before breakfast this morning.

'Like we have any snow around here.' Harper flops onto his bed.

'It's for my trip to Japan, duh.' Callum is fiddling with the settings on the snowboard. 'Which, may I remind you, starts tomorrow. I can practise on the VirtReal sim today.' He holds up his PA. 'Downloaded the app.'

'No one gave me a snowboard,' Audrey says, looking nervous at the prospect of her first mission.

'Probably because you said you can't snowboard.' Callum stands up. I swear he's grown at least two inches since we met six months ago. He's full of confidence after a successful mission in London with no bloodshed, as if unmasking two students with what turned out to be no more than a pipe bomb was hard.

'Well, maybe next time I'll get to use my gun,' he says, after I make no attempt to hide *that* thought.

'I'd be happy never to have to use one again.' I exit the room, my blood simmering. Callum isn't just green, he's cocky and dangerous with it.

Bruno intercepts me before I can duck into the cafeteria. 'Marlow and Bauer want to speak with you.'

'Now?' My gut emits a mutinous gurgle. After a twenty-kilometre run last night, I'm starving.

What are you training for? Harper had asked me the other day. *One of Dash's ultra-marathons?*

Yeah, I'd said, although the thought hadn't occurred to me before. It sounded better than *I'm running because it stops me going crazy.*

Bruno is already striding off. Mumbling beneath my breath, I follow him to the Oval Room. I'm not surprised to see Bauer and Marlow inside. Bauer has been here ever since he arrived for Violet's debriefing a few days ago.

I wonder how that went. It's not like I can ask her.

Bauer is wearing his usual black suit, but the spectacle frames are new: the left half white, the right half black. Marlow is looking more casual in a blue polo shirt, his sunglasses sitting on top of his head.

'Mr Fletcher, how are you?' Bauer greets me.

'Starving.' It almost comes out as a growl. Maybe I'm turning into a wolf after all.

'Bruno, bring the boy some breakfast, will you? And coffee for three.' Marlow gestures at the seat opposite him. I sit, automatically registering the blocking device each man wears in his right ear. I haven't quite figured out how they work, but I'm pretty sure they emit some kind of frequency that prevents us telepaths from intercepting their thought-streams. Ethan managed to get through them a little ... when he was alive.

'So, Mr Fletcher,' Marlow says. 'We thought it was time to discuss your ... aspirations. Your goals.'

I could stare at them, ask them if they're joking or being sarcastic. Pretend I have free will. Pretend I have *choices.*

What the hell, why not play along with them? What have I got to lose?

'Well,' I say, hoping Bruno will hurry up with the food, 'I'd like to get out of here more often. In fact, I'd rather not be here at all.'

To my surprise, Marlow nods. 'That's a reasonable request. I would hope we can come to a mutually beneficial arrangement. We'd be very keen to continue to employ you for your services.'

Employ me? I guess that's one way of putting it.

'Of course,' Marlow continues, 'we need to ensure that your abilities have been optimised first.'

Double-speak for *we're not letting you go yet.* It's no surprise.

'How long do you think that's going to take?' I ask.

'We're hoping you'll be ready by the end of the year. But we wanted to talk about the terms of the contract now.'

Marlow glances at Bauer, who is tapping on his PA.

'Contract?' I ask. One of the kitchen staff wheels in a trolley and begins placing items on the table—pastries, fruit, yoghurt, a coffee pot, cups and plates. Temporarily distracted, I'm not aware the screen at the front of the room has lit up until I've devoured two pastries and a banana.

I focus on the screen, my eyes skipping past the formal language at the top to the number with the euro sign in front.

'Five hundred thousand euro per annum,' I say, trying to sound casual.

'Along with a furnished apartment and car,' Bauer says. 'In return for your services, and, of course, your understanding that all work undertaken for the ITA must remain completely confidential.'

Thumbing a flake of pastry off my bottom lip, I say, 'How about seven hundred and fifty thousand?'

'Done,' Bauer replies, and I nearly choke on my croissant. Maybe I should have asked for more. Whatever, I have no idea what I'm going to do with seven hundred and fifty thousand euro a year anyway—buy a yacht? My own private plane? How much does a private plane cost?

'If you read on,' Marlow says, 'you will also see that the terms of the contract include no contact with anyone from your former life.'

'Well.' I try to keep my voice even. 'That shouldn't be too hard since my whole family's dead. But how come the secrecy?'

Marlow's eyes flicker. 'The very nature of your job will mean you have to keep a low public profile, or others could seek to ... eliminate you.'

'Right.' I'm not buying it, and I think Marlow knows it, because he adds, 'As time goes on, you'll be entitled to higher-level security clearance so we can reveal more about our mission to you. But one step at a time, Phoenix. Can you live with that?'

'I can live with that,' I say. Still playing along. Still pretending I have choices.

What if I turn down their offer of a job? What if I ask to return to New Zealand, to return to the army? It could be complicated, I guess, since I'm meant to be dead and all.

'Good,' Bauer says briskly. 'We'll give you a chance to read the whole contract before you sign it, of course.'

'In the meantime,' Marlow says, 'we'd like to discuss your next level of training.'

'OK.' Distracted by sugar and caffeine and a promise of a hefty salary, I'm only half-listening.

Marlow adds milk to his coffee, followed by a lump of sugar. 'We've been doing some computer modelling on the way the virally optimised brain works. As you know, for reasons we don't completely understand, the M-fever has opened up pathways previously inaccessible to humans. Interestingly, experiments on monkeys show that administering certain medications also leads to increased activity in some areas of the brain, such as the hippocampus, which is important for—'

'Learning and memory,' I say.

'Yes.' Marlow doesn't even look surprised that I know this. 'So we're hoping, with your cooperation, to see what effects these medications have on the virally optimised brain.'

'You mean *my* virally optimised brain.' Why doesn't he ever just come out and say what he means?

'That's right.'

'And what's the medication?' I ask.

'Lysergic acid 25,' Marlow says. 'Otherwise known as—'

The pastries-yoghurt-fruit-coffee curdles in my gut. 'No,' I say.

Marlow drains his coffee and pats his lips with a recycla-serviette. 'This will be delivered in a controlled setting, Mr Fletcher. You have nothing to be worried about.'

'No.' I stand up, knocking my coffee over. 'No, you're not putting that bloody L25 anywhere near me, do you hear me?' It's just another drug my parents used to trip on whenever they got the chance.

'Now, now, no need to be upset,' Marlow says, and at that moment, for the first time in months, I feel a twinge in my arm, followed by the all-too-familiar heaviness in my arms and legs that comes after the implant has released its sedative. And as I sink to the floor, I realise I've made a fatal error in my gaming strategy.

Because once you have hope then you have everything to lose.

FOUR

VIOLET

Tonight we're having a birthday dinner for Callum. The cook has prepared vegetarian moussaka, a wild rice salad, an apple strudel for dessert.

Phoenix isn't here. I glimpsed him in Callum's room first thing this morning. I don't care—the less I see of him, the better—but over the apple strudel, Callum says, 'Man, Phoenix must be feeling really sick to miss out on this.'

Harper wrinkles her nose. 'Hope it isn't contagious.'

'What's wrong with him?' Audrey asks. 'Gastro?'

Callum helps himself to a second serving of strudel. 'Dunno. I asked Bruno, and he said Phoenix had a fever so they decided he should go to hospital.'

'A one-bed room is hardly a hospital,' I say, remembering the infirmary Ethan was nursed in when he arrived from New Zealand, not long after his first cardiac arrest. The cardiologist had said his heart was dangerously weak. But I also remember the feeling of our hearts connecting. I remember Ethan telling me how mine somehow beat with his, *for* his.

Until I nearly died, that is. A new wave of grief threatens to drown me. If Phoenix hadn't told Ethan to let me go, to break our connection, then maybe Ethan would still be here now.

Audrey gives me one of her sensible looks. 'Still, it sounds like more than just a cold.'

I contemplate saying, *How sick can he be? He's a fit, healthy nineteen-year-old.* I know Audrey will shoot me down as soon as the words leave my mouth, though. If we hadn't all nearly died from M-fever, we wouldn't be here. If the M-fever hadn't weakened Ethan's heart, he'd wouldn't have...

Irritated, I push my plate aside. I wish my mind would stop doing useless loops like that. If only, if only. It doesn't help.

As I leave the dining room, I feel the pink hue of Audrey's concern. *Hey, Vi, if you want to talk...*

I don't, I think-say, then add, *But thanks.*

*

In my room, I flop onto my bed and aimlessly surf the net on my PA. The M-fever epidemic is over and barely makes the news anymore. A tourist rocket has crashed while orbiting the moon, killing all twenty passengers on board, and yet another Fijian island has officially disappeared due to rising sea levels. In New Zealand, a little blue penguin has been found on Stewart Island, after five years of everyone believing they are extinct, and an old woman has just celebrated her one hundred and fiftieth birthday.

What's your secret? the journalist asks her. The old woman says: *Swimming in the Pacific Ocean every day for the last one hundred and ten years.* Wow.

Not much chance of me doing that around here. Not much chance of me doing anything around here.

Stop being so weak. You've got a deadly weapon buried out there, so when are you going to use it?

I set my PA aside. Truth is, it's one thing to imagine holding the Foundation staff to ransom with a jar of Javier-infected broth, but quite another to carry it out. Truth is, I don't think it's something I can do on my own, and I'm not entirely sure I'll get full cooperation from the rest of the VORTEX members. Phoenix and I aren't on speaking terms, Callum seems positively delighted with his new role in life, Audrey is a super-cautious, semi-nervous wreck, and Harper's just moody. I've been blocking anything to do with Javier from the others since my return, although I'm not sure how successful I've been. Whatever, no one has brought it up.

'Hey.'

I look up, feeling guilty at my uncharitable thoughts, and see Audrey standing in the doorway, holding an e-reader.

'Can I come in?' she asks.

I shrug. 'Sure.'

Audrey sits on the chair by my desk, glancing around the corners of my ceiling. We'd be stupid to think our rooms weren't bugged, even if we can't see the cameras; stupid to think that our conversations—the audible ones—aren't recorded.

Audrey takes a deep breath, *Um, so you know how I'm going to Japan tomorrow...*

Yeah, Callum's only been mentioning it every five minutes.

She flushes. *Well, anyway, I wanted to ask a question about when you went to Berlin.* Obviously sensing my tension, she says, *Just a general question.*

OK ... The memory of the three days I spent in Berlin is enough to make me feel like puking.

No, not all three days. The first two days were fun, as much as I hate to admit it now. And Phoenix and I—

Block, block, block. From myself as much as Audrey. I don't want to remember that. His feelings for me are what got us into trouble in the first place, in all sorts of ways. I can still hear Phoenix now: *Jesus, Vi, when did you dream that up? Are you crazy?*

If I hadn't decided I had to get my hands on the vial of Javier virus, at all costs—

If Phoenix hadn't tried to save my life by having Ethan sacrifice his own—

Audrey's frowning at me, puzzled. I try to relax my block, at least partially.

Sorry. It's not easy for me to think about this, I think-say.

I know, and I'm sorry. I was wondering if you tried to contact anyone when you were away, like your family or friends.

I rub my forehead. *I thought about it a couple of times. But the minute I even got close to doing it, I had this intense reaction.* I can see I don't have to show her, because she's nodding like she's experienced it before, too. The racing heart. The dry mouth. The white-white fright, as if she's going to die.

I thought it might be different when I was on the other side of the world. Her disappointment is dull yellow. *I guess not.*

They've done something to us, haven't they? I ask.

I think so. Audrey taps on the e-reader and passes it to me. *I've been reading this psychology textbook, and I think it's got something to do with this.*

Frowning, I look down at the screen. *In classical conditioning,* I read, *a conditioned stimulus becomes paired with a previously neutral stimulus to produce a conditioned response.*

The old Violet would have given up halfway through that sentence. My new brain grasps it immediately, reinforced by the example at the bottom of the page.

The most famous example of conditioning is the case of Little Albert, a nine-month-old infant. In an experimental setting, Albert was shown a range of stimuli, including a white rat, a rabbit, a dog, and cotton wool. Albert showed no fear during any of these baseline tests. For the second part of the experiment, Albert was placed in a room with a white rat. At first he showed interest and tried to play with it. However, every time he tried to touch the rat, a loud noise was created behind his back. After several such pairings of the rat and the noise, Albert was shown only the rat and became very distressed, reacting by crying and crawling away.

I look up. *Oh my God, that's horrible.*

Audrey's mouth twists. *Wait until you read the rest.*

Reading on, I learn how Albert's rat phobia began to extend to other furry, white objects, until he was even scared of white beards.

No sitting on Santa's lap for Little Albert, then, I think-say.

Definitely not.

I can't believe scientists are allowed to do that.

Well, it was over a hundred years ago, Audrey replies. *They're not meant to be allowed to experiment on humans like that anymore.*

Unless you're a virally optimised telepath, like us?

I guess so. But I don't know for sure. She fiddles with the earrings in her left ear, a hoop and three studs. *I mean, how could they know if I buy a new PA and message my parents once I get to Japan? Or write them a letter? How are they going to track that?*

Even though what she says makes sense, knowing Audrey is contemplating contact with her family is enough to send a surge of adrenaline hurtling through my arteries. I can feel *her* fear too, purple and spiky.

I'm not sure, I say. *I don't know exactly what these are capable of.* I run a thumb over the underside of my left wrist, where I know my implant is. *If you're really serious, then maybe you need to try and get rid of this.*

Audrey's terror increases, her emotion-stream so intense I feel as though *I'm* going to die. As much as my brain is trying to tell me that's completely irrational, it's all I can do not to climb under my bed and curl up in a ball.

Audrey's whimper is barely audible. *I can't even feel the implant anymore. I have no idea how to even begin to remove it.*

I hug myself. *Maybe I'm wrong,* I manage.

Audrey raises her hands to her flushed cheeks, lowers them again. *I have to try. If I don't, then I may never get another chance.*

I know, I think-say. *I understand.* I do, I do.

Audrey stands up. Her whole body is trembling, just like mine. When she reaches the door, I say, 'Audrey?'

She turns, squeaks as I hug her tight. 'Good luck,' I say aloud, before think-saying,

Cut it out. Before you try and contact anyone, you have to cut the implant out.

Audrey whimpers again. I release her, shut the door behind her. Collapse onto my bed, trying to breathe my way through the fear.

What if she's right? What if this is just some stupid conditioned phobia? What if she manages to get a message through once she reaches Japan? It could mean her freedom, and eventually ours.

It's all too much to deal with. Exhausted, I strip down to my underwear and crawl beneath my bedcovers.

I miss you, Ethan. I miss you, I miss you.

For the first time in weeks, the tears flow.

FIVE

PHOENIX

I'm drifting, rainbow colours swirling around me, blue-purple-indigo-pink. My limbs are so heavy I can barely move them, can barely even twitch.

When I frown, I feel my skin moving beneath the electrode dots on my forehead.

Lysergic acid 25. Otherwise known as

I'm going to teach you a lesson, boy, going to show you who's boss around

No, no, no

Lysergic acid 25. Otherwise known as

L25

She tasted like maple syrup and I

Think you're smarter than me but I will always, always be stronger than

We did everything we could for your sister but she

I reach for Tilly but her image dissolves, to be replaced by a girl with honey-blonde hair. She's holding me by the wrists, her laughter rippling through me, the snow melting behind my neck and I

Am holding her as the blood pools beneath her, so much blood I've never seen

Oh God oh God Violet don't move

Prisms hurtling through my brain

(L25 no no no)

And I open my dream-flow, and I'm flying high

Above my body, above the spiral-shaped configuration of the Foundation and in a wing-beat I'm a

Wedge-tailed eagle

And as I swoop over the ochre-red desert I call out hoping that someone, anyone will hear me

Johnny Johnny Johnny

Before

Snap

I ricochet back into my weak-weak body, restrained at the ankles and wrists, my virally optimised telepathic brain

(VORTEX)

Writhing in a fog of

Lysergic acid 25. Otherwise known as

Acid death.

SIX

VIOLET

I wake suddenly, my heart thudding. Darkness presses around me. When I check my PA, I see it's 3.02am.

Johnny Johnny Johnny.

I sit up, reaching for my water bottle. Cool water slides down my throat. Dream images linger: an eagle, banking high above the Foundation, its eerie call echoing in my ears.

Johnny Johnny Johnny.

Johnny. Johnno. Jonathan.

The memory of reading our own death notices comes to me now: *The bodies of Ethan Wright, Violet Black, Audrey Spelling, Harper Mehta, Callum Templeman and Jonathan (Johnno) Fletcher were laid to rest today.*

An eagle, banking high above the Foundation. A wedge-tailed eagle, the form Phoenix likes to assume when travelling away from his body.

I lie down again, draw my sheets up to my chin. *Get out of my dream. I told you I didn't want to talk to you.*

He doesn't reply. And yet, the eagle's cry weaves in and out of my dreams for the rest of the night.

Johnny Johnny Johnny.

*

Only Harper and I turn up for breakfast the following morning. Callum and Audrey departed for Japan first thing, before I even woke up.

'How do you think Phoenix is doing?' Harper asks.

'Who cares?' I reply, but my resolve not to care is wavering. I avert my eyes, watching a pair of housekeeping staff walk past, their laughter trailing behind them.

Johnny Johnny Johnny.

A cry for help? Or just a figment of my imagination?

You heard that too? Harper think-asks.

I tighten my grip on my spoon. *Heard what?*

Someone was calling out Johnny in my dreams last night. Over and over, Johnny-Johnny-Johnny.

Oh. That.

Her brow wrinkles. *Do you think someone new is trying to contact us? Someone like us?*

No ... I hesitate. *I think it might have been Phoenix.* I show her the death notice, the memory from Berlin.

(Me: *Who's Jonathan?*

Phoenix: *That's me. Or was.*)

Huh. Harper sips on her smoothie. *Do you think he was delirious or something?*

How am I supposed to know? I wish I didn't have to think about this, but I am. What if Phoenix is really sick, like in a dangerous way? As much as I hate him—at least, I think I do—I don't want him to die. I stand up. *I'm going to the gym. Do you want to come?*

Ugh, no, Harper says. *Think I'll go for a swim instead.*

OK, catch you. I hurry towards the door and hurtle straight into a broad chest.

'Hey, sorry.' Bruno clasps my arms. 'You OK?'

Twisting out of his grasp, I say, 'Fine.' I don't know why I peer over my shoulder as I exit the room, but when I do, Bruno is taking a seat at the complete opposite side of the room from Harper.

They used to be friends, maybe even more than that, before Berlin. Now they don't talk to each other at all.

*

I haven't visited the gym in weeks. When I arrive, I see I'm not alone. Melody is running on a treadmill, watching who-knows-what behind the tinted lenses of her Smart-Glasses. She slows and comes to a halt, taking her glasses off.

'Hi, Violet.' Sweat glistens on her brow. 'How are you this morning?'

'Same as always.' I climb onto the exercycle. 'Have you been looking after Phoenix?'

And why am I asking that, why?

Curiosity, I tell myself. *Nothing more.*

Melody's expression is blank. 'Not since last night, when we transferred him to a hospital in Alice.'

'Alice Springs? Did you fly him?' I don't remember hearing any planes or helicraft last night.

'Uh, no, they...' Melody strokes the side of her nose, 'transported him in an ambulance.'

'What's wrong with him?'

'We're not sure. He had a fever and a sore stomach, possibly appendicitis.' I'm sure she's lying, but I've got no way of proving it.

Or have I?

'Hopefully he'll be back before you know it,' she says.

I shrug and start pedalling. Melody walks out, leaving me alone in the gym. Faster and faster I pedal, until my vision begins to blur.

Leaving my body isn't a new experience, not anymore. Usually I'm able to do it if I'm lying down, hovering in the space between wakefulness and sleep, or if I'm distracting my earthbound self with a repetitive action such as cycling.

I cast my dream-flow out further and further, ripples on a pond. *Johnny,* I think-whisper. *Johnny Johnny Johnny.* I hover above the alabaster-white Foundation, watching the heat shimmer across the russet landscape.

Johnny Johnny Johnny, I repeat, and then, *Johnno.* A moment later, I feel a *shift,* and I have to concentrate really hard to see the images flowing towards me.

Towards me. Through me. Into me.

My vision fragments. Memories scud past me, not mine. *Johnny, where are you, when I find you I'm going to kick your arse* and I'm being dragged across the driveway and there's a pain in my arm *Mummy no no no*

(it burns)

Johnny Johnny Johnny

Sucking in a breath, I turn my head from side to side and see the curved walls of a pod and I realise I'm in his—

Snap.

I'm in the gym once more, swaying on the exercycle. I clamber off, fighting a surge of nausea so violent I think I'm going to throw up. Sink onto the track. Try to make sense of what I've seen, where I've been.

In Phoenix's body.

In Phoenix's memories, as someone presses a cigarette into his arm, over and over.

Mummy no no no

I try to send him a message—*Phoenix, where are you, can you talk*—but all I get is a kaleidoscope whirl.

He's close, but where?

'Violet?'

I jump. Harper is standing nearby, her black locks piled on top of her head.

'Are you all right?' She crouches beside me. 'You look as though you've seen a ghost.'

Maybe I have, I think-say, before showing her what just happened to me.

Harper's eyes widen. *I saw Melody a couple of minutes ago, and she told me he'd been taken to Alice Springs.*

So, she was lying. I get to my feet. *I don't know where he is, but he's somewhere in this building.*

I already checked in the hospital wing.

No, I say, striding out of the gym and into the corridor. *Not there.*

Harper is close behind me. *Then where?*

I don't answer, but I think I know. I think Phoenix is somewhere the rest of us have never been permitted to go.

I think Phoenix is in One Below.

SEVEN

PHOENIX

Time has turned into a series of meaningless units, past-present-future slipping around each other, a spiral, no, a vortex, no beginning or end.

Johnny Johnny Johnny, I call out, until one minute-hour-day later, my words loop back into me.

My words, but not my voice.

Johnny Johnny Johnny.

Johnno.

And it could be Violet, or it could be my imagination, and I'm trying to grasp the words but it's just too hard when I'm tripping-sedated-I-don't-know-what-else.

Am I dying?

Or worse, have I lost my mind?

Johnny Johnno Phoenix Wolf, can you hear me, where are you?

I try to open my dream-flow, but nothing happens. I open my mouth. Someone is screaming. Someone is screaming.

Someone who used to be me.

EIGHT

VIOLET

Of course, our attempts to take the lift to One Below get us nowhere. The retinal recognition scrambler app on my PA, the one I used in Berlin, isn't working—not that I really expected it to. Either the Foundation has disabled it, or their retinal recognition systems are much more advanced than the usual ones.

How do you know he's still here? Harper think-asks, following me outside. I detect the faint scent of smoke, a constant reminder of the fires that are raging out of control hundreds of kilometres from here. At least, I hope they're hundreds of kilometres from here. It's not as though there is much vegetation to burn around here, anyway.

I heard him, I say *Not just that, I travelled* ... I hesitate, trying to figure out what just happened. *I travelled* into him.

Harper kicks at a stone. *Ugh, how weird.* We wander along the fence line and through the open gates. They don't lock us in all day anymore. It's not as if we'd get too far if we decided to make a break for it—and, even if we did, the Foundation staff would soon track us down. I stroke the inside of my left arm, remembering the conversation I had with Audrey last night.

Cut it out. Before you try and contact anyone, you have to cut the implant out.

Harper grabs my elbow. 'Watch out.'

'Just a lizard.' I watch the reptile scuttle across our path. It must be at least a metre long.

'Maybe you should transport yourself into one of *those*.'

Ssh, I think-say.

Harper rolls her eyes at me. *Relax, no one can hear us out here.*

Want to bet? I say, still stroking my arm, still thinking about how to get to Phoenix.

God, you have such a one-track mind. I thought you hated him.

Yeah, I say. *But I hate* them *more.*

'Hey. Look.'

'What now?' I ask, looking for a snake, or an ant nest. Instead, I see a cloud of dust. It's getting closer.

'A car,' Harper says, and now I hear music, the faint sound of an engine. Red clouds, red dust. As the vehicle draws closer, I see it's a black SUV with large bull bars and a snorkel, which seems kind of hopeful, considering there's barely any water for a two-hun-dred-kilometre radius around here.

My albatross self knows this from when I used to travel with the others, long after we were meant to have gone to sleep, our earthly bodies safe inside the Foundation.

Or not safe, as the case may be.

I'm not entirely surprised when the SUV slows and comes to a halt only metres away from where we are standing. I am surprised to see who is behind the wheel, though—a woman, in her early thirties maybe, with short, raspberry-red hair and neon-green sunglasses. Next to her, in the passenger seat, is a skinny girl with ice-blonde hair and a nose-ring.

'Hey.' Raspberry Hair leans out of the window. 'Need a ride?'

Trying not to stare at Ice Blonde, I ask, 'Where are you going?'

Raspberry Hair points over my shoulder, towards the gate.

'In there.'

Oh. Very funny.

'We've only just started our walk.' Harper's tone is steely, but I can feel her disappointment too. 'Thanks anyway.' And, as the SUV trundles past us, I hear her think-ask Ice Blonde, *Where are you from?*

Ice Blonde doesn't answer, but like Harper, I sense the skinny girl's electrical hum long after the SUV has disappeared inside the gates.

Whoa, Harper says. *Did you hear that?*

Couldn't miss it. I pick up the pace, breathing in the sand-dry air. *Try speaking to her in German next time.*

What?

Woher kommst du? I think-ask, and almost immediately the new girl answers, *München*, adding, *Ich bin Mila.*

Mila, I echo, before continuing in German, *How did you get here?*

In a SUV, duh, Harper answers, but Mila knows what I mean, because she think-says, *I played a game, and I won.*

A game. Oh God. *What sort of game?* I think-ask.

A game called Eternity, Mila answers, right before a voice says, '*There* you are.'

I turn around. It's Bruno, his wide-brimmed hat riding low on his brow. 'What are you girls up to?'

'Just getting some fresh air,' Harper says, as my brain races to make the connection. Eternity is the game Ethan and his best friend Rawiri designed, the game that has recently gone viral—the game Ethan was convinced the Foundation had altered and put online to track down the only other people who could ever hope to solve it.

Others like us.

'Well,' Bruno says, his eyes darting between Harper and me, 'don't be too long, will you? You never know what could be lurking out here.'

I cross my arms. 'Yeah, you never know what kind of creep you could meet.'

'Come and say hi to the new girl,' Bruno says in a tone that has me wondering whether he'll activate our implants if we refuse, sending sedative racing through our bloodstreams the way they used to in the early days, before they trained us.

Before they *conditioned* us, I tell myself, as we follow him into the compound, like the sheep we've become.

What's that saying about wolves in sheep's clothing?

I send another message to Phoenix.

Johnno. Johnno, can you hear me? Are you OK?

There's no reply.

*

Bruno takes us to the common room, where Melody is sitting on a couch opposite Raspberry Hair and Mila. Mila is fidgety, her gaze wandering. I sit in a chair by the window, noting that in addition to the nose piercing, Mila also has micro-tattoos on her eyelids, something that was trending on ChinWag before I got sick. On the left eyelid, there is a rose; on the right, a crescent moon curving around a star. They're unusual, and very pretty.

The next thing I notice is the tiny scars on her arms, mostly clustered around the veins in the crooks of her elbows. Presumably they're from all the needles she had while in hospital, if that's where she's been.

I guess I can't assume anything, though. Nothing is ever what it seems.

Mila blinks, and I realise I'm staring. Flushing, I look away.

Melody says, 'Mila, I'd like to introduce you to Violet and Harper.'

Mila just hunches into herself. I don't blame her.

'Uh, welcome,' Harper says, shooting a *WTF?* look at me.

'And this is Greta.' Melody transfers her smile to Raspberry Hair. 'One of our neuropsychologists. She'll be spending some time with you all over the next week or so.'

'Awesome,' I say.

Not sarcastic at all, Harper think-says. I'm tempted to kick her, but everyone is watching me, so I don't.

'Well, we'll leave you to it.' Melody checks her watch. 'I believe you have a class with Dash at ten. Mila, I'll return in five minutes or so to show you to your room.'

'OK.' It's the first time I've heard Mila speak aloud. I guess she understands English after all.

Once Melody and Greta have left with Bruno, I say, 'So have you had M-fever, too?'

Mila nods. 'I was very sick. The doctors told my parents I might die. But I didn't, and when I woke up...' She hesitates. 'I could hear what people were thinking.'

'Are there others like you in Germany?' Harper asks.

'I don't know. Today is the first time I was able to speak to anyone else like that.'

Switching to think-speak I say, *You said you solved the Eternity game.*

Mila's pale gaze lights on me. *That's right, a couple of weeks ago. Two days later, I was walking to school when I felt a pain here.* She fingers the side of her neck. *I passed out and when I woke up I was in a—*Her forehead wrinkles.

Pod? When Mia appears confused, I show her an image.

Mila nods. *Yes. Apparently I had a seizure. The doctors said I needed to be tested and placed in quarantine. I don't remember much about anything that has happened since then, not until I woke up just before the plane landed this morning.* Her eyes are wide, scarlet fear rippling through her thought-stream. *What's going to happen to me? Are they going to experiment on us?*

It's not so bad, Harper think-says.

Before I can tell Mila that it *is* that bad, and yes, they *are* experimenting on us, Melody returns, holding a white towel.

'Your room's ready,' she says. 'Come with me. I bet you're dying for a shower.'

Biting her lip, Mila leaves with Melody.

'Why did you lie to her?' I ask Harper, not even bothering to hide behind think-speak this time.

'I was reassuring her. And it's not that bad most of the time.' Harper stretches. 'If this hadn't happened, there's no way I'd be signing a job contract for five hundred thousand euro a year.'

'You what? When?'

'Yesterday. Your turn will come, don't worry.'

'I'm not so sure about that,' I mutter, rising to my feet. 'I'm going to my room.'

'I'll come with you,' Harper says. The last thing I feel like right now is company. I want to make sense of my whirlwind thoughts, to work out why my instincts are telling me that something is off about the new girl. Maybe it's the marks on her arms, or the way she keeps hesitating when talking to us, like she's rehearsed what she's about to say.

We've just entered the section of the spiral that houses our living quarters when I hear voices coming from Ethan's old room, one of them with a German accent. I halt.

Oh. No. They're not putting Mila in there, are they?

I think they are, Harper think-says, touching my shoulder in sympathy. I jerk away and start hurrying towards my room, scared if I don't get there soon that I'll scream or cry or both. As I do, I send a final, semi-hysterical message to Phoenix.

Johnno, Johnno, are you there? Are you going crazy like me?

The reply is so rapid, so loud, that my skull feels as if it's about to split in two. I clutch my head, and I hear Harper yell, '*Violet,*' just before my vision turns inside-out, outside-in and I

We

Fall and fall and fall into

The vortex.

NINE

PHOENIX

How long have I been here? One day? Three? My mind has begun to reassemble. The images from my past, which have been flying around my mind, a confetti nightmare, begin to fade.

Except for one. Violet is glassy-clear in my head, and I'm seeing her in three different planes. Across a table in Berlin, her brow furrowed in concentration. On the firing range in Central Australia, gazing through the sights of a gun. In a small room in New Zealand, where I met her for the first time—Violet Black, her hair falling like raven's wings over her molasses-dark eyes. Before they changed our identities. Before they tattooed our irises and tried to take our souls.

I am Wolf Black, Black Wolf. I am lost, lost, lost.

Violet's voice comes to me again: *Johnno, Johnno, are you there? Are you going crazy like me?*

My heart *leaps* and I reach for her, *don't go, don't leave me here,* and in an instant (but what is time? A microsecond? An eon?) it is as though every cell in my body is buzzing, so intense it's almost painful.

Almost.

Johnno, oh my God, Violet think-says, and I can feel her behind my eyes, in my chest, and it no longer hurts to breathe, to think, to be.

'Phoenix.' An external voice this time.

My eyes fly open. Who is this woman with bright red hair? Am I still in Australia, or have I been flown back to New Zealand?

'Phoenix,' the woman repeats. 'I'm Greta. Welcome back.'

Someone else is helping me sit up. Someone else is feeding a metal straw into my mouth.

And someone else, someone *within* me, is guiding my eyes around the room. Someone else is taking in the visual clues that tell me—us—where I am. The spiral symbols on the door, the scanner boxes on the walls. The lack of windows. The featureless corridor, the lift bank with the sign that confirms exactly where I am.

Because now I—we—have left my body behind.

One Below, Violet think-says, as we fly up, up, into the blue.

One Below, I reply.

Somewhere beneath us, we hear an alarm, raised voices. We are soaring above the Foundation, a wedge-tail eagle and an albatross, while the staff panic over our unresponsive bodies.

We could leave, I think-say. *Never go back.*

I don't know if that's such a good idea. For the first time in two months, Violet doesn't sound as though she wants to tear my throat out. *Losing our bodies forever could be like a version of hell, don't you think?*

Limbo, I reply. *Maybe.*

I know where you are now, she says. *I'm going to get you out.*

Don't do anything dangerous. Like she's ever listened to me before. Like she'll listen to me now.

We have to go back. Violet sounds almost regretful. *In case they do something weird with our bodies.*

I think they already have, I think-say, and *whack,* I'm writhing in my pod, my mouth opening and closing like a fish.

Someone is rolling me onto my side. Someone is holding a bowl beneath my chin while I throw up.

The buzzing, swollen-cell feeling has gone, but Violet's promise lingers.

I know where you are now. I'm going to get you out.

It's all I have to hang on to.

*

Time returns to me, meted out in small packages. Twenty minutes later, I'm standing in a shower, water streaming over my trembling limbs.

Once dressed, I sit on a single bed in a room with shiny white walls, flexing and extending my fingers, taking deep breaths. The shaking has stopped, at last. I've returned to my body, and my body has been returned to me.

For now.

'Phoenix.'

I look up. It's Bruno. I'm tempted to rush at him, tackle him to the ground, but I'm not sure I can rely on my limbs yet.

'Come with me. The doctors would like to speak with you.'

Bruno takes me to a room that looks like a study, with lime-green armchairs and a rug patterned with purple and red shapes. There's even a fire crackling in the corner, as if it's minus ten outside rather than thirty-something degrees. Marlow and Greta are already in there, waiting for me. I don't return their smiles.

There's food, coffee, water. I'm not hungry, but I eat. I drink. I'm in survival mode. I need to regain my strength, and as quickly as possible.

'How are you feeling, Mr Fletcher?' Marlow asks. He's wearing his usual bone-white suit. Me, I'm wearing black trousers and a black t-shirt. Wolf Black. Black Wolf.

'Like I've been raped,' I reply, in my most polite tone. 'Thanks for asking.'

Marlow's upper lip curls. 'That's a bit dramatic, don't you think?'

Struggling to control my fury, I say, 'You knocked me out and forced me to take a Class A drug. In most countries, that's illegal.'

Marlow strokes his chin. 'Mr Fletcher, your claims are most outlandish, but understandable. I'm not sure what you remember, but yesterday morning we asked you to sign a contract. Do you remember that?'

I clench my fists. 'Of course.' Was that really only yesterday?

'Good. And what do you remember after that?'

'I remember you telling me you wanted to experiment on me with L25.'

Marlow's eyes widen. 'Really? No wonder you're so upset.'

Are they serious? I look at Greta, but she's tapping on a mini-Tab, as if recording everything we're saying.

'I can assure you that no one has given you anything of the sort.' Marlow reaches for his coffee. 'We did give you medication, but only because you had a seizure. We had to sedate you and give you an infusion of anticonvulsants. You've been in a state of delirium until only a couple of hours ago.'

I hesitate. 'I don't believe you.' Every nerve in my body is telling me that he is lying to me ... But what if Marlow *is* telling the truth? How am I supposed to know? I point at Greta. 'Why is *she* here?'

Greta crosses one long leg over the other. 'Phoenix, Doctor Marlow is concerned you may have had a psychotic episode. I know this is all dreadfully confusing, but I'm here to make sure we get the balance of medications right.'

I stare at her, unable to say anything else. What's the point? Either they're lying, or they're right, and my mind is loopy, unreliable, feeding me incorrect information.

Greta leans forward. 'Phoenix, we're going to monitor you for a few days. There's a good possibility the psychosis was a one-off incident.'

'I want to go back to my room,' I say. 'My old one, up there.' I point at the ceiling.

'And you will, soon,' Marlow says. 'But we have scans to run, tests to give you.'

I give up. I cross my arms, look away even as I make an almost certainly futile attempt to get a fix on Greta, to reach into her thought-stream.

The familiar flicker is almost instantaneous. She's thinking *WEB scan.* She's thinking *smaller dose next time.* She's thinking of a girl with white-blonde hair and micro-tattoos on her eyelids. I have no idea who this girl is, but I think I'm about to find out.

'Mr Fletcher.' Marlow's voice breaks in. 'Have you got anything else to say?'

I blink. Check out the blocking device in Greta's ear, which somehow I've just rendered useless.

'No,' I say. 'Nothing at all.'

TEN

VIOLET

When I return to my body, razor-like pains shooting through me, I'm lying in a bed with electro-dots on my chest and temples. A plastic tube snakes out of a needle in my vein. Great, I've been hauled off to the infirmary.

'Violet.' Melody's concerned face appears in front of me. 'How are you feeling?'

'Fine.' I sit up, wincing when another pain shoots through my belly. 'This is a bit OTT, isn't it?'

Melody presses a button on the monitor beside my bed. 'Hardly. You lost consciousness. Your heart was going so slowly we thought we were going to have to start CPR.'

'But you didn't, right?' I start peeling dots off my upper chest. 'I think I was just dehydrated. I've been known to faint sometimes.'

'Really?' Melody doesn't look convinced. 'Since when did you become a doctor?'

'I don't need to be a doctor to know my own body.' Is a healer a doctor? I'm not sure. It's not something I want to let the Foundation staff know about, anyway. They don't know about the times I've eased Harper's menstrual cramps by laying my hands on her back, or the time I healed Callum's broken ankle by wrapping my hands around it for a few hours.

I don't know why I'm the only VORTEX member capable of doing that, any more than I can understand how Phoenix managed to yank me out of my body just before.

'I'd like you to keep those on for another twenty-four hours,' Melody says, stopping my fingers before I can take off another dot. 'Especially after what happened to Ethan.'

I swallow. 'That was nothing like what happened to Ethan.'

Melody gives me one of her no-nonsense looks. 'Leave them on and I'll let you go to your room. Otherwise I'll be obliged to keep you here for the next twenty-four hours instead.'

Deciding there's no point in arguing any further, I let her put the dots back on before escorting me to my room.

'Rest up,' she says. 'I'll have lunch brought to you.'

Lunch? Once she leaves, I check my PA and see it's almost eleven am. Surely Phoenix and I weren't away from our bodies for that long ... were we?

And now I've made a promise I don't know if I can keep.

I know where you are now. I'm going to get you out.

With a soft groan, I turn onto my stomach and type *Eternity game* into the internet browser on my PA. There are lots of links, mostly with players giving each other tips on how to get to the next level.

This game is practically impossible, someone called *Whatev* has commented.

Yeah, but two people have solved it, and I'm going to be next, Wassup has replied.

Only two people? I type *how many people have solved Eternity* into the search bar. It's true. Every post I can find says the same thing: only two people have ever solved the game. The first was a player who called himself *Kill Bill.*

'Ethan,' I whisper, remembering how he once told me that he and his sister used to call each other Bill and Jill.

The second person to solve the game was *Aufreizend Katze,* which is German for slinky cat. It was only two weeks ago. Yet when I search *Mila Eternity,* all I get is a few random photos of German girls called Mila, but none look like Ice Blonde, and one looks like a porn star promising an eternity of pleasure to her customers. Gross.

Giving up, I download Eternity onto my PA and give myself an alias: *Purple Albatross.* It's the best I can come up with at short notice.

I don't know if playing the game is going to achieve anything, but it's not going to hurt me.

At least, I don't think it is.

*

Melody returns to see me that evening, after my dinner tray has been collected. I've been confined to my room all day, which would normally drive me crazy, but I've been busy.

When not playing Eternity, which I cast to my mini-Tab, I've been thinking about how to gain access to One Below.

'Any headaches?' Melody asks me. 'Chest pain, shortness of breath?'

'No, none of that. Can I go for a swim?'

Melody hangs her stethoscope around her neck. 'As long as someone else is with you. And make sure you get an early night, all right?'

'OK,' I say, not intending to do anything of the sort. After changing into my swimsuit, I stop by the common room, where Harper and Mila are painting their toenails and chatting like they've been friends for months rather than a few hours.

'A swim?' Harper pouts. 'My polish isn't dry.'

'Just hang out by the pool then. Come on, I'm going loopy here, and Melody won't let me swim without a babysitter.'

Mila stands up. 'I'd like to swim. I don't have anything to wear, though.'

'You can borrow my bikini.' Harper runs a cotton bud around the edges of her big toenail. 'I'll just sit by the pool and look beautiful.'

Mila laughs. Rolling my eyes, I make my way outside, where the surface of the pool is rippling in the breeze. I sit on the side and drop my feet into the water. Leaning on my hands, I close my eyes, letting my mind drift.

Violet.

I sit upright. *Phoenix? Are you all right?*

Kind of. Can you talk? As if we're having a phone conversation.

For now. I splash water over my arms and belly. The air is still hot, thirty degrees at least. I show him where I am, tell him I'm waiting for Harper and Mila.

The girl with the white-blonde hair? Phoenix think-asks.

You know about her?

Sort of. Look, I've kind of got a fix on Greta.

Seriously? How did you do that? Behind me, I hear voices, laughter.

I think they've done something to my brain. With the drugs they gave me yesterday, he think-says, as Harper and Mila come through the doors.

Anxiety prickling beneath my skin, I plunge into the pool. *I'm coming to get you.* Tonight, I hope, if I can work out how to disable the retinal ID.

No, Vi, that's what I need to tell you. I think I can get out myself.

I start swimming, long strokes, not willing to lose contact with him just yet. *But when?*

Soon, I hope. But I need you to start getting ready to leave. You and Harper and Mila.

Leave? Where are we going to go?

I don't know, but we need to get out of here as soon as possible.

I touch the end of the pool, execute a tumble turn, and start churning through the water again. *Why?* I'm picturing him hurting someone to get away, maybe even killing them. It's giving me a weird feeling in the pit of my stomach.

No, Vi, that's the thing. Phoenix's voice is rapid, urgent. *Soon they'll be hurting* us, *way more than they have already. If we don't leave soon, none of us will be leaving here alive.*

Before I can ask him how he knows that, he's gone. I stand up, running my fingers down the sides of my face. Mila is standing at the edge of the pool, raising her arms above her head. The needle marks on her skin are barely visible in the glare of the floodlights.

She catches my eye, gives me a nod. Dives into the pool, her angular body cutting through the water like a blade.

I climb out and wrap my towel around myself.

'That wasn't much of a swim,' Harper says from her deckchair.

'Yeah,' I mumble. 'Guess I didn't really feel like swimming after all.'

'Where are you going?' Harper calls after me.

'Early night,' I call back.

Yeah. Right.

ELEVEN

PHOENIX

That night, I lie in bed in my newly appointed room in One Below. Greta says I can return to my old room once she's satisfied that I've recovered. She's lying.

Greta spent two hours with me this afternoon. First, she escorted me to a room with the now-familiar box-like objects on the walls—the WEB scanner—and asked me to solve a series of problems, each more difficult than the last.

I could have pretended I didn't know how to solve the problems, but I stupidly thought that the better I performed, the more likely it was that I'd be hanging out in the common room with Harper and Violet by early evening.

Wrong, wrong, wrong.

I'm not sure if Greta knew I was dipping in and out of her brain to access the answers. It wasn't as if I hadn't done it before, in New Zealand before the Foundation staff had improved their blocking devices. At least, I assume that's why I stopped being able to do that.

Perhaps she did, because next she gave me a series of problems that she didn't know the answers to, either. Mathematical proofs, mostly.

But this is the thing. I solved them anyway, and I don't even know how.

Prove that $2 - 2.7 + 2.7^2 - \ldots + 2(-7)^n = (1-(-7)^{n+1})/4$ *whenever* n *is a nonintegrative integer.*

Show that the function $f(x) = \sqrt{x}$ *is continuous at every* $x_o > 0$.

Show that $n^2 \geq 2n$ *for all* $n = 2,3\ldots$

It sounds weird, but for an hour or so I was actually having fun. Not just that, I was relieved that my brain hadn't been fried by L25 and whatever else they gave me yesterday.

After that, we moved on to the ink blots. That was when things started to get really weird.

'You're kidding me,' I said. 'Aren't these, like, really last-century?'

'They still have their uses.' Greta passed the first card to me. 'What do you see here?'

I stared at the shapes. 'Two bears fighting.'

'And this?' Greta asked.

I hesitated. 'Two people. In a fire.' When I accessed her, I got: *Childhood trauma, yes, that fits.*

I didn't want her to know any more about me, didn't want her pulling apart the ropes I'd woven around my inner self over the past several years. When she held up the next ink blot (a melting skull, like something out of my worst nightmare), I accessed what *she* thought it resembled, and said, 'Flowers.'

'Flowers.' Greta wasn't expecting that.

'Don't ask me what sort.' I crossed my ankle over my knee, feigning casualness, even though my pulse was racing. 'I'm not good on plants.'

Greta smiled. 'Fair enough.' She dispensed with the ink blots after that.

That's when I realised I wasn't leaving there in a hurry. Maybe ever.

*

She was recording me. I know that because I was accessing her the whole time; when she was sneaking her fingers into her trouser pocket to start the recording on her PA, when she began her carefully rehearsed questions.

I guess, when she played it back, it would have gone something like this.

It would have gone exactly like this.

Greta: Phoenix, I'd like to ask you a few questions about your childhood now.

Phoenix: Why?

Greta: It might help explain what happened yesterday.

Phoenix: I don't see how.

Greta: Sometimes trauma we've experienced in childhood can return to haunt us years later.

Phoenix: Trauma we've experienced? What trauma have you experienced?

Greta (laughing): Luckily for me I had a very settled childhood. I didn't lose any parents, or end up in and out of foster homes.

Phoenix: Yep, you're lucky all right.

Greta: I wonder, Phoenix, if your response to what happened yesterday was driven by what happened to you in childhood.

Phoenix: My response to being drugged, you mean?

Greta: The only drugs you received were the medications we gave you to stop the seizures, and then to calm you down. But I can understand why you're so fearful of drugs, after what you went through with your parents' addictions.

Phoenix: I don't want to talk about that.

Greta: It might help you going forward.

Phoenix: Talking about the past never helped anyone go forward.

Greta: Tell me about the scars on your arms and legs, Phoenix. How old were you when you got those?

Phoenix (crossing arms): I'm guessing you're going to tell me.

Greta (gently): I don't know how old you were, Phoenix. But your records tell me that you were abused from an early age. Cigarette burns, being beaten with cricket bats, broken—

Phoenix (standing up): I said, I don't want to talk about this.

Greta: The sooner you talk about this, the sooner I can clear you for release. Do you understand?

Phoenix (sitting down): Fine. What do you want to know?

Greta: Tell me about your mother. What's your first memory of her?

Phoenix: I remember taking her a cup of tea in bed.

Greta: How old were you?

Phoenix: Four, I think.

Greta: And?

Phoenix: I spilt it. She got angry.

Greta: And?

Phoenix: She tipped the rest over me.

Greta: That's the scar on your right foot?

Phoenix (teeth gritted): Yes.

Greta: And your father, what's your first memory of him?

Phoenix: Riding on his shoulders. When I was maybe three.

Greta: And?

Phoenix: Then he spun around and around until I felt like I was flying.

Greta: Can you remember anything else about that moment?

Phoenix: I was happy. I thought he would always protect me from all the bad things.

Greta: Did he ever abuse you?

Phoenix: Can we stop now?

Greta: What about your sister? Did he ever hurt your sister?

Phoenix: I'm not—

Greta: You don't have any family left, do you?

Phoenix: No.

Greta: Have you ever had thoughts of self-harm? Of ending your life?

Phoenix: Sure I have, haven't you?

Greta: Thank you, Phoenix. We'll reconvene tomorrow. Have you got any questions?

Phoenix: Yeah, when can I go back to Ground Level?

Greta: Once we've finished your psychometric testing. Your full cooperation will be very helpful in this regard.

I guess the recording is too clumsy to pick up on the subtleties of the interview. If only it were capable of picking up on our internal thoughts, Greta's and mine.

Phoenix: This is bullshit. She already knows most of this, and doesn't care about the answers to the rest of the questions.

Greta: I'd like to see what a second dose of L25 will do, whether he'll be able to access the memories he's kept locked inside all these years.

Phoenix: I have no idea why she wants to access my so-called repressed memories, and I'm not letting her anywhere near them.

Greta: Once we can access those, I'd like to see if we can...

Phoenix: She doesn't care if she drives me crazy. Maybe that's exactly what she wants. But why?

Greta: ... control new memories, create new memories.

Phoenix: This isn't psychometric testing. This is ... this is...

Greta: And once we know how to control his memories, his cognitive pathways, then we can apply our research to the rest of our virally optimised subjects, so we can create a...

Phoenix: Brainwashing.

Greta: Virally optimised army.

I get out of bed. Pace around my darkened room, chewing my fingernails. Sit on the mattress again. Rub the inside of my forearm, feeling the implant's contours beneath my thumb.

Violet? I think-say. *Can you hear me?*

Her reply is quicker than I expected. *Yes. Are you OK?*

No, I reply. *Listen up. I need you to do exactly what I say.*

There's no reason why Violet should care if I live or die. But if she doesn't do what I say, then we're both going to wind up dead, or worse, lose our minds.

TWELVE

VIOLET

When I walk outside, the moon is large and yellow, surrounded by an infinitude of stars. I don't have time for star-gazing, though. I have jobs to do.

Task number one: locate the weapon.

The box containing the Javier broth is buried beneath a gum tree on the outskirts of the property, near the fence, where as far as I can tell there are no cameras. It takes me at least ten tense minutes to locate it, not surprising when all I have to dig with is a stick and my hands. I take the metal cylinder out and stow it in my bra, then bury the box again.

'You all right?' the lone guard asks when I wander past him, thirty seconds and several panicked heartbeats later.

'Yes. Lovely evening, isn't it?' I don't duck inside, even though every nerve in my body is urging me to return to the safety of my room.

Task number two: check the escape vehicle.

Greta's SUV is parked at the north end of the Foundation, not too far from the swimming pool. It's locked, of course. I shine my PA torch through the windows. The interior is relatively sparse, but I find what I need in the back: four large plastic containers of water. There's probably about twenty litres of water in each. There's a smaller, red container, too, with a yellow cap—spare petrol, I'm guessing.

Task number three: check on water and fuel.

Tick.

I pick up a couple of rocks and stow them in my pocket before looping into the building and down to the common room. Someone, probably Harper, has left the e-screen on. The theme song for *Teen Island* is playing: a bunch of teenagers fighting for survival. They have no idea.

I rifle through the kitchenette drawers for a minute or so before giving up on task number four. There's nothing sharper than a fork in there, which is no surprise. I put as much food as I can into an empty box, though, including a block of cheese, Marmite, crackers and six packets of Two Minute Noodles.

My next stop is the dining room. The entrance to the main kitchen is locked. No surprise there, either. Task number four isn't vital for our escape, anyway; at least not immediately.

The final stop is Phoenix's room, across the corridor from mine. The door is unlocked, as he said it would be. I pause for a moment after entering, taking in the bed made with army-sharp corners and the books on the desk, one of which is the Nietzsche Audrey was reading before we went to Berlin. A quote she'd read out to us has been echoing in my mind ever since: *If you gaze long enough into an abyss, the abyss will gaze back into you.*

A tiny shiver rippling through me, I drop to my knees and pull a box out from under the bed. Inside the box is a slingshot, homemade by the looks of it, and a snow globe. When I pick up the globe, I see a fairytale-style castle inside. I make a show of looking at it to fool anyone watching on monitors. I shake the globe, watching the fake snow swirl within. That makes me feel shivery too, so I put it back and retreat with the slingshot in my pocket, next to the rocks.

It's midnight when I return to my bedroom. After locking my door and turning off the light, I tug a backpack out from beneath my bed: the same backpack I took to Berlin.

Task number six: pack what you can.

After stuffing in a couple of t-shirts, jeans, socks and underwear, I add the food. Doing up the zips and buckles is a struggle. Trying to work out where to stow the backpack in the event of a quick getaway is even harder. It's not as if I can leave it by the door. In the end, I push it beneath the bed again. I'll work it out later.

Now for my final task, or the last one I can complete before trying to get some sleep. I lie on my bed, searching for Harper's thought-stream. It's slow, undulating.

'Sorry,' I whisper, before think-saying, *Harper, can you hear me?*

I have to repeat myself three times before I get an answer.

What the hell, Vi, can't you tell I'm asleep?

Not anymore.

Smart arse. Can't it wait until tomorrow?

No, it can't. Listen up, I think-say, before realising I sound just like Phoenix. Whatever, it's easier just to show her exactly what Phoenix showed me a few hours ago. I don't know what I'm expecting—shock? Panic? Instead, I'm getting something else entirely.

How do you know Phoenix isn't having a psychotic episode? Harper's disbelief is aubergine tinged with brown. *He could have made all of this up.*

Why would he make it up? And even if he is having a psychotic episode, why did Melody lie to us and say he had appendicitis?

Maybe she didn't want to upset us.

Frustrated, I leap up and start pacing the room. *Fine. If you don't want to come with us, stay behind. If all you're interested in is your five hundred thousand euro a year contract, then I guess that will suit you just fine.*

If the alternative is to be a poor, hungry fugitive, then I know what I'll take. I sense she's blocking me, divorcing herself from me already. Unbelievable.

Were you even paying attention before? I snap. *There's no five hundred thousand euro a year contract. We're just the first part of a massive experiment to create a virally optimised army they can sell off to the highest bidder. They don't care if they destroy us in the process.*

Harper's colour has morphed, red-orange. *Yeah, and what you're suggesting might get us killed a whole lot sooner. Like, tomorrow.*

It's already tomorrow, I bite back, before blocking her and going to have a long shower. It's not as though I'm going to get to sleep anytime soon.

*

I do go to sleep, eventually, but probably only for about three hours. I wake just after five am. The world outside is still dark. When I reach for Phoenix, I find he's awake too, his thought-stream rapid-fire and spiky.

Did you get everything done? he think-asks.

Except for the knife.

Yeah, I didn't rate your chances on that one.

When will you see Greta?

She said we'd have another session this morning. Phoenix's colour flares green. He's anxious, excited, scared ... just like me.

Do you really think it'll work? I ask.

It has to. Are you ready?

I move into my ensuite and flip open the top of the toilet cistern.

I'm ready. I close my fingers around the jar of Javier broth. *See you on the other side ... Wolf.*

Later, Liesl.

*

Melody joins us for breakfast, her skin flushed and shiny from her usual early-morning work-out.

'Heard you went for a run this morning, Violet,' she says.

I place my spoon in my cereal bowl before my trembling hands can betray me. 'I did.' The guard who greeted me on my return must have told her. Nothing we do goes unnoticed.

Melody sprinkles nuts on her porridge. 'Pretty early for a run.'

I meet her gaze. 'It's too hot later in the day.' To Harper, I add, *Stop looking at me like that.*

I wasn't.

Have you changed your mind?

Harper hesitates. *No.*

Are you going to dob us in?

No, why would I do that? But you're crazy, you know that? She spreads peanut butter on her toast. I'm so nervous I feel like I'm going to puke, but I force myself to finish my muesli before downing a berry smoothie and two pieces of toast. Depending on how this goes, it could be a while before I eat a decent meal.

'Have either of you seen Mila this morning?' Melody asks.

Harper shrugs. 'Nope. Guess she's still in bed. Jet lag and all.'

For a moment, I consider asking Mila if she wants to come with Phoenix and me. No, too risky. Besides, if Phoenix and I are successful in our escape, then we can alert the authorities, tell them where Harper and Mila are.

That's when I realise that Phoenix and I haven't factored Audrey and Callum into this. Should we contact them, tell them not to return from Japan? Remembering Audrey's last words to me, I wonder if she is halfway to doing that already. *I have to try. If I don't, then I may never get another chance.*

Phoenix's voice makes me jump. *Violet. Ten minutes.*

I gulp. *Ten minutes?* I'm not ready.

See you soon. He's gone again. Crap. I take my tray up to the counter, peering through into the kitchen. The knives are hanging on the opposite wall. Not a chance.

'Greta wants to meet with you at ten,' Melody says when I walk past the table. 'Don't forget.'

'I won't.' I take a deep breath. 'Um, I was wondering if I can speak with you. In private.'

'Now?'

'Yeah.' I shuffle my feet. 'It can't wait.'

Melody wipes her lips with a tissue before following me out of the dining room. 'What's up?'

'It's private,' I mumble. 'Like, a girl thing. I might need you to look—' I gesture towards my groin.

'Oh, I see.' Melody has switched to the clinical tone she uses whenever anything medical comes up. 'Would you like to come to the infirmary?'

Two minutes later, we're in the same room I was in yesterday. The bed is freshly made, as if I had never been there in the first place. There is no nurse today, just me and Melody. My heart is thumping.

Melody closes the door and slides on a pair of gloves. 'Have you got an itch? Discharge?'

I reach into my bra and very slowly, very deliberately, say, 'No. I've got this.' *Now,* I think-say.

Got it, Phoenix replies.

'This?' Melody asks, staring at the cylinder. From the way her mouth has dropped open, I can see she knows exactly what it is.

(Bauer: *A metal cylinder went missing from the lab, just like the one in this photo.*

Me: *I've never seen anything like that before.*)

'The temperature inside is still thirty-seven degrees Celsius, can you believe it?' I adopt a conversational tone, even though my body has gone into fight-or-flight mode: my mouth dry, my heart going so fast I can barely concentrate. 'The virus has had the perfect environment to replicate in. A cocktail of Javier, I guess you could call it.'

'Violet.' Melody holds her hands up, like I've just pointed a gun at her. 'Come on, you can't have me believe you would be so stupid as to release that.'

'Wouldn't I?' I step closer to her, lower my voice. 'Take your earpiece out.'

'What?'

'Take it out.' Since she won't do it herself, I reach forward and pluck it out before stomping on it, hard. 'Now, look,' I murmur. 'I want you to take me to One Below.'

'I—'

Pushing the cylinder into her belly, I whisper, 'I need you to act for me. Do you think you can do that?'

'Yes,' Melody says quickly.

'Good. You don't have the equipment to examine me here, so you're taking me to One Below. And when you get there, you're going to take me to—' I hesitate.

Clinic room two, Phoenix think-says. *And hurry.*

'Clinic room two,' I continue. 'Tell Greta there's been a security breach and that you need to speak to her immediately. Tell her she needs to remove her earpiece, too.'

Her nostrils flaring, Melody says, 'Violet, I don't have the equipment I need to examine you here. Come with me.'

Gripping the cylinder, I follow her out of the infirmary and toward the lift bank. Melody moves in front of the retinal ID sensor and presses the button for One Below.

We're on our way, I think-say.

We sure are, Phoenix replies.

THIRTEEN

PHOENIX

It's 8.13am and I've been sitting with Greta for eight minutes while she messes with my mind.

Little does she know how much I'm looking forward to messing with *her* mind.

'So,' she's telling me, 'unfortunately we've had to have you sectioned. Do you know what that means?'

'No,' I stall, even though I know damned well what it means. My mum was only sectioned about three times before she and Dad had their accident.

Greta adjusts her earpiece. Pity she doesn't know how useless it is. 'It means you are being detained under a section of the Mental Health Act until such time as you are competent to make your own decisions.'

I don't say anything because (a) there's no reply for that and (b) I'm busy intercepting her thought-stream. She's about to try a smaller dose of L25 on me. If I don't take it willingly, then she'll sedate me with the implant and administer the drug while I'm out to it. Who knows what repeated doses of L25 could do to me? I'm not willing to find out.

'If and when you can prove you are competent to make your own decisions,' Greta carries on, 'we can let you go back upstairs, so you can carry on with your life.'

'Carry on with my life? That would mean you'd let me return to New Zealand. I can't see that happening.'

'If that's what you want to do...' Greta spreads her hands, her gold-painted fingernails sparkling beneath the lights, 'then so be it.'

She's lying, but there's no point in arguing with her. I just need to string her along for five more minutes until Violet shows up. When she takes a pill container out of her pocket and unscrews the lid, I say, 'Wait. There's something I forgot to tell you yesterday.'

Greta shakes a tiny pill into her palm. It's red and shiny. 'Yes?'

Violet think-says, *We're on our way.*

See you soon, I reply.

'Your medication,' Greta says, softly, insistently. She's holding out her hand, nodding at the glass of water sitting on the table between us.

I take the pill. Place it on the table. Reach for the glass of water. 'You asked if I'd ever had thoughts of self-harm. Don't you want to hear more about that?'

Greta's long eyelashes quiver. 'Yes.'

'I think about it all the time,' I say. Violet is getting closer, so close it's almost unbearable, like the feeling I get when I'm about to snap back into my body.

'That must be very distressing for you.' Greta, distracted, reaches for her own glass of water. 'Have you ever tried to harm yourself?'

'Not until now.' I pick up the pill, just before the intercom beeps and a familiar voice echoes around the room.

'It's Melody. And Violet Black.'

Greta's head snaps around. 'Violet Black? What is the purpose of your visit?' She half-rises to her feet.

'There's been a security breach,' Melody says, and the door swings open. Melody is standing in the corridor, with

Violet close behind her. 'I need you to remove your earpiece.' Melody glances up at the ceiling, in the direction of the micro-camera. 'As I said, there has been a security breach.'

Damn it, I need to get rid of the camera right now, I tell Violet.

Slingshot's in my right pocket, Violet replies as Greta, frowning, removes her earpiece.

Things move fast after that. Violet pushes Melody inside, closing the door behind them. I snatch the earpiece off Greta, then nod at Violet to throw me the slingshot and rocks she has just taken out of her pocket. Rock number one hits its target, smashing the camera. After following up with a second rock to be sure, I loop my arm across Greta's chest.

'Didn't realise you could move so fast.' Violet is holding Melody in exactly the same way, her thumb hovering over Melody's left carotid artery.

'Well, I am a wolf, after all,' I say, taking an absurd pleasure in the waves of fright-disbelief coming off the two women.

'What's going on?' Greta tries to wriggle free. I press, ever-so-softly, over her carotid artery and hear her gasp.

Violet's tattooed-blue eyes glitter at her. 'Some might call it Biological Warfare. Guess that concept won't be too unfamiliar to either of you.'

'It's Javier,' Melody says in a strangled voice as Violet waves the metal cylinder beneath Greta's nose.

Greta coughs. 'You're lying,' she says, but I can tell from her thought-stream that she isn't so sure.

I force a laugh. 'What was that you were saying about a psychotic episode, Greta?'

'You can run, but we'll track you down,' Melody spits. 'And when we do, you'll be sorry you were ever born.'

Violet pushes the cylinder into the side of Melody's neck. 'Nice to have it confirmed.'

'Have what confirmed?' Greta's wheezing beneath my arm. If she wasn't panicking before, she certainly is now.

'That we have nothing to lose,' I say. 'Now, I think I could do with some fresh air. How about you?'

*

The guards barely look at us when we drive through the front gates, Melody in the driver's seat. In the rear with Violet is Greta, still wheezing, although less so since we let her retrieve her spare asthma inhaler from the glove box.

Melody grips the steering wheel. 'You won't get far. They'll hunt you down faster than you can blink.'

'I don't know,' I drawl, still taking a vicious pleasure in poking fun at her and Greta, even though I know she could be right. 'We're so much smarter than we used to be. Isn't that right, Greta?'

Greta just takes another toke from her inhaler. We bump over the dirt road, brick-red dust billowing behind us.

'Turn left here,' Violet says.

Melody scowls. 'That's not a road.'

'No kidding. Turn left, or we'll dump you even further away.' To me, Violet adds, *I hid the backpack about a kilometre from here.*

OK, but we need to drive them in further, ten k at least, I reply.

What if no one finds them?

Do you really care about that?

Violet doesn't reply, but I can tell she's conflicted.

We'll let Greta keep her inhaler, I think-say. *That's humane, isn't it?*

'Here,' Violet says, and when Melody doesn't do anything, 'Stop. Now.'

Melody brakes hard, throwing the rest of us forward in our seats. Violet, still holding the metal cannister, points at the blue backpack leaning against a termite mound.

'So that's why you went for a run this morning?' Melody asks. She's thinking about how she'll get the security guard fired for missing the fact that Violet went running with a backpack this morning, and returned without one.

'That's why I went for a run,' I hear Violet say as I leap out to grab the backpack.

The rest of the drive is conducted in silence. I watch the odometer like a hawk (no, a wedge-tailed eagle) until we've reached ten k exactly.

'Stop,' I say.

Melody brakes, not quite as abruptly this time. She knows what's coming. She knows, and she doesn't like it. One. Bit.

'Get out,' Violet says, after making Melody and Greta hand over their PAs. There's no reception out here, anyway.

Greta, clutching her inhaler, says, 'What, here?'

Unwavering, at least externally, Violet says, 'It's as good a place as any.'

'But ... it's thirty-eight degrees out here.'

Melody is close to tears. I know, because I'm getting the bluegrey waves she's throwing out. I'd be more empathetic if I hadn't been treated like a lab rat for the past few months.

'There's a tree over there.' Violet points at a leafless ghost gum, which is casting a thin oblong of shade. 'We'll even leave you a cannister of water.'

'No.' Greta is shaking. 'No, you can't leave us here.'

'Watch us,' I say. I push her out of the SUV and deposit one of our precious containers of water at her feet.

Melody climbs out on her own, her expression stony. 'After all I've done for you,' she says to Violet.

'My point entirely,' Violet replies. I climb into the driver's seat and plant my foot on the accelerator.

Neither of us looks back.

FOURTEEN

VIOLET

'We need to find a service station,' I say, about fifty kilometres from where we've dumped Melody and Greta. It'll take them several hours to reach a phone, which gives us several hours to disappear.

'Yeah, eventually.' Phoenix slows for a rut in the road. We haven't seen another vehicle since we left the Foundation, which is no surprise, considering we're in the middle of nowhere. In the distance, I see a faint plume of smoke. For all I know, we could be driving straight into a bush fire.

'We need to find one soon. Before someone tracks us down.'

Phoenix turns up the air con. 'Sure, but do you have any idea where this service station would be?'

'No, but returning to the main road would be a start.'

'And do you have any idea where *that* would be?' He detours around a pothole. 'We still don't have any reception in case you didn't notice.'

As patronising as ever. 'Luckily one of us thought ahead.'

'Let me guess, you memorised a map?' *FYI,* he think-adds, *I was stating a fact, not being patronising.*

Rolling my eyes at him, I say, 'You didn't guess that.'

'Then I guess I must have read your mind.' Phoenix gives me a half-grin, and I return it before remembering that I hate him.

Mostly.

By the time we reach the main road, it's quarter to midday. The sun boils above us. Melody's PA starts pinging soon after we hit the tarseal.

The first message, from Bruno, reads: *Where did you take off to? Is everything OK?*

The second, also from Bruno, says: *Just saw the camera footage re the breach of*

I can't read the rest of the message, because the screen is locked. 'Crap.'

'What?' Phoenix accelerates, sending the speedo needle up to one hundred and forty k's an hour.

'They're onto us.'

There's been a breach of security.

No kidding.

'Had to happen sooner or later. What about our PAs, are they working?'

I take my PA out of my pocket and press the home button, over and over. 'Crap,' I say again. 'Where's yours?' Phoenix hands his PA over. It's dead as well.

'Surprise, surprise,' he says, before grabbing it off me and chucking it out of the window.

'What did you do that for?'

'What do you think? It's useless. And even if they do switch it back on, it'll only be used to try and track us.'

Knowing he's right, I throw the other three PAs onto the road, watching them shatter one by one. When I look forward again, Phoenix is slowing and I see something shimmering in the distance, a mirage.

No, not a mirage, a service station.

*

A couple of minutes later, we stop beside a petrol pump. The only other vehicle is a Jeep parked around the side of the station. Excitement-hope kindling in my belly, I stride into the store, Phoenix following me. There's no one behind the counter, so I ring the bell and wait, watching the e-screen to the left of the till.

'With you in a sec,' someone calls out from the rear of the store, at the same time as Phoenix think-says, *Shit.*

Oh, I say, taking in the images on the screen. *Oh. No.*

Because there are our photographs, me with my dyed hair and tattooed blue eyes, Phoenix with his new grey irises and distinctive Japanese characters above his left eyebrow. The text scrolling beneath our images reads: *If you see either of these youths, keep your distance and notify the police immediately on the number below. They are armed and dangerous and should not be approached.*

Armed? I think-say, before remembering the Javier stowed in the tool box in the rear of the SUV.

Phoenix plucks the remote off the counter and turns the screen off. *Quick. Go fill up the SUV.*

But we don't have any—

He gives me a look. *Just do it, OK? And let me know when you're behind the wheel. Leave the passenger door open for me.*

'How can I help?' The forecourt attendant appears behind the counter, his beer gut straining over his belt.

'Do you sell pocket knives?' I hear Phoenix ask as I exit the store. I unscrew the fuel cap on the SUV and take the fuel pump off its cradle, acid searing my gut.

I want to cry. I want to scream.

But I won't. I can't. If I fall apart now, then we might as well be dead.

And as I stand at the pump, miserably watching the litres tick up, a voice comes to me: my own. It's a memory, an echo from several weeks and a lifetime ago—a quote I read aloud to the rest of the VORTEX members from Victor Hugo's *Les Misérables*.

Even the darkest night will end, and the sun will rise.

But when? When?

I take the pump out and screw the fuel cap on. *One minute,* I tell Phoenix.

I get behind the wheel. Turn the ignition on. Wait for Phoenix to come out and prove that we are, indeed, the armed, dangerous, duplicitous fugitives portrayed on the e-screen.

It's what we've been trained for, after all.

*

'Call the police,' I say ten minutes after we've peeled out of the service station, the forecourt attendant yelling exactly that. 'Isn't that what we want?'

'Not if they're going to hand us straight back to the Foundation.'

'Why would they do that?' I slow for a rut in the road, speed up again. We're off tarseal again, heading into the middle of nowhere. 'Once we tell them who we really are...'

'But that's the thing.' Phoenix pounds his fist on the dashboard. 'Violet Black and Johnno Fletcher were buried months ago. We don't even look like them anymore. Shouldn't have let them tattoo our irises, what were we thinking?'

'They could do DNA tests on us...'

'Yeah, Violet, they sure could, and guess who'll process those results?' He turns his grey gaze on me, and I recoil before focusing on the road. My brain is whirring.

'A genetics lab.' I slow for a corner, speed up again. 'A genetics lab controlled by the Foundation.'

'You got it. And even if it isn't, I bet our original DNA was destroyed when the Foundation erased our identities. We're screwed, don't you get it?'

'You're talking like you want to give up.'

'I didn't say that. We just need to hide out for a bit, try and work out what to do next. Do you want me to drive?'

I glare at him. 'Why, is there something wrong with my driving?'

'I didn't say that either. Settle down, will you?'

'I will if you stop treating me like your kid sister,' I flare.

'You should be so lucky,' he snaps, and then, 'Sorry. Look, fighting isn't going to help, OK?'

'No kidding,' I mutter. I take a deep breath. 'Did you get the knife?'

And Phoenix says, 'Yeah, I got the knife.'

*

'Do you think they'll come straight out?' Phoenix asks.

'I have no idea.' I take another swig of water from the bottle he swiped from the service station. Every second out here seems to strip another layer of moisture from my skin, my eyes, my mouth. Sweat is gathering in all my creases: behind my knees, in the crooks of my elbows, carving a sticky trail between my breasts.

Phoenix takes the Cellophane off the roll of bandages and sets it on the tree stump beside him. 'There are some tweezers in here,' he says, poking around in the first aid kit. We found the kit in the glove box, along with a box of tampons and roll-on sunblock.

'I'm a healer, not a surgeon.' At least, I think I'm a healer, but what if I was imagining it? I haven't laid my hands on anyone for ages, not since Ethan—

Stop. I can't distract myself with that, not now.

'No harm in branching out.' Phoenix levers the blade out of the red handle and tests it on the tip of his finger. 'Do you want me to do it, or do you want to do it yourself?'

I swallow. 'I don't think I can cut myself.' I'm starting to feel ill already at the thought of having my forearm sliced open.

Phoenix looks at me for a moment, then reaches into his pocket. 'This might help.'

I squint at the glass bottle. 'Where did you get that from?'

'Service station, where else? Thought it might come in handy.' He unscrews the lid and passes it to me.

'Smells gross.'

'It's brandy. It'll take the edge off, I promise.'

I hesitate, then gulp the brandy. It burns going down my throat, but after a few more gulps my head starts to feel floaty, and everything seems softer around the edges.

'Ready now?' Phoenix asks, surveying our surroundings. I'm not so drunk that I've missed how twitchy he's getting. We've parked a hundred metres or so off the road, but they could still be tracking us.

Not for much longer, though.

I take a deep breath and hold out my arm. 'Ready.'

Phoenix is hesitant, barely scratching my skin at first.

'Faster,' I say, closing my eyes, then jump.

'Don't move, OK?'

'I'm trying.' When I look at my arm, I see there's a thin cut already, but it's nowhere near deep enough and now I'm starting to feel really gross.

'Put your head between your knees,' Phoenix says, his voice fierce but his face pale.

'Don't you faint as well,' I say, before giving up on trying to stay upright. I lie down, clutching my water bottle harder and harder as the pain intensifies, *oh no oh no oh no,* and just when I think I can't stand it any longer *no no they'll just have to track us I don't care I don't* Phoenix says, 'Done,' and starts winding the bandage around my arm.

I think I'm going to throw up. 'Where is it?' I ask. Phoenix drops it into my palm. I stare at the metallic object, which is no bigger than a matchstick and glistening with blood. Just as quickly, he takes it off me and smashes something down on it. My vision greys. When I open my eyes again I'm staring up at the blue-domed sky, but the ground beneath me is no longer hard.

'You all right?' Phoenix strokes my forehead, and I realise my head is in his lap. I don't want to move, but we haven't finished yet. I sit up, holding my bandaged left arm to my chest.

'Of course,' I say, fighting nausea. 'Let's do yours.' I pick up the knife, lying on a square of gauze inside the first aid kit. The blade is clean.

'I poured brandy over it.' Phoenix holds out his arm.

'Are you going to drink some of that too?'

'I already did,' he says, before lying back, just as I did a few minutes before. I don't feel drunk anymore, barely feel the stinging-throbbing in my own arm as his skin parts beneath the blade.

He screams when I remove his implant. It's nestled deep in his flesh, and I have to twist it to get it out. I clamp one hand over his wound and with the other smash the implant with a rock.

'Sorry,' I say, registering his blue waves of pain, which are so much worse than mine. 'It was really deep.' *Sorry, sorry.*

'It's all right,' he says faintly, and we stay where we are for a few more minutes, as his blood surges beneath his skin, as our hearts begin to slow. I'm thinking about the cylinder containing the Javier broth, hoping it's safe in my latest hiding place—the SUV's tool box.

Phoenix sits up, passing his right hand through his sweat-damp hair. 'Sorry for bleeding all over you.'

'Ditto.' I'm still holding his arm. His blood is no longer oozing through my fingers.

'You can let go now. If you want.'

I loosen my grip a little. 'It's not ready yet.'

'Yeah, but we'll get heat stroke if we stay out here. We can bandage it up, finish the healing later.' He reaches out a finger, our blood already faded to rust on his skin, and touches my cheek. 'Do you think you can heal yourself too?'

'I don't know.' My arm is throbbing, but somehow it doesn't feel so bad when I'm touching him. I guess it's something to do with the healing.

'Guess it is,' he murmurs, and I have to look away.

Don't think I've forgiven you for Berlin, I think, before blocking him, just as he is blocking me.

Some wounds never heal.

FIFTEEN

PHOENIX

It's early evening, dusk, and we've set up camp in the middle of nowhere. It's hardly a camp. We have no tent, no sleeping bags, nothing to cook with. We'll be eating out of cans tonight, sleeping in the SUV.

'We're not really in the middle of nowhere,' Violet says. We're sitting on a blue-and-white checked blanket I found in the boot, watching the wallabies and kangaroos forage for food now the heat of the day is fading.

I snort. 'If this isn't the middle of nowhere, I don't know where is.'

'It's not nowhere if you know where you are. The Gibson Desert is that way.' She points over my shoulder with her spare hand. The other one is still wrapped around my wrist. I took the bandage off a couple of hours ago to check it, and realised I wouldn't have to put it back on. The pain from this morning is a dim memory, although I'm not sure Violet can say the same.

Violet lowers her bandaged arm. 'It's not hurting that much.'

'It's not healing like this, though.' I slide my arm from her grasp and hold it up. The edges of the wound have closed, as if it's been two weeks since my implant was removed rather than six hours.

Violet shrugs. 'I'll have to heal the old-fashioned way, I guess.' She stands up and moves around to the rear of the SUV. 'Do you want tinned algae or baked beans?'

'Whichever.' I close my eyes, trying to tune in to anyone who might be nearby. No doubt Greta and Melody have acquired new blocking devices by now, but those are no deterrent to me. Not anymore.

Remembering my session with Greta that morning, I forage in my pocket. By some miracle, the tiny red pill is still there.

'What's that?' Violet passes me a can of baked beans and a plastic fork.

'Lysergic acid triethylamine,' I say. 'Otherwise known as L25.'

She sinks down beside me. 'Is that what they were giving you?'

I roll the pill between my fingers. 'Only once. I wouldn't recommend it.'

Violet gives me a thoughtful look. 'If it weren't for that, you wouldn't have been able to overcome the blocking devices ... right?'

'Maybe it was going to happen anyway.'

'You don't really believe that.' She pulls the tab on her spaghetti can and peels the lid off. 'Is there anything else you can do that you couldn't before?'

'I don't know yet.' And when she snatches the pill off me, 'Seriously, don't take that shit unless you want to risk losing your mind.'

'Only if you're non-VORTEX.'

Red flashes behind my eyes. 'You have no idea if that's true or not. And the last thing I feel like doing is looking after a tripping user.'

'How does taking one of these make me a user? Wait, does that mean you're a user as well?'

'I didn't have a choice!' I roar, and stomp off to eat my baked beans in peace beneath a desert oak.

Violet doesn't come after me, but a few minutes later she think-says, *Don't you think you over-reacted slightly?*

My parents died because of drugs, so no, I don't, I snap, then wish I hadn't. It's not the kind of information I like to share with anyone, partly because I don't want them to feel sorry for me, but also because I don't want anyone to think I might have inherited their druggie tendencies.

Violet appears and sinks down beside me. We watch the sun set in silence.

'Sorry,' I say, once the russet sky has faded to indigo. I seem to be saying that a lot lately.

'S'OK.' She hugs her knees to her chest. 'I'd love to have a shower, wouldn't you?'

'Might be able to work out something with one of those cannisters and a tree.'

'No, it's a waste. Although...' She swivels her head. 'There are waterholes scattered around here. We could find out where the nearest one is, head there tomorrow.'

'Find out how?'

'With our dream-flow, of course. Want to go for a trip?'

'As long as it doesn't involve any mind-altering substances, sure.' I lean against the tree. 'We should go inside the SUV before we do it. Don't want to risk being eaten by a dingo while we're out.'

'Ugh.' She shudders. 'Yeah, that'd be really gross. And stupid.' She touches my wrist. 'Um ... about your parents. I thought they died in a helicraft crash. Did I hear that wrong?'

'No. It just sounded better than *my parents were driving when they were stoned and didn't take the corner.*' I think about kissing her on the forehead and dismiss the thought almost as fast, because I'm pretty sure she'd punch me. 'Are you sure your arm doesn't hurt?'

'I've had worse. Remember?'

'Of course.' Now it's me shuddering, remembering how I held her in my arms in Berlin as the snow fell outside, as the pool of crimson beneath her grew and grew. My thoughts are clashing like cymbals, and Violet says, 'I didn't ... I couldn't...' and then she leaves me there, and I don't go after her because she's crying and there's nothing I can do about it.

*

A couple of hours later, we fold down the rear seats in the SUV and lock the doors before settling in for the night. I'd be lying if I said I didn't enjoy being close to Violet, the checked blanket draped over us. I'd be lying if memories of what it was like to kiss her in Berlin didn't keep chasing themselves around my brain—how she'd tasted like maple syrup from the pancakes I'd made for breakfast, how her breathing had sped up, and her heart, too. I'd be lying if I said I didn't feel a surge of exhilaration when Violet's arm came to rest against mine as we slipped out of our bodies.

Being an eagle is almost as good as sharing a blanket with Violet. When I'm flying, I'm free and strong and nothing else matters. Tonight Violet has assumed the form of a kestrel rather than her usual albatross, her black eyes fierce and intent.

There, she think-says after we've been flying for an indeterminate time; soaring in the updrafts, then plummeting towards the ground at speeds that would scare me witless if I were in my human form.

Yes, I think-say, circling the molasses-black surface of the waterhole. *Do you think we'll be able to find it tomorrow?* I have no idea how far we've come, how far away our bodies are.

If not tomorrow, then the next day. Violet alights on top of a rocky outcrop. *If our petrol lasts that long.*

It should do, I think-say, not wanting to think about the alternative, which is certain death. *We can camp out here while we figure out what to do next.* While we figure out how to outwit the Foundation. It seems like an impossible task.

Violet lands on a ledge above me and preens her feathers. *It's not impossible. We're already smarter than they will ever be ... right?*

Right. I'm not going to argue with her, despite my misgivings. I just want to enjoy our freedom, to feel the night air flowing over my wings. We do that for a while longer, taking in the rocks and the stars and the many animals that have become so familiar to us on these journeys—thorny devils, massive snakes, darting mice and skinny-sly dingoes, to name a few. I wonder how many other species we would have seen if we were here fifty years ago, and how many species will still be around in fifty years' time. Australia is burning, burning, and the temperature is set to rise by at least two degrees in the next ten years, the desert expanding as the vegetation shrinks.

I return to my body before Violet does. It's as painful as ever, the going back, but it's a relief, too. I roll onto my side, blinking at Violet's motionless form with my inferior human vision. She's barely breathing. When I touch the side of her neck, her pulse is so slow that I can see why the Foundation staff thought she was having a cardiac arrest the other day. A minute passes, then two, and I start to freak out a little. What if something has happened to her? But what could possibly happen to a wandering dream-flow?

I'm about to go looking for her when Violet sucks in a deep breath, then moans.

'Are you all right?'

She coughs. 'Of course. Are you?'

'Yeah, but where were you?' I ask, aware I sound like a nagging parent.

'I went to check out the road.'

'And?'

'I saw a road train. Nothing else.' She's holding her stomach, breathing fast. 'Hey, remember what happened at the Foundation, when I entered your body?'

'That was weird.' I frown, wondering if there's some way we could use that to our advantage.

'Yeah,' she says. 'I was wondering about that too.'

'We could give it a go.'

'Another night, when we're not so tired,' she says, which makes me feel strangely melancholic, because what happens once all this is over? What if I never see her again?

Of course I want to be rescued, along with the rest of the VORTEX members and any other poor bastards the Foundation staff have been experimenting on. I want the Foundation staff to be arrested and made to suffer the way we've been made to suffer. I want all this to end before someone else dies.

But for now, for tonight, I don't want to be anywhere else but beside Violet, listening to her fall into sleep, feeling her thought-stream slow and merge with mine.

SIXTEEN

VIOLET

The next day we follow the road deep into the desert, follow it until my head aches from juddering over the uneven ground. My wrist is aching, as well, but I'm trying not to think about that too much. We've turned off the air con and wound down the windows to save fuel, and now everything is coated in red dust.

I want a shower. I want a bed. I want a drink of ice-cold water.

We are a long way from having any of those things.

'This looks like a perfect spot for lunch.' Phoenix brings the SUV to a halt.

'Perfect,' I reply, with an equal measure of sarcasm. It doesn't look any different from the past three hundred kilometres. We might as well be on the surface of Mars. Thank God I memorised the map before we lost our internet access, or we'd be even more screwed than we are now.

As in, fatally screwed.

There's nothing taller than a knee-high bush out here, so we flip the boot and sit in the shade to eat our stolen cabin bread and cheese. Dopey flies swing around us, barely moving when we try to bat them away. They're even after the fluid in our eyes, although mine feel dry and gritty. The ever-constant scent of smoke hangs in the air.

'Just think of that waterhole,' Phoenix says.

'What if we were imagining it?'

'Both of us at once?' He raises the water bottle to his lips. The incision on his forearm is a pink scar rather than a wound, unlike mine, which bled when I bumped it this morning.

'No,' I say. 'Not both of us at once.' I try to focus, to work out if there are any foreign thought-streams nearby. All I get is Phoenix's craving for a beer.

'Sorry.' He passes me the bottle.

I take a sip of lukewarm water. 'Maybe you could turn this into beer. Who was it that turned water into wine?'

'Jesus.' He stretches. 'I'll be pissed off if we get to the waterhole and it's turned into wine.'

'I don't know, we might die happy.' I slide off the SUV, keen to give my butt a break after hours of sitting. 'What kind of animal survives out here, anyway?'

Phoenix's dove-grey eyes flit over me. 'Snakes. Mice. Flies. Reptiles. Kangaroos.'

'And birds.'

'Some birds. What are you thinking, Vi?'

'Have you ever tried hunting in your eagle form?'

He squints at me. 'No.'

'Do you have a shadow when you fly?'

'I don't know,' he says. 'I've only travelled at night time.'

I'm trying to think outside the square, outside the inconvenient constraints of my human form. 'How fast can a cheetah run, a hundred k's an hour?'

'At least.' Phoenix's thought-stream is rapid and viscous, his curiosity a rainbow. 'But what about our human bodies? We can't just leave them here to rot.' And yet, I realise he's thinking of my body when he returned before I did last night, of how my heart was going so slowly he could barely register my pulse. If our metabolism slows to a tenth of normal, then surely our energy needs should reduce as well?

'Like going into hibernation,' he says, picking up on my logic. 'You could be right. Pity there isn't a snow cave to park up in.'

'True. Still,' I say, 'when it's cooler tonight, we should see what we can do.'

'Yes.' His thought-stream darts this way and that, quicksilver.

That's when I have my second idea, one I daren't show to him.

He'd never agree.

*

Night falls, and we haven't seen any sign of the waterhole. For all I know, we could be driving in the complete opposite direction. We spread out the blanket beneath a spindly ghost gum and eat cheese and bread as the sun slips below the horizon.

'What do you think Harper and Mila are doing?' I ask. I feel guilty for leaving them, although it's not as if I didn't give Harper a choice.

Phoenix rolls his bread into a ball and starts plucking tiny pieces off it. 'Either they're enjoying a pleasant meal, or they're sedated and tripping on L25.'

'Maybe they won't do that to the others. Maybe it was just you they were after.'

'That's not the impression I got,' he says. 'We could try and contact her, I guess. Harper, I mean.'

'I tried.' Earlier today, during our endless drive.

'And?'

'Nothing. Maybe we're too far away.'

'But you talked to Ethan when we were in Berlin.'

'That was different.'

'Different, how?'

I stand up and pace around the tiny patch of desert we've claimed for the night. 'We were linked. My heart was beating for both of us.'

Phoenix is watching me, wary, as if afraid I'm going to lash out at him, or worse, start crying again.

'So, you guys had some sort of synchrony going on, is that what you're saying?'

'I guess.'

'Last night, I—' He hesitates.

'Yeah,' I say, recalling how our dreams had blurred and merged, although I can only recall fragments of them now.

I'm pushing my sister on the swing and she says, higher, Johnny, push me higher.

And my father is saying, Violet, we buried you, don't you understand?

You're dead. Dead.

And she jumps off and for a few seconds she is flying and then she is a bird, we are both birds—

And I'm writhing beneath the earth, and it's all dark, I'm blind, and there's soil in my mouth and my throat and my—

I clap my palms over my eyes. Feel Phoenix's hands on my arms, detect the salt'n'vinegar tang of his sweat.

'Yes,' he says. 'Like that.'

'It's because of you.' I lower my hands, try to blink the dream-images away. 'Do you think the L25 made you more able to do that?'

His irises are flinty, his mouth downturned. 'No. Greta's whole purpose was to fragment my brain, to empty out my memories and replace them with whatever they wanted. It's a miracle I got out of there intact.' His voice softens again. 'Because of you.'

'You would have figured it out without me,' I say uncertainly. And we're standing so close to each other, and I wish I smelt better than two days of sweat and dirt and blood. 'I'm sorry I never thanked you for saving my life.'

His Adam's apple bobs up and down. 'Any time, Liesl.'

'I'd rather not repeat the experience, Wolf.'

He takes hold of my wrists, presses his forehead into mine. Our thought-streams are tangling together again, and there's a juddering in my chest, like when you go over a speed bump.

'Call me Johnno,' he says.

'Johnno,' I whisper, and then he releases me and we're separate once more.

Separate, but not.

Maybe Ethan gave me his heart, but it seems as though Phoenix—Johnno—has just given me his soul.

*

The waterhole is closer than I thought, one hundred wing beats away. From my perch on the bank, I gaze into the water through my kestrel eyes. The surface breaks, and what looks like a very large dog swims towards me.

No, not a dog. It's a wolf, a black wolf. He emerges, water streaming down his flanks, before turning to drink, his delighted shiver rippling through me.

An overwhelming longing fills me. I close my eyes, concentrating, and when I open them I'm in my new form. I plunge in, the water closing over my head, and start paddling. When I emerge on the other side, dripping, satiated, the black wolf is there to meet me.

Do white wolves like to swim? he asks.

This one does. I shake, delighting in the sensation of my muscles, my hair, my canine brain.

The black wolf moves away swiftly, and I hear a squeal, followed by a soft, wet, masticating noise. Saliva floods into my mouth.

Mouse? I think-say.

Mouse, he confirms. Sensing movement in the periphery of my vision, I turn. There's something quivering in the bushes nearby, something flooding into my nostrils.

Wallaby, I think-say, my muscles coiling.

It struggles, but not for long. We feast on it together, Johnno and I, and when we've filled our bellies we lie panting on the riverbank.

We should go back. I lick one of my paws.

Soon. Johnno shuffles closer, and I feel his tongue on the top of my head. *Blood,* he think-says.

I return the favour, washing the tip of his nose. My heart is thundering, the blood-scent still thick in my nostrils. We curl up together, listening to the desert wind stir above, listening to each other's breathing.

When we snap back into our human bodies who knows how many

minutes-hours later, they are curled together, too, Johnno's arm draped over my shoulder. We shudder and twist, as always, before settling into sleep once more, Johnno's chest rising and falling against my back.

SEVENTEEN

JOHNNO

Just before noon the following day, we finally reach the waterhole. Recognising the surrounding rocks and trees as we get closer, I wonder if we'll see any evidence of last night's kill.

I still can't believe we did that. Perhaps it could have passed as a collective dream, shared by Violet and myself, except for the fact that I wasn't starving when I woke up.

Neither of us ate breakfast. There was no need.

Violet pulls into the picnic area and turns off the ignition. 'No one else here.'

'No one else,' I echo, wondering what the chances of someone else turning up are. I'm thinking pretty low, considering we've only seen two cars in the past twenty-four hours.

Violet jumps out. 'I'm so grimy, this waterhole will look like a dirty bath by the time I get out.' Within seconds, she has stripped down to her underwear and is diving in. Smiling, I follow her, gasping when the cold hits my groin and belly.

'Felt different when you were a wolf, didn't it?' Violet is grinning, droplets glistening on her eyelashes.

'Most things feel different when you're a wolf.' I swing my hand through the water, sending a wave across her torso. She laughs and swipes me back, and then we're kicking and splashing at each other, and it's not until I see the trail of crimson between her fingers that I remember her wound.

'Hey.' I gesture at the adhesive dressing on her arm, which is bright red. 'Looks like you're—'

Scowling, she begins wading toward the shore. 'Great. I should have known not to get that wet.'

'Wait.' I go after her, my feet sliding over rocks. 'I thought you wanted to wash your hair. The soap's in the car.'

'Yeah, well, maybe it'll have to wait.' She raises the boot and takes the first aid kit out.

I take the kit off her. 'I'll do it.' I stick another adhesive dressing on, noting there are only two more of those and about six plasters. 'I can wash your hair for you, if you like.'

She hesitates, glances away. 'OK. Thanks.'

*

Violet sits on a rock, cradling her arm, while I lather her hair, then rinse it using an empty spaghetti can to scoop up the water. When she tilts her head back, for some reason I'm reminded of last night, of how she looked after she brought down the wallaby.

She'd torn the throat out first, fresh red blood gushing over her snowy snout. The memory of the smell is fresh, too, even though all I can detect now is soap and the faint, almost metallic scent of the water.

'I'm not hungry yet,' she says, obviously intercepting at least some of my thought-images. 'Are you?'

'No.' I tease out the tangles in her locks, reluctant to finish. 'How do you think that works?'

'No idea, but it means we'll be able to survive for as long as we need to out here. Or anywhere, really.' She turns. 'Are you going to wash your hair now?'

'Sure.' I lather up, then dive in, head towards the bottom until I realise the waterhole must be really, really deep. By the time I return to the surface, my lungs are ready to burst with the effort of holding my breath for so long.

Violet, still sitting on the rock, her feet dangling in the water, says, 'Maybe you should travel as a fish next time.'

I flip onto my back, my breathing slowing. 'Guess that could be fun. But...'

Yeah, she think-says, our communication interspersed with thought-shapes and colours. *Being a wolf was awesome. I felt so ... powerful.*

I stand up, treading water. *You are powerful.*

Not like you.

What makes you say that? You're the healer.

Not a very good one. She pushes wet locks off her forehead. *You're the best at solving the problems they're always giving us.*

I swim towards her and prop my elbows up on the rock. *How useful do you think that really was?*

It means you can figure out other stuff. Her gaze is distant, but I'm remembering the blaze of her wolf eyes. *If you put your mind to it.*

By 'other stuff', you mean convincing everyone that Violet Black and Jonathan Fletcher really have returned from the dead, and that the Foundation is experimenting on other people like us?

Violet inhales. *Yes. Obviously. But not just that. I had this idea.* Her brow wrinkles. *I don't know, maybe it's crazy. But what would you say if someone told you that the M-fever epidemic was manufactured?*

I frown. *What do you mean?*

I mean, what if M-fever was an engineered virus, one that was released on the unsuspecting public?

You mean by the Foundation? Why would they want to do that?

She gives me a thin smile. *They created us, didn't they?*

I'm starting to shiver, so I clamber up beside her, the sun-heat of the rock soaking into my skin. *Alternatively, I* think-say, *they could have created a virus and released it by accident.*

The same virus they're trying to alter to create more of us? Doesn't sound like an accident to me. Her thigh is very close to mine. So close, but so far. Last night, while we lay curled together, we created our own shared dreams. Wolf dreams.

I try to focus. *Maybe you're right. But how are we going to prove that?*

Violet touches me, gently, between the eyebrows. *Before we left the Foundation, you overcame their blocking devices ... right? I mean, all you need to do is access the right people. Greta. Marlow. Melody.*

But that means I'd have to go...

Back to the Foundation, yes.

'No,' I say aloud. 'No, no, no. We only just left.'

'But ... last night, didn't you hear her? Harper was calling out.'

'I don't know.' But it's coming back to me too, a faint memory of a cry for help. Could that really have been Harper? 'I thought I was just dreaming, but now I'm not so sure. I've never communicated with anyone over that sort of distance before.' I shake my head. 'Even if it was Harper, we need to find another way. If they get us again, we'll never leave. Not alive, anyway.'

'But, Johnno,' Violet says, and the sound of my real name is enough to make me feel hot all over again, 'we don't have to return. Not like this.' She spreads her arms, nearly toppling off the rock. I grab her by the shoulders, steadying her, and stare into her ice-blue irises. Images scud across her—our—consciousness. A wedge-tailed eagle. An albatross and a kestrel. Black wolf, white wolf.

'Like you said, we're already so much smarter than they are,' she continues. 'We're getting smarter every day. If we can bring together the VORTEX members, if we can join our collective consciousness together just like you and I already have, then don't you think we can bring them down?'

'Bring them down,' I repeat. I'm still holding her by the shoulders, but any desire to kiss her has been replaced by a white-hot, excited terror. 'I hope you're right. Because if Greta gets her talons into me again, I think she'll melt my mind.'

'That won't happen.' Violet's eyes change, ever-so-subtly, and the dream-scent returns, fresh blood and flesh and wolf.

'We're changing,' I whisper. 'Aren't we?'

'Yes,' she says. 'We are.'

*

That night, we change into our wolf forms and go hunting again. What a joy it is to run and run and run and not get tired. To bring down small animals and feast until all I want to do is sleep.

When we've finished feasting, that's exactly what we do; our wolf-selves wound around each other on the banks of the waterhole, while our human bodies survive on the barest of heartbeats, the smallest of breaths, safe in the confines of the SUV. We stay like that, our hot flesh-and-blood exhalation mingling, until the sun breaks over the horizon.

And I dare to think that we might do this all over again tomorrow, and tomorrow, and tomorrow.

But of course, nothing ever stays the same.

EIGHTEEN

VIOLET

I wake to the crackle of tyres over dirt-gravel. With a growl, I sit up before realising I'm still in wolf form. Johnno springs up too, and as one we plunge into the waterhole. Down and down and down, until *snap,* we're writhing in the rear of the SUV.

'Crap.' I sit up, peering through the dusty window at the camper van that has just rolled into the picnic area. 'What shall we—'

'Just act natural.' Johnno opens the boot and jumps out into the dirt. The newcomers are driving one of the new-release Fuse vehicles, a thin stream of water spilling out of the exhaust pipe.

A rangy guy with a trimmed blue beard, in his early thirties maybe, leaps out of the camper van. 'Hey, watch out.' His accent is American, his syllables long and drawn-out.

'What for?' Johnno asks. I tug on a t-shirt and jeans before venturing outside, at the same time as a woman with dyed-gold hair climbs out of the passenger side of the van.

'We saw two big ... dog things. Dingoes?' She looks at her boyfriend.

'Those weren't freaking dingoes, more like coyotes. They dove in there.' Blue Beard points at the mirrored surface of the waterhole.

Johnno fingers his hair. 'No coyotes around here.'

'Someone's dogs, maybe?' the guy asks.

'Maybe.' I hug myself. 'We never heard anything.' I wonder if they have any weapons. Seems unlikely, especially if they're tourists.

Blue Beard shakes his head. 'I'd keep an eye out if I were you. They looked kind of wild.'

'Sure,' Johnno says, while simultaneously intercepting my ponderings. *Are you kidding? We can't leave them stranded out here.*

There's spare fuel in the SUV, I say. *Enough to get them back to civilisation, if you can call it that.*

'I'm Conrad,' Blue Beard says. 'And this is Kelly.'

'I'm Wolf,' Johnno says. 'And this is Liesl.'

'Nice to meet you.' Kelly eyes up the waterhole. 'We were going to stop for a swim, but I'm not so sure now.'

Conrad shrugs. 'Well, they've either drowned or taken off, whatever they were.'

'Probably more scared of us than we are of them,' Johnno agrees, while continuing our think-conversation. *Let's just hang out with them for a bit first, OK?* Aloud, he says, 'We were about to go for a morning swim ourselves. Are you camping?'

'Yeah. Thought we might stop here, but...' Conrad scratches his chin. 'God, maybe it was some sort of mirage. I mean, they were huge.'

'They must have been dingoes,' I say. 'That's the only doglike thing that would survive out here. Maybe not even that.'

'Well, I'm getting my trunks on then,' Conrad says. 'Coming, Kel?'

'Yeah, maybe...' Kelly says, still reluctant, but when I sift through her thought-stream, I can tell she's hot enough to put her worries aside, as long as someone else gets in first.

Johnno obliges by diving in, still wearing his boxers. Conrad appears from around the other side of the Jeep a couple of minutes later in a pair of red boardies, and follows him in.

Kelly glances at me. 'Are you going in?'

'I can't.' I hold up my arm. 'Cut myself a few days ago.'

'Yeah? Is it deep?' Kelly asks. When I probe further, into her subconscious, I realise she's a doctor. She and Conrad are having their first holiday together, and she's already having second thoughts about their relationship.

'It is quite deep,' I admit, while trying not to delve too much further into her feelings for Conrad. None of my business, really.

'Want me to take a look? I'm a doctor.'

'OK.' I smile. 'Thanks.'

In front of us, Johnno is jumping off a rock, his wet skin glistening in the steely glare of the sun. If I squint, he could almost be a fish, the way he's slipping through the water.

Not even close, he think-says. *Keep an eye out for the car keys. We'll have to be fast.*

I will, I reply, while feeling guilty at the prospect of robbing such a nice couple and leaving them stranded in the middle of somewhere that is close to...

*

'Nowhere.' Kelly moistens a square of gauze with saline. 'But Conrad wanted to try out his new toy, the Fuse Camper. He says we'll make it all the way to Darwin without having to refuel.'

'Really?' I try not to jump when she starts cleaning my wound.

'Wriggle your toes,' she says. 'Wow, this is really deep. What happened?'

'I was trying to open a can with a knife. Dumb, huh?' I'm trying to sound calm, while inside my emotions are all over the place. What if Conrad and Kelly aren't who they say they are? What if they're from the Foundation, lulling us into a false sense of security until the back-up comes in with their helicrafts to take us back to the Spiral? No, there's no way they'd be coming anywhere near us without blocking devices, I think, my emotions segueing into gratitude that Kelly is helping me, and then horror-guilt at the thought of what we're about to do to her and Conrad.

'Just unlucky. Well, it should heal up OK with some glue.' Kelly takes a tube of something that looks like superglue out of her first aid kit. 'Just try not to get it wet for the next twenty-four hours or so.'

'Awesome, thanks.' Watching the glue ooze into my fish-mouth flesh is grossing me out, so I look away. Johnno and Conrad are still horsing around in the waterhole, snatches of conversation drifting towards us. 'Must be at least a kilometre deep' ... 'amazing we haven't seen any snakes yet' ... 'So how does that work, not having to refuel for so long?'

'Conrad's team have worked out a way to super-compress the hydrogen, so the tanks last for up to five thousand kilometres. Don't ask me for any more details than that. I was never very good at physics. How about you guys, where have you come from?'

'New Zealand,' I say. 'We're having a gap year; travelling around.' When I look down again, I see that Kelly has drawn the edges of the wound together with the glue. 'Wow, that was fast.' Does she have to be so nice? God, I don't know if I can go through with this.

She smiles. 'Got pretty good at it after a year in the Emergency Department. So, are you guys sleeping in your car?'

'We couldn't be bothered pitching our tent last night,' I improvise. 'We arrived late.'

'Fair enough.' She applies a clean dressing. 'There you go. You should change the dressing in a couple of days. Maybe get your boyfriend to do it for you.'

'Oh, he's—' I bite my lip. Not my boyfriend, no, but I can feel the water sliding over his skin, can taste the kangaroo-blood on his tongue, can still hear his wolf-breath in my ear and I—

'Good like that,' I say, forcing a smile as the guys walk toward us. 'Thanks again.'

Johnno returns my smile. *Liesl, don't forget.*

I won't forget, I reply, blinking away the blood and snow and Berlin, Berlin, Berlin. He sits next to me and slides his fingers beneath my mended arm.

'Wow,' he says. 'You were lucky.'

'So lucky,' I say, melancholy seeping through me.

*

The Americans share their brunch with us, store-bought waffles and yoghurt and fruit. I'm not really hungry after last night's hunt, but who knows when we'll next get to eat something that isn't either stale food or fresh kill?

'Man, it must be ninety-five degrees in the shade.' Kelly stows the leftover yoghurt in the chilly bin. 'I'm going to have that swim.'

'Yeah, I'm almost ready for another one.' Conrad flashes his teeth at me. 'Pity you can't come in, Liesl.'

'One more day,' Kelly says. 'You should be fine to swim after that.'

I shrug. 'It's OK, I've got some tidying to do. Are you going in, Wolf?' Another wave of guilt-misery assails me.

Kelly and Conrad have been so nice to us, and we're about to throw it in their faces. Not just throw it in their faces, but rob them and leave them in the middle of one of the harshest environments in the world.

I feel awful about it, too, but it's not like we have a better option, Johnno think-says, before saying aloud, 'Definitely going for a swim.' Rising to his feet, he think-says, *Just like at the service station ... OK?*

OK. I return to the SUV and gather up our few items of clothing, the pocket knife and anything else I can fit into my backpack, including the leftover cheese and cabin bread. I look at the cannisters of water—two left—and hesitate. It's way too obvious, hauling those over to their camper van ... isn't it?

Kelly's laughter spikes into me, making me jump. No, I'll have to leave the water. I approach the van, keeping the SUV between myself and the view of the others from the waterhole. The electronic key is where I spotted it before, sitting in the drinks compartment in front of the handbrake.

The ignition button is to the left of the steering wheel. With any luck, it'll start as soon as I press it.

But what if it doesn't? What if I give Johnno the signal and he runs for the van and then nothing happens?

Just act casual, Johnno think-says. *I'm getting out now.*

My heart pounding, I glance at the waterhole, where Kelly and Conrad are floating with their noses turned to the sky, their eyes closed. They look so serene, so trusting.

'Sorry,' I whisper, feeling shaky all over. 'Sorry, sorry.'

I grab a stick and use it to etch a message in the sand, one they won't see until the van has departed: *we left the key, keep looking.* As I watch, the letters begin to blur in the breeze. I don't know if they'll ever see the message, but at least I tried.

What are you doing? Johnno think-says, as impatient as ever. Ignoring him, I climb into the driver's seat. *Now,* I say, as I press the ignition button and Johnno, ever-so-casually, climbs in beside me. The engine starts immediately, no noise, because of course it's an electric vehicle, *yes,* and as I slam my foot down on the accelerator, I look in the rear-vision mirror and see the Americans are still floating, still oblivious. Too easy.

NINETEEN

JOHNNO

'Do you think here is far enough?' Violet's cheeks are flushed despite the air con, her thought-stream clouded with guilt and worry.

'We've been driving off-road for two hours,' I say. 'There's no way they're going to find us now. I reckon they'll be heading for somewhere they can call the police, and we know that's at least eight hours away.'

Violet chews her lower lip. 'I hope they're OK. I feel like scum.'

I do too, but there's no point dwelling on it. 'What's done is done,' I say. 'And look, there was enough water in the SUV to last them for a few days, and enough fuel to drive out. We did what we had to.'

'Maybe we can make it up to them when it's all over.'

I stare into the heat shimmer. 'Yeah,' I say, although I'm starting to wonder if this is ever going to all be over.

Violet glares at me. 'You can't think like that.'

'I didn't say anything.' Damn, sometimes I wish I could go back to the old me, when no one else could hear my thoughts. I touch her wrist. 'All we can do is keep going, right?'

'I guess so,' she says, her colour changing from worry-mauve to the more determined navy blue I've become accustomed to.

'We need to find somewhere to hide the van,' I say. 'A place where our bodies will be safe if we need to leave them for a while.'

Violet's gaze becomes distant as she consults her memorised map. 'There's none for ages,' she says after a minute or so. 'The closest I can find is a small settlement at the base of some large rocks about six hundred k's northwest of here.'

'A settlement means people.' People who could recognise us, who could report us to the police.

'I guess people have to make the most of what they can find out here.'

I huff through my nose. 'Don't know why you'd live out here in the first place.'

'Some people don't have much choice. The alternative is to drive during the day and park up at night, do what we can while it's dark. That way our bodies will stay cool.'

'That might work.'

'Do you want to stop for lunch?'

'I'm not hungry, are you?'

Violet glances at me. 'No.'

So we drive. We drive on and on, making the most of the air-conditioned interior of the camper van, further and further into the middle of nowhere.

*

Nowhere is red and dusty and hot.

'You know what,' I say, several hours and a couple of short rest stops later, 'if I die and go to hell, it will look just like this.' I've been in the driver's seat for the last four hours, while Violet navigates.

'Mine will look like the inside of a spiral building.' She drains the last of the water from the bottle we've been sharing. 'Shall we stop for the night?'

'It's as good a spot as any, I guess.' I park up next to a sand dune. 'Thirty-three degrees outside, in case you were wondering.'

'Could be worse.' Violet gets out and slides open one of the rear doors. 'I can't wait to sleep in a real bed tonight.' She hesitates. 'Do you think they got out OK?'

I walk around to her side. 'We can try and get a fix on them later, find out.' I follow her into the main body of the van, which we haven't explored fully yet. There's a double bed, a small kitchenette, and a small bathroom behind a sliding door.

'A toilet. A *shower*.' She's twirling, her arms stretched up to the roof.

'And beer,' I say, peering inside the small fridge.

'Even I could drink a beer right now.' She sits on the bed, jiggling up and down.

'Go on, then.' I take a can out. The hiss when I pull the tab back is almost too good to be true. 'Are you sure we're not dreaming?' I take a long sip and pass it to her. Violet does the same, her eyes closed.

'Wow,' she says. 'I never liked beer much before, but this is...'

'Heaven.' I take another can out and sit beside her. I guess I must be really thirsty, because I drink it way too fast. The second goes down slower, and the whole time, I sit beside Violet and watch the sunset colours blaze across the sky.

'Looks like the sky is on fire,' she says.

'It probably is, somewhere.' I deposit my empty can next to the first one on the windowsill, then stretch out on the bed.

'Not much to burn here.' She lies down beside me. 'We should eat.'

'Soon.' I pull out a tangle in her hair, then another. 'You could have a shower,' I add, remembering how she couldn't swim this morning.

'Are you saying I smell?'

'Not badly. That wasn't what I meant,' I add quickly when she narrows her eyes at me.

'Too late,' she growls, before leaping on top of me and we wrestle for a moment before I flip her over.

'Watch it, Liesl,' I say, and her thought-stream goes all hazy again, just like when we were in Berlin, tussling in the snow. I'm about to apologise, Jesus, am I ever going to learn, when she curls her fingers into *my* hair.

'No, Johnno, you watch it,' she whispers, and her mouth is warm and wet and she tastes like beer and something sweeter and I feel an ache in my belly and groin.

(oh)

And I pin her arms above her head, gently, gently, and kiss her back, slowly, deeply. It is hot, so hot I can feel sweat soaking through my t-shirt. I have fleeting thoughts of turning the engine on for the air con before Violet tugs my t-shirt up and off, and I don't want to ruin this moment, don't want to break the momentum, so I help her out of her t-shirt and then her bra.

'Gorgeous,' I whisper, and our thought-streams are tangling together in the most beautiful way, and after that we don't say anything, at least not aloud.

(Vi, are you sure)

(yes, I)

(oh)

And we slide over and around until I forget we are fugitives and I forget we are lost and I forget we were ever anything but Johnno-Violet-Wolf. Afterwards I hold her and she cries and I tell her what I've wanted to tell her since she was trying to die in my arms in Berlin, and she says it back, once, twice, three times.

TWENTY

VIOLET

We sit outside, later, eating our first cooked meal since we left the Foundation—risotto from a packet with corn, peas and canned tuna. It's cooler now, maybe eighteen degrees, and the breeze is refreshing. Once we've eaten, we return to the strange new thing that's been creeping up between us.

Although, really, I guess it has been creeping up on us all along.

In Australia, after our first flight together. (*Me: Are you coming? Johnno: Right behind you, kiwi bird.*)

In Berlin, after a snow fight that turned into a confusing cacophony of emotions. (*Johnno: Watch it, Liesl. Me: No, you watch it. And suddenly my heart was beating way too fast, and he was blocking me but not fast enough. Not. Fast. Enough.*)

And then thoughts of Ethan flood in. (*Ethan: Don't leave me. Me: Don't leave me.*)But I *did* leave him, and then he left me. Forever.

No. I can't think about Berlin, can't think about what has gone before. All I have is the here and the now.

'Are you sure that was safe?' Johnno asks me once we've finished eating. 'What we did before?'

'It's a bit late *now*,' I reply, then feel bad, because he'd asked if it was OK to carry on, and I'd said yes.

'Melody gave me an injection before I went to Berlin,' I say. 'So I wouldn't have to worry about getting my periods.' Which is true, but it's not the *whole* reason she gave me the injection. Not that Ethan and I ever got a chance to take advantage of the contraceptive properties. When I thought about losing my virginity, I never dreamed it would be in a stolen Fuse Camper in the middle of the Australian desert, let alone with Johnno instead of Ethan.

'Well, then,' Johnno traces the inside of my thigh with his forefinger, 'thank God for *that*.'

We're lying on top of the bed, exploring all the different ways we can kiss each other, when really we should be thinking about other things.

'Johnno,' I say, when he inches my top up. I'm thinking of maps and driving distances. Johnno is thinking of skin on skin, of repeating what we did in the camper van a couple of hours ago. I know because his mind, for the first time since I met him, is wide open, blinding me so I can barely see.

'Sorry,' he says. 'Sorry, I can't—I don't know how to block you when—'

'No,' I say. 'No, I don't want you to.' Even though it's almost overwhelming, the strength of his feelings for me. 'But ... we need to talk.'

Johnno sighs, kisses me between my breasts. 'OK,' he says.

'Later,' I promise, holding him close, until he groans, and says, 'Is it later yet?'

'No.' I plant my palm on his chest. 'We need to talk about strategy.'

'So, I take your clothes off and then you take mine off. That worked quite well last time, didn't it?'

I laugh, touch my fingers to his smile. 'You know that's not what I mean.'

'Yeah.' He rolls off me and sits up. 'Strategy. So, we need to return to the Foundation, or at least get close enough to see if we can communicate with the others.'

I sit up, too, crossing my legs beneath me. 'And see if we can intercept the minds of the staff, see what they're planning.'

'And then what? Leak documents to the government?' He stares out of the window, at the star-speckled sky. 'What if the Foundation *are* the government?'

'Do you really think our government is that corrupt?'

'Maybe not the whole lot of them. Does your father have any links to politicians?'

'I don't think so. He knows a few journalists, though.' Just talking about my dad makes my heart race, my stomach clench.

After several such pairings of the rat and the noise, Albert was shown only the rat and became very distressed.

Johnno squeezes my thigh. 'Sorry.'

'It's OK. It's not a bad idea. It just seems as though there are so many steps before we can do that.'

He goes silent for a moment, then says, 'How far can a godwit fly, Violet?'

'Eleven thousand kilometres,' I say, recalling an earlier conversation with Audrey, who'd always assumed the form of a godwit when using her dream-flow. 'From one side of the Earth to the other.'

'Well, then,' he says. 'The world is our oyster, or should I say, our godwit's oyster.' He kisses the tip of my nose. 'Is it later yet?'

I wind my arms around his neck, press my mouth against his. 'Yes,' I say. 'It's later.'

Then we repeat what we did that afternoon, slowly, stealthily. And maybe we leave our bodies at some stage, maybe we do, because when we've finished my heart is pounding the way it does after a hunt, and my neck is grazed, as if I've just been play-fighting with a wolf.

Did you feel that? I think-ask.

Johnno's pupils are wolf-wide. *I sure did,* he says, touching his own neck, where twin blood-spots glisten.

*

Johnno makes a pot of tea and we drink it before returning to bed, lights off this time. We lie spooned, our thought-streams eddying around each other.

We need to talk about Berlin, Johnno think-says. I know he's right, but it's giving me a similar feeling to when he mentioned my dad before. Fight-or-flight, no, no, no.

Johnno layers his fingers across my forehead. *You bled so much I didn't think there could be any more blood left in your body.* His heart is pounding against my back, his terror-grief rising to meet my own. *I didn't know what else to do.*

I know. The memory of Johnno pleading with me when all I wanted was to escape the agony of breathing returns to me, a tsunami threatening to drown me. (*Hang in there Violet do you remember asking me if you could heal yourself concentrate.*) He's showing me his memories, too, of how I looked with my grey-white skin and my breathing so quick and shallow and the blood soaking into his lap, running over his thighs and all over the floor.

Stop, I say. *Please, stop.*

Johnno blocks the images, holds me tighter. *If you'd died, then Ethan would have died, too.*

I don't answer, at least not with words. I don't have to. I can't keep blaming Johnno for something that was out of his control.

(*Ethan her heart can't keep up with both of you, she's lost so much blood.*)

I curl into a ball. Johnno curves around me, his lips on my ear.

If you'd died, he think-says, *I would have died too. I would have had no reason to carry on.*

No, I say. *No, you can't ever think like that.* Because it could still happen. It could. I grip his wrists. *Please, can we stop talking about it now? It's over. What's done is done.*

What's done is done, Johnno repeats.

I inhale. 'Tell me about you,' I say, aloud now, because it's all so intense, almost too intense for think-speak. 'Tell me about your parents.'

Johnno laughs, a short, harsh sound. 'What do you want to know, Vi? They were drug addicts. It's like that nursery rhyme about the girl with the curl in the middle of her forehead. When they were nice, they were very very nice, and when they were trashed they were horrid.'

I turn, stroking the inside of his forearms, where the small, circular scars form depressions in his skin. 'Did they do this to your sister, too?'

'Uh-huh.'

'And this, how did you get that?' I touch the scar beneath his mouth.

'From my father's ring,' he says. 'When he hit me one day. I flushed the ring down the toilet a few days later after I found it on the floor next to his bed. He never knew.'

'How old were you when they died in the accident?'

'Eight.' His tone is inflectionless, almost robotic. 'We were placed in foster care after that.'

'What was that like?'

'Better than home. Not always by much, though.' He takes a deep breath. 'That's why I joined the army, so I'd never have to rely on anyone else again. No student loans, no landlords chasing me for rent. All expenses paid, including a uni degree. Not that I'll ever finish that, I guess.'

Remembering how I used to tease him *(Me: Big words for an army guy; Johnno: Now who's being patronising?)*, I feel bad. Not just bad—like a spoilt rich kid. I guess I was, before I got sick.

'I wish that hadn't happened to you.' I trace his brow ridges, the line of his nose, his lips.

'I'm glad *you* happened,' he replies, before kissing me until all the hurtful, spiky memories are pushed away, deep into our virally optimised brains.

We should go to sleep. We should, but we don't, not until we've explored every inch of the other's body, in both our human and wolf forms.

Our boundaries are slipping and blurring, and it's the most exhilarating and terrifying feeling I—we—have ever had.

TWENTY-ONE

JOHNNO

The next day, I drive while Violet navigates. If only we could take the main road. We'd be at the Foundation in ten hours, maybe less. But if we take the main road, it will only be a matter of time before we're arrested.

The good news is that the waterhole, when we return, is deserted. No SUV, no Conrad and Kelly. The sun is rapidly sinking below the horizon.

'We shouldn't stay here too long,' I say after we climb out of the camper van.

'A ten-minute swim,' Violet says, already shedding her clothes. 'I can't detect anyone nearby, can you?'

'No.' I hope my newfound ability to bypass the blocking devices isn't going to fail me now. What if they've developed new ones?

Violet tugs on my elbow. 'Are you going to stand there worrying, or are you going to come for a swim?'

'I can't argue with you when you're naked,' I mutter.

'I'll remember that.' Laughing, she twirls away from me and runs into the water. I follow her in, and we dive and twist through the water, slippery-slick.

We should try travelling as dolphins, Violet think-says. *Or seals.*

Yes, I say. *We should. But not right now.* I hook an arm around her neck and kiss her and we go under, briefly, before bobbing up again.

'Time to go?' she says, flicking her hair out of her eyes.

'Unfortunately.' The sun is melting into the horizon. Above us, a hawk arcs, its cries echoing around the waterhole. 'I don't trust this place.'

Violet clambers over the rocks and up onto the bank. 'Nowhere is safe.'

'Nowhere,' I agree, stooping to pick up a couple of rocks of just the right size and weight for my slingshot.

It pays to be prepared.

*

That night, we park well away from the dirt road, at least five kilometres in.

'We're about six hundred k's from the Foundation,' Violet says over a dinner of vegetarian pasta. 'So ... we should be around four hundred k's away by midday tomorrow.'

'That's close enough for me.' An easy distance for a pair of birds, but not so close that we risk exposing ourselves. I push my plate aside and take my slingshot out of my pocket. 'Ever used one of these?'

'No.'

'Time for a lesson, then.'

She frowns. 'It's dark.'

'You never know when you might need it. We can take this out.' I tap the LED lantern on the table between us. 'I'll make another slingshot tomorrow.'

Violet takes the slingshot from me. 'Where'd you get the elastic from?'

'Bought it in Berlin. And I found the stick beneath that gum tree near the fence at the Foundation. Remember that tree?'

She looks up, her eyes flickering, as if remembering something. 'Yeah,' she says, before closing me off, but not before I get an image-sensation of her kissing someone who's not me.

Is it wrong to feel jealous of a dead person?

'OK, let's go.' Violet picks up the lantern and moves outside. After taking the rocks off the windowsill, I follow her out.

'So,' I say, standing behind her, 'you want to hold it like this.' I show her how to hold the slingshot with her right hand at shoulder height, then how to take aim at her target, which is currently a can I've balanced on a tree branch. 'Aim slightly above the can,' I say. 'Keep both eyes open.'

'I can't see my target,' she complains.

'I'll take the torch over,' I say, unable to resist kissing the base of her neck first, just under her ponytail.

'How am I meant to focus when you're doing that?' She turns. 'How about you go first?'

I shrug. 'Sure.' I take the slingshot and rock off her, and take a step to the right. 'Here goes.'

'Whoa,' Violet says after the can clatters to the ground. 'That looked pretty deadly.'

'That's the idea.' I squeeze out the dent before placing it on the branch again. 'Your turn.' After placing the torch on a branch above the target, I move well away.

'Urrgh,' Violet says after a few minutes. 'I think I'm too uncoordinated for this.'

'Practice makes perfect.' I'm sitting on the top step of the camper van, having just dodged the last stone, which shot off at a forty-five-degree angle. 'Try flicking your wrist forward slightly after releasing the band. That's better.'

'In cricket, they'd call that a wide.' She moves towards me and presses the slingshot into my palm. 'I'm done.'

'OK,' I say when she wriggles onto my lap. 'I hear you.' Because I can't resist her when she's kissing me like that, when she's touching me like *that*.

Violet pushes me until I'm lying on the camper van floor, straddles my belly. 'Let's go travelling tonight.' She leans forward to kiss me again.

'Sure,' I say, my breath short. 'Where do you want to go?'

She nips my lower lip with her teeth before peeling her t-shirt off. 'Back to the waterhole.'

'Back to the waterhole,' I echo. *Yes. Yes, why not? As wolves.*

We can sleep beneath the stars. Violet unzips my trousers. *We can hunt.*

No slingshots required, I think-reply, and she laughs into my mouth. We start to move together, slowly at first and then faster, faster, our hearts pounding in synchrony.

'I love you, White Wolf,' I whisper, once we're lying tangled on the floor, our pulses still exactly matched.

'I love you too,' she whispers back. 'Are you ready, Black Wolf?'

'I'm ready.'

We lock the door, move to the bed. Lie between the sheets and cast our dream-flow out, ripples on a pond. We travel as an eagle and a kestrel, morphing into our wolf forms once we reach the waterhole.

I smell wallaby, I think-say.

Violet turns, a front paw raised, her eyes shining through the darkness. *Me too.*

I sit on my haunches, waiting. *Do you think it can smell us?*

I can smell you, she says, lying on her belly, her front paws stretched out in front of her. Behind her, the water shivers in the wind. Above us, a three-quarter moon. In the bushes, a rustle.

I dart forward, and a kangaroo bounds to the right. So does Violet. In seconds, I'm there too, sinking my teeth into the gamey flesh. Blood arcs into my mouth my eyes my nostrils. We drink. We eat. We sleep.

Practice makes perfect.

*

It's one pm the following day when a pair of eagles sets off from a camper van in the middle of nowhere. Inside the van, two bodies lie intertwined, their hearts beating half-time, thirty per minute, their chests barely rising and falling. Hundreds of metres below, I spot our fellow animals: wallabies and kangaroos and camels.

And *there* is the spiral structure I hate so much. I hear the hum of the electric fence. I see the guards patrolling the perimeter, their guns slung over their shoulders.

Maybe we should have come as wolves, Violet think-says, as we alight on the roof.

No, I reply. *Those guys would shoot us without even hesitating.*

What happens if someone shoots a figment of my imagination? I don't want to find out, not when I can feel the roof tiles beneath my feet, when I can feel the cool breeze stirring my feathers. Instead, I turn my focus to the hum of a thought-stream other than Violet's. Not just one thought-stream, but one-two-three; Harper and Callum and Audrey.

Audrey didn't get away, then, Violet think-says.

Did you think she would? I focus on Audrey. From the pattern of her brain waves, I can tell she's asleep. No, not just asleep, deeper than that.

Violet think-says, *They're not asleep, they're comatose.*

Harper and Callum too. I strut across the roof, my talons clicking on the tiles.

And listen to this.

I open my dream-flow as wide as I can, so Violet can sense it too: Greta, her thought-stream a triumphant torrent.

No, Violet think-says. *No, no, no.*

I told you, I reply, while wishing I didn't have to be right.

Because two words keep bobbing to the surface, like foam on a beer in hell.

The first word is *deconstruction.*

The second word is *complete.*

TWENTY-TWO

VIOLET

It is late, almost midnight. Johnno and I are sitting in the camper van, trying to make a plan with very little information, no tools, and no weapons apart from two slingshots, a pocket knife and a cylinder of Javier virus.

I think the latter is probably dead. The digital temperature read-out on the side has disappeared, the screen blank. I don't know what kind of conditions Javier needs to survive, but I'm guessing the scientists were keeping it warm for a reason.

'Deconstruction complete,' Johnno says, for about the twentieth time since we flew back. 'What's the point in rescuing them now?'

'We don't know that's actually happened yet. What if Greta was just having a fantasy?'

'She seemed pretty happy for something that was just a fantasy.' Johnno levers the blade out of the pocket knife, tests it on the tip of his finger. 'We need to try and get a message to your old man, see if he can help us.'

I can almost taste the adrenaline flooding through me at the mention of my father.

'We can't,' I say. 'They'll know. They'll track us down, take us away to be deconstructed too.'

Johnno sighs, rubs the back of my neck. 'They really messed with you, didn't they?'

I hunch into myself. Maybe my fear is irrational, and maybe it isn't. How am I supposed to know?

Little Albert became very distressed, reacting by crying and crawling away.

'Maybe I should try and contact him,' Johnno says.

Trying to control my trembling limbs, I say, 'But how? We've got no way of communicating with anyone, in case you hadn't noticed.'

'We could return to the main road. Flag down a passing car and ask to borrow a PA so we can call for help.'

'What if someone recognises us?'

'What if they don't?' He leaps up. 'We should ditch the camper van, hitch into Alice and make some phone calls.'

'Are you crazy?'

'No, Violet,' he flares. 'I'm desperate. Just like you.' He flings open the door and I hear a low moan, followed by retching.

They messed you up too, I think-say, once the retching stops. *Didn't they?*

I don't remember. Do you?

I'm not leaving this van, I think-say. *And I'm not leaving the others in the Foundation either. OK?*

Johnno doesn't reply. It's several minutes before he comes in from outside, several more minutes before he crawls into bed and turns his back to me.

It's not our first argument. I've got a feeling it won't be our last.

*

We may not be talking to each other, but our dreams mingle anyway, thought-fragments drifting through our merged minds.

Maybe it was some sort of mirage. I mean, they were huge.

Eternity. Asclepius. Spiral. Tattoos.

After my sister died. I guess I was trying to ... forget. Reinvent myself.

Phoenix rising.

Eternity. Ethan and Rawiri's game.

The woman who stabbed you. I never heard her, never got her thought-stream. And after I shot her I saw why.

Conditioning. Intensification. Bavaria. The prototype.

Mila. How did you get here?

Johnny Johnno Phoenix Wolf can you hear me where are you?

I played a game. I played a game, and I won.

I sit upright, my brain whirring. Mila. The woman who stabbed me. A game called Eternity.

Johnno stirs, touches my hip. 'Violet?'

Mila. The woman who stabbed me. Eternity.

'The woman who stabbed me,' I say. 'What did she look like?'

'I don't know.' Johnno's voice is blurry, half-asleep. 'It was dark. Why?'

I shake my head, prod the rubbery outline of the veins on my arms. No scars, not like on Mila's arms, despite all my time in hospital.

'Track marks,' Johnno says, grasping my think-image and turning it around, as though holding it up to the light.

'But...'

He sits up too. 'Trust me, I know track marks when I see them.'

'So, she was a user?'

'A user,' he repeats. Like me, he's trying to put the pieces of the puzzle together, but they don't. Quite. Fit.

'She said she was really sick. And that after she recovered, she played Eternity—Ethan and Rawiri's game—and the next thing she knew, she was a captive, just like us.'

Johnno examines my memory, front and back, side to side. 'You know what I think? I think she was a user, and the Foundation staff offered her money in exchange for an experiment, like those drug trials university students volunteer for.'

'But why would she lie to us?'

'Maybe her job hadn't finished yet.' He pulls me down beside him. 'Maybe she was sent to the Foundation to infiltrate VORTEX, to flush out any traitors.'

'She didn't get very far.'

'Not with us. But Harper...'

Fresh guilt assails me. 'We should have taken her with us.'

'She didn't want to come. You asked her, didn't you?'

'Yeah, but I don't think she really understood how much danger she was in. Or didn't want to.'

Johnno rolls his lower lip between his teeth. 'Or she couldn't bear to leave Bruno.'

'I don't know, I don't think that lasted long.' I frown, recalling the words that came to us when we were dreaming last night. 'There was something Ethan wrote in his notebook before he...' I hesitate, unable to say the word *died.* 'Well, anyway, he'd written *Bavaria,* and *prototype.* And before that, *conditioning* and *intensification.*'

'And Bavaria is in Germany,' Johnno says slowly. 'Do you think Mila is the prototype, the first one of us?'

'Maybe,' I say. 'But I'm not sure how that helps us. She was the only one I didn't hear this afternoon.'

'Who, Mila?'

'Yeah.' I chew a fingernail. 'What if *she's* the one who has been deconstructed? What if the fact that we could hear the others means they're still intact, still able to be rescued? Like you?'

Johnno is silent for a moment. Then he says, 'No matter how hard we try to get away, they're just going to keep reeling us back in, aren't they?'

'We need to help the others,' I say. 'Look how much we've been able to do together. Imagine what five of us could do.' I wind my arms around his waist, feeling his warmth seep into me. 'You overcame Greta's blocking device, right?'

'Right.'

'So you could do it again.'

'Yeah, and?'

'So, what if we mess with *her* mind?'

His breath stirs into my nostrils. 'I don't know if that's possible.'

'None of this is possible.' I kiss him. 'Together, we are infinite. Remember?'

'I remember,' he murmurs. Reluctant. Resigned.

I kiss him again. 'When do you want to go?'

'Never.' He turns me until I'm lying beneath him, licks the base of my throat.

'Johnno,' I whisper, and then I don't say anything else, because he's moving his lips lower, lower, lower, and my thought-stream is dissolving, kaleidoscope colours.

I am a bird. I am a wolf. I am a girl-boy. I am the wind whistling around the camper van. I am the bottomless depths of the waterhole. I am endless and infinite. I am a promise, circular and unbroken.

I am Violet Black, and I am going to win this game if it kills me.

TWENTY-THREE

JOHNNO

When I wake the following morning, it's with an echo resonating inside my skull, low and eerie, like a whale song.

Violet is up already. She's sitting on the top camper van step, brushing her hair. I wander off to pee on a nearby shrub, then return to wash my hands with alcohol gel.

'I don't know why you don't use the loo,' Violet says, when I sit beside her.

'Call it getting back to my roots. Speaking of which, I can see yours.' I stroke the dark regrowth close to her ears.

'It's going to look gross once it's half black, half blonde.'

'Like trailer trash, yeah,' I agree, and she punches me.

'Ow, that hurt.'

'Liar. Anyway, I'd be quite happy to be trailer trash right now, wouldn't you?'

'If it's with you, sure.' I kiss her earlobe. 'With six kids under the age of five,' I tease, then feel super-awkward, because what if she thinks I seriously want that? I mean, not to say I don't one day, but...

Violet smiles. 'I knew you were kidding.' She prods her biceps. 'As long as the injection is working, that is.'

'Melody said it would stop your period, didn't she?'

'Yeah, although she said it might take a few months. Fingers crossed for this month.' She stands up, stretching. 'Are you hungry?'

I lean against the door frame, one foot propped up on the other side. 'Definitely not. Think I ate enough for the next twenty-four hours at least.'

'Good. We need to make sure we drink lots when we're out to it.' Violet squeezes a stripe of toothpaste onto one of the spare toothbrushes we'd found in the bathroom. 'I know wolves are carnivores and all, but do you think we'll get scurvy if we stop eating fruit and vegetables?'

'I don't know what the rules are. Pity it's not the kind of thing you can look up on your PA.' I stand up and drink out of the water bottle on the table, grimacing at the lukewarm temperature. 'I'm going for a run, are you keen?'

Violet gives me one of her *are-you-kidding* looks, and I give her a *no-I'm-not-crazy* look in return.

'Our muscles are going to waste away if we carry on lying around in bed all day and night. Come on, before it gets too hot. What do you say?' And, when her expression doesn't change one bit, 'OK, I'll take that as a no.' I pull on a pair of Conrad's shorts, which are a little tight but will have to do, and leave my chest bare. 'I'll see you in about twenty minutes, OK?' I should be able to knock off five k in that time, easy.

'Sure. Actually, wait.' Violet retrieves the metallic Javier cylinder from a drawer beneath the bed and hands it to me. 'I baked this in the sun all afternoon yesterday. Can you bury it while you're out?' When I hesitate, she says, 'No one will ever find it. And if they do, it won't matter, because it's dead. Right?'

'Right.' I slip the cylinder into my pocket. 'See you soon.'

'Don't get lost,' she calls after me. 'You can come rescue me if I do.'

*

The heat seems more intense away from the camper van, the sun closer. The shoes I was wearing when we escaped the Foundation are more suited to skateboarding than running, but it's refreshing to be pounding the earth again, to let my mind drift for the first time in over a week. We've been fugitives for seven days, seven long days. As uncertain as I feel about everything right now, I'm starting to feel as if I'm getting my old self back.

But who was the old me, anyway? I won't be that person ever again. Phoenix is gone, dead and buried. Still, I'm starting to regain some control over my life, some direction ... I think.

As I run, I take note of the land-marks—termite mounds, a rock shaped like a hedgehog, a dead gum with three branches. Violet will kill me if I get lost. And if she doesn't, then the desert sure will.

Sweat is running into my eyes already. I swipe an arm across my forehead. I'll have to wash when I return to the camper van or I'm going to stink. Should have thought of that. We need to conserve our water, we probably only have enough to last a few more days.

Remembering the cylinder in my pocket, I halt and crouch to dig a shallow hole with my hands. After dropping the evil object into the hole, I cover it over with sand, pack it down hard, then put a rock on top for good measure. Violet's right. The chance of anyone finding it is low, and even if they do, the broth inside will be inactive, dead.

Still, I'm glad not to be carrying one of the deadliest viruses known to humankind in my pocket anymore. I've had more than enough of those.

I straighten up and take off again, my breath quickening. I'm rounding a shoulder-high termite mound, thinking I must have done two k already, when something explodes behind my eyes, a red-black

(*Johnno come quick there are*)

It's *her* heart I feel pounding behind my ribs, *her* ragged breath in my lungs.

I think-shout, *Violet, what's wrong,* because it has to be her, no one else would call me Johnno, but her thoughts are so scrambled, her colours so intense, it's hard to make out what she's trying to

(*Men two men and I think they're going to—you need to come as Black Wolf Black Wolf Black Wolf*)

I start to sprint. I start to sprint, and as I do, I throw my dream-flow towards her and I've never done this before, I don't even know if it's possible but there's no time to question her. (*They're holding me down and I*)

Am running on all fours, a howl ripping out of my throat, running so fast I could almost be flying.

I'm coming, I send to her. *Tell them if they hurt you, they're dead. Tell them now.*

Violet screams.

TWENTY-FOUR

VIOLET

After Johnno leaves for his run, I realise it's the first time I've been alone in nearly a week. I make the bed, which is probably stupid considering we're going to be lying on it for most of the day while we travel, then check on our supplies. Forty litres of water, counting what's in the shower reservoir, which we've been careful not to use, as tempting as it is. That's probably enough for two weeks if we're careful. A few tins of food, dried pasta, one more box of crackers. I'm less worried about food, and know we can do without water, too, if we really have to. As long as we can fly, we can source whatever we need to keep us alive.

I wander outside, thinking again about Mila and the woman who stabbed me in Berlin. There's a connection there, I'm sure of it, but I have yet to figure out what that is.

That's when I hear it.

An engine, music, tyres whirring over dirt-sand. Before I can blink, it's there, a silver Jeep. It's slowing, the passengers in the front looking straight at me: two ruddy-faced men. One is wearing a red cap that says, *Who Shot Donald Trump?* The other guy has a full-faced tattoo that extends all over his bald head, like a rash.

I duck inside, closing the door behind me. *Go away, go away.*

I hear doors slamming. I hear voices. I hear a rap on the door.

Should I ignore them? Maybe they want help, directions or something.

My gut knows this isn't true. My gut has contracted into a tiny, hard ball. If I were in wolf form, every hair on my body would be standing on end.

'Little pig, little pig, let me come in,' one of them calls out, followed by a rasping duet of laughter.

J—I go to think-say, just as the door flies open.

'Oh, hello.' It's the man with the *Who Shot Donald Trump?* cap. 'Sorry to intrude. We weren't sure if anyone was here.' He peers over my shoulder, no doubt taking in the fact that I'm alone.

Very, very alone.

My nostrils flare. I smell cigarette smoke and something sickly sour—alcohol? It's barely eight am. 'What do you want?' Trying to remember where the pocket knife is, I realise it's on the windowsill above the bed. I inch backwards.

Red Cap ascends another step, hitching his jeans up. 'Well.' He scratches his chin. 'We were having some trouble with our engine.'

'I don't,' I say, before realising he hasn't yet verbalised what's in his syrupy thought-stream, which was *We were wondering if you had PA reception.* Because I've got a fix on him now, and what I'm streaming is so scary I can barely concentrate on trying to send a message to Johnno.

Johnno come quick there are

And suddenly the bald man is in here, too, how did he move so fast, and Johnno think-shouts *Violet what's wrong* his panic spiking into me and I think-yell *Men two men and I think they're going to—you need to come as Black Wolf Black Wolf Black Wolf.*

And Red Cap hits me hard across the face and I go down on my knees and then he's holding me down and the bald man is yanking at my underwear and I'm trying to wriggle but I can't and I call out again

They're holding me down and I

Can't hear what Johnno is saying anymore and I scream and someone hits me again and I bite him and then I hear a snarl and I don't know if it's coming from inside me or outside

And someone is forcing my legs apart and I gulp and snarl and crouch and *leap*

Just as a dark shadow flies over me and I hear a scream-yell-gurgle and one of the men yells, *Oh my God,* and the other one just gurgles and the Black Wolf has him by the throat and I think-say, *No, Johnno, no, don't kill him,* even as I sink my teeth into Red Cap's thigh and Bald Man is crawling and falling out of the door and Red Cap is running and blood is streaming down his leg and down my chin and I'm staring at the girl on the floor, her eyes wide open, her chest barely moving, and what if she's dead what if I'm dead and *snap.*

I'm lying on my side, shivering and retching, and Black Wolf is licking my face and Johnno is think-saying, *Oh my God, Violet, oh my God, I shouldn't have left you, I should have torn his throat out.*

An engine rumbles, tyres skidding-squealing, and they're gone, their thought-streams scrambled together *What the fuck were those how did you miss those dogs I swear they weren't there when we arrived I told you we shouldn't have* and then they're gone.

Gone.

I reach for Black Wolf, my arms around his neck, his blood-breath in my nostrils.

'No,' I say, trembling all over. 'No, it's not your fault, those men were evil, but Johnno, where's your body? Where's your body?'

It's safe, he think-says, although I don't know how he can know that. *But I'm not leaving you. I need you to come with me.*

I can't. I'm still shaking. *I can't.*

Yes, Violet, you have to, please. I shouldn't have left you in the first place. It's not far, I promise.

That's how I end up walking through the desert with a Black Wolf at my side, until we come across a body sprawled in the dirt, the flies already settling on his eyes-mouth-ears, but when I touch my fingers to his neck I feel the pulse bounding beneath his skin.

When the Black Wolf goes I feel the sickening *snap* within me, too, as if I've broken a rib. Johnno inhales and coughs and I fall down beside him, and we hold each other as an eagle circles overhead, crying, *Blood, blood, blood.*

TWENTY-FIVE

JOHNNO

In the camper van, I prepare a bowl of warm soapy water to wash the blood off Violet's face. At first I think it's all from her nose, until I see the split in her lower lip. It's all I can do to push down my fury, bury it deep so I don't upset Violet even more than she is already.

'I don't think anything's broken.' I prod the slender line of her nose, the high arches of her cheekbones. 'Did he—' I can hardly bear to ask.

'No.' Violet winces, whether from my cleaning efforts or the memory of what I saw, I'm not sure. The tattooed guy's trousers were down, Violet's underwear, too. Jesus, I should have torn his throat out when I had the—

'Stop,' she whispers.

'Sorry.' I shut down the image. 'I just can't stop thinking about what would have happened if I'd walked in a second later.'

'You didn't walk, you *pounced*.'

'You were doing a pretty good job of defending yourself when I arrived,' I say, remembering the White Wolf, its teeth sinking into the fish-white flesh of the tattooed guy's thigh.

Violet shoves me away, her colours red-orange-purple. 'I was not and you know it. If you hadn't turned up, the guy with the red cap would have got his gun out of the Jeep.'

'He had a *gun?*'

'I heard him thinking about it when he was holding me down.' She shuffles away and shrinks into the corner of the couch. 'If you hadn't turned up, he would have shot the White Wolf to get him off the tattooed guy. What do you think happens if someone tries to kill our dream-flow selves?'

I'm not sure, but I'm guessing it wouldn't be good. For the hundredth time, I wish I hadn't left her. What was I thinking? Violet is crying again. She feels dirty and violated and helpless, and I don't have a clue how to make it better.

'Look,' I say once she has calmed down, sort of, 'let's have a shower.' I wait for her to tell me it's a waste of water. She merely lowers her head, defeated, which only fuels my worry.

There's shampoo and conditioner in the shower cubicle, body wash too. After checking the water temperature, I turn the tap off again and go to get Violet.

She's not there. My heart leaping, I hurtle out of the door, just in time to dodge a rock travelling at an almost certainly fatal speed.

'Jesus! Are you trying to kill me?' If it weren't for my virally optimised reflexes, I'm pretty sure I'd be lying in a heap on the ground right now.

Violet stares at me, the slingshot dangling from her fingers, her mouth rounded into an O. 'I misfired,' she says in a small voice.

Keeping my expression carefully blank, I pick up the stone from where it's lying next to the front tyre of the van and press it into her palm. 'Here.' I turn her around, so she's facing the tree. 'See that knot there? That's the tattooed guy's—' The word *face* has barely left my mouth when the stone hits the tree, sending bark flying.

'Practice makes perfect,' Violet says, leaning into me.

'Perfect,' I agree, before leading her up the steps and into the shower. There's hardly any pressure and the water is lukewarm, but when I see the tension begin to leave Violet's body, when I see the blood running into the drain, I know it is the right thing to do.

'Vi,' I say, once we're lying on the bed, our bare skin glistening, 'you know what we have to do now, don't you?'

'We have to rescue the others,' Violet says, as I knew she would.

'No. I mean, yes, we need to do that but not right now.' I sit up, peering out of the window. 'We need to get the hell out of here,' I say, as she knows I will. 'If those pricks have a gun, then they might return, try and put bullets in us.' Us, and the creatures they thought were dogs.

Violet rolls onto her stomach, burying her face in the pillow. I want to hold her. I want to kiss her all over. I want to be somewhere, anywhere, other than in this soul-destroying desert.

I get up and pluck my trousers off the floor, where I left them last night. 'I'll drive.'

*

We've been driving for two hours when charcoal clouds start pushing across the sky. Within minutes, the light is dusk-grey rather than noon-bright.

'Going to rain soon,' I say, like it isn't half obvious. When I wind down the window, the air feels electric, heavy with the promise of a storm.

'We should collect rainwater.' Violet is sitting next to me, her still-damp hair flowing over her shoulders. When I inhale, I can smell the coconut scent of her shampoo. It's making my chest ache to look at her, with her swollen lip and the bruise blooming across her right cheekbone.

Should have torn his throat out, I think, for what must be the hundredth time. *Or, at the very least, an ear.*

Violet touches my thigh. I shut down the images. 'Good idea,' I say. 'We'll park up, put the cannisters outside.' I'm not too averse to the thought of having a rest stop. Every kilometre is taking us closer to the place I thought I'd escaped. But until we've sorted out this mess, there's nowhere else we can go—not with a stolen camper van and no money, not with our photographs splashed across the media. Armed and dangerous, yeah, right.

Actually, yeah.

Raindrops are splatting against the windscreen now, huge mothers that a whole community of microbes could take refuge in. Seconds later, there's a flash, followed by a deep rumble.

'Whoa, I've never seen forked lightning before.' I don't know why I'm so excited. Maybe it's the electricity sparking through the air, or that I haven't seen a good storm in months. The next thing, rain is lashing the van, so thick it's impossible to see.

Violet jumps out as soon as I bring the van to a halt. I follow her, the rain instantly soaking me to the skin. She's unpacking all available containers and laying them on the ground to collect rain. Stepping back, she spreads her arms and starts to spin, her hair flying out behind her. I copy her, feeling like a little kid. Tip my head back. Open my mouth. Let out a whoop.

And then I turn and see that Violet has stopped moving, that she is standing with her hands over her face, her shoulders shaking. Guilt spiking me again, I help her up the stairs to the camper van, where I undress her, just as I did a few hours ago, and towel her dry.

'You're OK,' I keep telling her. 'You're OK. We're going to be OK.' I take her rain-cool body into my arms. 'I won't leave you alone again. Let's take a nap, wait for the storm to pass.' I'm exhausted. Violet must be, too, but she's blocking me—why?

She shivers, pushes her forehead into mine. 'OK.' She takes a deep breath. 'OK, let's do that.' And still, her thought-stream is blurry, like the world outside the window.

I join her beneath the covers, holding her close. She's trembling, her thought-stream all over the place. I don't blame her. I wish I could take the memory of the morning's events away; wish I could lock it away in the place where I keep all the bad things that happened to me when I was a kid.

(*you're too old to be wetting the*)

(*I'm only doing this for your own*)

(*your own*)

(*it burns it burns it burns*)

Instead, I stroke her brow, as one of my foster mothers used to do when I woke with a nightmare, and sing, low and soft, in her ear. *Hush little baby don't say a word.* But I don't say anything about buying her a mockingbird. *No,* I tell her, *soon enough you'll be flying, free as a bird.*

The rain eases, until it's no more than a patter on the window and a gradual plopping into our row of containers outside. Violet's thought-stream slows, too, and begins to merge with mine. We soar, free, if only in our dreams.

I wake to find a damp space in the bed next to me, every one of my hair follicles prickling. *Something is ... something is...*

'Violet?' I sit bolt upright so fast a muscle twinges in my neck. Wincing, I massage it and call her name again. Am I always going to be this freaked out every time Violet disappears from my sight? I can sense her now, though, can hear the toilet flushing.

She appears from behind the sliding door and sits on the end of the bed, her hair shielding her face. She's wearing an oversized t-shirt, one of Conrad's. *Something is...*

'Are you OK?' I venture.

She inhales. 'Johnno, I need you to ... take care of me.'

'What do you mean? Of course I'll take care of you.' Is she getting at me for leaving her this morning? Black guilt floods through me yet again.

'No. I mean for the next few hours. Or as long as it takes.' That's when I figure out what's wrong, at least partly. Violet is blocking me, her thought-stream barely discernible, but when she lifts her eyes to mine, I get the full blast of it.

Oh. No. 'What have you done?' Her pupils are huge, her skin flushed. I thought I'd thrown the L25 away, but I remember now. She took it off me, and I yelled at her, but I never asked for it back. I never did.

No, no, no.

Violet's speech is sluggish, as if she's struggling to form words. 'I know for our previous bodies this would be the path to self-destruction, but I'm not Violet Black any more, I'm White Wolf, virally optimised, soon to be L25 optimised. I thought I might need it one day. Because you have to admit, since you took it—' She plucks at the air, looks wide-eyed at me. 'Did you see that?' At nothing: she's plucking at nothing.

I know, because I've seen my parents do it so many times before.

I could yell at her. I could tell her she's out of her mind, but of course that's exactly what she wants—to leave the boundaries of her brain.

Violet starts to shake. 'No,' she moans, shrinking against the window.

I steel myself. If my memories of L25 are correct, as both an external observer and an unwilling participant, we're in for a long, agonising night.

TWENTY-SIX

VIOLET

I'm lying on a bed, the mattress bobbing up and down, like I'm in the middle of an ocean. I feel sick and dizzy and the world won't stop moving. When I open my eyes, I see that's exactly where I am, floating in a soft-pink sea—the same colour as the sky above. *Lie still,* someone says. *Lie still,* just as the Bald Man had, except he'd added, *And it won't hurt so bad.* I strike out and show my teeth, just as I did when the Bald Man tried to

(*rape me, he was trying to rape me*)

The ocean disappears and I am White Wolf, running across a blood-red desert. My paws bleed into the soil. I am so thirsty my tongue is sticking to the roof of my mouth. Someone is calling me and I twist, looking for my mate, but he is nowhere to be seen. I bare my throat to the death rays of the sun and howl.

Vi, the voice says. *Vi, please, you need to drink.* I'm writhing on the mattress and the ocean has turned to blood, too, with disembodied limbs and heads floating past. And oh no, there is Ethan, his pupils fixed on mine, his lips moving. *You cheated on me,* he says. *You cheated on me, and then you left me to die.*

No. Acid tears carve a path down my cheeks. *No, it's not true. He kissed me in Berlin, but it didn't mean anything, not then.*

Liar, the Ethan-head says. *Liar, you're such a liar.* More body parts float past—a pink pair of lungs, inflating and deflating, and a huge heart with drainpipe-sized blood vessels arching out of the top. Is it my heart, ripped from my body? The heart is beating so loudly I can feel my bones vibrating. I lunge for it, intending to give it to Ethan, and topple off the mattress and into—

A pair of arms. The voice says, *Vi, what have you done, please, just calm down, you're safe, I won't let anyone hurt you.*

The ocean evaporates and I am in the desert again, running for my life. Heat sears my eyeballs. The sand burns the soles of my feet. My head aches. I am human and naked and all around me are Bald Men with tattoos and men in red caps, all yellow teeth and fetid breath, and they are coming for me, they are going to hurt me hurt me hurt me.

And the voice is in my ear, it won't let me go, and it's saying, *Hush little baby don't say a word, soon you'll be flying, free as a bird.*

And I *leap,* and I am soaring high above all the laughing heads with their tattoos and red caps and *there* he is, my wedge-tailed eagle, and we dip and whirl, whirl and dip, until *snap,* I'm curled in a ball on the floor and the heat is pressing all around me.

Violet, don't, the voice says, when I try to escape my thirsty-hungry-throbbing body. *You have to stop doing that. You might not be able to find your way back next time.*

But, of course, I'm not listening because I've escaped the nightmare. I've escaped the nightmare, and now I need to escape myself. I fling my dream-flow out, out, out ... and, very faintly, hear someone say, *Oh shit.*

TWENTY-SEVEN

JOHNNO

It is early morning and Violet's thought-stream has finally reassembled. Not into a wakeful state, though. She's asleep, exhausted from almost eighteen hours of tripping. Through it all, I've held her and stopped her running from the camper van countless times. I've lost track of the number of times she's travelled out of her body, over and over until I wasn't sure she'd return. I don't remember doing that when I was given L25. But then, that was probably the last thing she was thinking about before the drug took hold, the ability she was determined to master.

The last time was the scariest. The scariest because, for the first time, I wasn't able to track where she was going. Either consciously or subconsciously, she was blocking me, her earthly body corpse-like, her dream-flow a black hole.

Oh shit, I'd said, and Violet had twitched, ever-so-slightly, before settling into the comatose position I knew so well. Her heart going thirty beats a minute, if that, her lungs taking in two breaths a minute, at the most. We were on the floor by then, Violet having fallen off the bed an hour or so before. I'd lain next to her, sending my own dream-flow out, but she was nowhere to be found.

I nearly freaked out then. What if Violet had travelled somewhere beyond the pull of her earthly body? What if she couldn't find her way back? All I could do was wait. So I did. All night.

It's seven am when I sense the jolt of her return. I prop myself up on my elbow, watching Violet's breathing speed up, watching the colour diffuse into her skin. At first her thought-stream is pulsating and phosphorus-bright. It flares, briefly, before settling into the delta rhythm of sleep.

I scoop her into my arms, her head lolling against my shoulder. *Hush, little wolf,* I say, transferring her to the bed. Outside, the sky is blue and endless. We sleep.

TWENTY-EIGHT

VIOLET

To say Johnno isn't too happy with me would be an understatement. We're on the road again, and he's gripping the steering wheel so tightly his knuckles are white. I don't think he's ever been this angry with me.

'You could have killed yourself.' His tone is a low growl. Wolf Black. Black Wolf.

I flip the sun visor down. 'But I didn't. That's why I asked you to take care of me. Thank you.'

'Well, don't ask me to do that ever again, because I won't. We've wasted a whole day.'

I grit my teeth. 'It wasn't a waste.'

'Yeah? What can you do now that you couldn't before?' We jolt over a rut. My head feels as though it's going to split open, but I don't want to admit to my L25 hangover, or whatever you call it when you come off an acid trip.

'I heard ... stuff.' I prod the scab that has formed on the split in my lip.

'They're called auditory hallucinations. Like when you have schizophrenia.'

'There you go again, as patronising as ever.'

Johnno's voice rises. 'No, Violet, I'm being *realistic*. In case you haven't noticed, all we've done for the last few days is drive around in circles.'

Swallowing a scream of frustration, I fling open the passenger door, waiting until Johnno slows before leaping into the dirt. Johnno slams on the brakes and jumps out after me.

'Trying to kill yourself again?'

'No. I'm not.'

'Could have fooled me. I'm not going to keep rescuing you every time you do something stupid.' His thoughts are so loud. *Javier virus. L25.* And then, *But it wasn't her fault she got attacked yesterday, it was all mine.* A stricken expression crosses his face.

I stamp my foot. '*You* rescuing *me?* If it weren't for me, you'd still be at the Foundation being deconstructed. If it weren't for me, we'd keep driving in circles until we're dead or taken prisoner again. Believe me, I'd rather be dead.'

'Yeah?' Johnno points at me. 'Tell me one thing you achieved by taking that stupid drug, just one.'

I swat his finger away, and for a moment I think he's going to swat me back. A split second later, I feel his self-control kick in, his mind closing over like a steel trap.

'Yeah, block me, why don't you?' I say. 'Fine, but why don't you try listening to me for just five minutes?' Clenching his jaw, Johnno leans against the van. Batting away a fly, I say, 'I did have hallucinations, OK? For a while I thought I was going crazy.'

He raises a tattooed eyebrow at me, as if to say *no kidding*. Ignoring him, I carry on. 'But towards the end, I heard a voice. A real voice. Not yours, not any of the VORTEX members. There was someone else.'

I have his attention at last. His steely gaze on mine, he says, 'Like who? Greta? Melody?'

'No.' I hesitate. 'Did you ever hear Ethan talk about a friend called Rawiri?'

'The one who designed Eternity with him?' Johnno wipes his brow. 'The news reports said he'd died, right?'

'Sure, just like they said we died.'

He huffs through his nose. 'Yeah, OK. So what, you talked to Rawiri?'

'I'm not sure. It could have been.' I wait for Johnno to mock me again, but his anger-frustration seems to be receding. 'He said he'd designed a game and he wished he'd never done it, because it killed his friend. But when I tried to quiz him further, he shut me down. I don't think he trusted me.'

'Designed a game and it killed his friend,' Johnno says slowly.

'Who else could it be?'

He shakes his head. I slump next to him, the warm metal of the van seeping through my t-shirt. 'I'm sorry I put you through that,' I say.

'You're not sorry you took the L25, though.'

'No.' I turn to face him. 'There might be others out there, too. If we can get enough minds working together, and harness our collective consciousness, then imagine what we can do.'

He squints at me. 'That's the thing. I can't.'

'What, so you're giving up?'

'No. Look, let's try travelling again, see what we can scope out at the Foundation. But if the others have been deconstructed, or if they're dead, then we need to give up on that. We need to find someone out here who will believe us and help us expose *them* for what they are.'

'I don't know who that someone is,' I say.

'Neither do I. But as you say, maybe there are others like us who have had the sense to evade the Foundation.'

I inhale. 'OK. But first, we need to see what's happening there. When do you want to do it?'

Johnno gives me one of his half-smiles. 'If I didn't know you better, Violet, I'd think you were propositioning me.'

'Later,' I say, and he kisses me, holding me tight until I almost change my mind. Almost, but not quite.

*

We turn the engine on again, set the air con to twenty-two degrees.

'I'm so sick of the inside of this van,' I say, flopping down on the bed.

'Cabin fever.' Johnno stretches out beside me. 'Me, I've got desert fever.' He strokes me behind the ear, as if I'm a cat. 'Or a panther,' he says, obviously picking up that thought. 'You'd make a pretty sexy panther, by the way.'

'Johnno.' I still the motion of his other hand, which is sliding beneath my top. 'Focus.'

He blinks, and for a moment I could swear he's looking at me through wolf eyes, deep brown rather than tattooed grey. I'm trying to remember what his untattooed irises looked like when he says, 'Blue. Just ordinary blue.'

'You're not ordinary.' I trace the Japanese characters above his eyebrow. 'Although I think I'd take ordinary right now.'

'Violet, focus,' he whispers when I nuzzle the side of his neck, although I can tell he'd rather exploit my moment of weakness. He kisses the corner of my mouth, taking care to avoid the split in my lip.

'OK.' I clasp his shoulder. 'Do you think you can repeat what you did yesterday, after I called out for help?'

'I have no idea. Let's give it a go, shall we?'

We lie spooned, Johnno behind me, and close our eyes. I slow my breathing, picturing the hateful spiral curves of the Foundation. Deep within me, I feel Johnno's dream-flow coiling, tighter and tighter. I do the same, concentrating everything I have into a spring of potential energy.

Go, he think-whispers, and we hurl our dream-flow out, as if from a slingshot. There's a blur, an almost sickening *shift,* and then I'm squinting, reassembling, inhaling desert air through my eagle-lungs.

The world floods in. The scent of eucalyptus, the woody feel of the branch around which my talons are curled, red earth, azure sky. And directly in front of us, the alabaster curves of the Foundation.

Johnno's eagle-gaze meets mine. *Success,* he think-says.

Success, I reply, taking in the twin SUVs parked around the rear of the building, a pair of armed guards prowling along the fence line. I can hear the hum of the electric fence, but there's another hum, too.

Audrey? I try. *Harper? Callum?*

At first there is no reply, but gradually the hum intensifies until all of the outside-world sounds are obliterated.

Are you there? Johnno think-asks.

And there's something, so faint I can barely make it out. Thought-fragments. *Sarah ... don't want ... sedation...*

Harper, Johnno and I think-say in unison. There is a surge in the thought-stream, and we hear her more clearly now, although the words and images are coming very slowly.

Where are ... you? Harper think-asks.

We're close, I reply, not wanting to launch into a long explanation when our conversation could be cut off at any time. *Where are you? Are you hurt?*

There is another surge, so strong and desperate it makes me want to cry. *Audrey is gone, Mila too.*

You mean they're dead? Johnno think-asks.

No, they've been ... deconstructed. They're alive but not ... alive. Do you get it?

We get it, Johnno says grimly.

I can hear Callum too, his signal so faint, as though he's a thousand kilometres away. *Sarah,* he says. *It's all ... Sarah.* He's hallucinating, at a guess.

We're going to get you out, I promise, even though I still have no idea how we're going to achieve that. But Callum and Harper are alive, and Harper, at least, is intact—for now. *Who else is there with you?*

Bruno, Harper replies, her thought-stream fading in and out.

Bruno? Yeah, sure, but we're not asking about the staff, Johnno think-says, his tone dismissive.

And Harper replies, *No, Greta is...*

She's almost gone, and I have to strain to catch the words before she slips into a fog of sedation. I could be wrong. I could have misheard. But I'm pretty sure she says, *taking him apart too.* If I didn't know better, I'd think she was crying.

Jesus, Johnno think-says, before launching into the air.

I follow him, riding an updraft until we're so high the Foundation looks like the Lego bricks I used to play with when I was little.

They're punishing Bruno, I think-say. *But why?*

I don't know. Johnno swoops and dives, dives and swoops. We circle the Foundation a few times before alighting on the roof.

Should we return to the camper van? I think-ask.

Not yet, Johnno replies, and I can tell he's listening in again, searching for Greta. I try fixing on her, too, but it's not Greta's consciousness I slot into.

No, it's Bruno's. A memory, from just over two months ago.

TWENTY-NINE

BRUNO

DEBRIEFING
COMMENCED: 10.00AM
PRESENT: DR BRUNO HOFFMAN (JUNIOR DOCTOR), DR NOEL MARLOW (NEUROLOGIST),
DR HANS BAUER (CHIEF OF INTELLIGENCE,
INTERNATIONAL TERRORIST AGENCY, ITA),
DR GRETA ZIEGLER (NEUROPSYCHOLOGIST).

Bauer: I would like to welcome everyone to the meeting. For the record, it is 10.00am Australian Central Standard Time. Doctor Hoffman, could you please state your name for the record.

Hoffman: You already know my name.

Marlow: I'd be careful if I were you. You're in enough trouble as it is.

Hoffman: Bruno Hans Hoffman.

Bauer: Thank you. As you're aware, the first VORTEX mission was successful, overall, but encountered an ... obstacle.

Hoffman: Is that all she was to you? An obstacle? An inconvenience?

Bauer: I don't know, Doctor, I'm waiting for you to tell me.

Hoffman: Why don't you call her by her name? Sarah Schumann, your precious prototype, managed to get herself killed. It's nothing to do with me.

Zeigler: Sarah Schumann seemed to think she had rather a lot to do with you, judging from the messages being exchanged between you two before she went AWOL.

Hoffman: She was crazy. You said that yourself in her psychiatric evaluation. What were the words you used? Borderline personality disorder with psychotic features?

Bauer: Let me remind you of Sarah's last text message to you.

Hoffman: You don't need to remind me.

Bauer: For the record, I'm going to read out Sarah's last text message to you, which we've obtained from her PA. It said—

Hoffman: For God's sake, these are the ravings of a psychotic teenager.

Zeigler: She was twenty-one years old, which is technically no longer a teenager. A university student majoring in physics.

Hoffman: With borderline personality disorder.

Marlow: If you'd please control yourself, Doctor Hoffman, then this will go a whole lot faster for all of us.

Bauer: Thank you. The last text message read: I know you've been cheating on me. It's over, you bastard, for us AND your slutty VORTEX girlfriend. *Tell me, Mr Hoffman, who might Sarah have been referring to?*

Hoffman: Like I said, she was deluded. Perhaps you should add stalker to your list of diagnoses.

Marlow: And then, days later, Sarah tracks down Violet Black and stabs her, almost fatally. So, Doctor Hoffman, we have two questions for you. The first is, did you have sexual relations with Sarah Schumann?

Hoffman: I told you she's a liar.

Bauer: Doctor Marlow, could you please read out the relevant parts of the autopsy report on the deceased, Sarah Schumann?

Marlow: Certainly. The cause of death, as you know, was a gunshot wound to the head, resulting in irreversible brain injury. However, I'd like to refer to the swabs taken from the vagina post-mortem.

Hoffman: For God's sake, what sort of sick pathologist does a vaginal examination on a dead person?

Bauer: Doctor Hoffman, this conversation is being recorded, and the evidence may be used for any future proceedings that may be required to continue or terminate your employment with the Foundation. I'd encourage you to keep quiet unless directly spoken to.

Hoffman: (clenches fists)

Marlow: Due to the nature of the recent text messages, and the fact that this is now a police investigation with a chain of evidence, a full examination was performed. The vaginal swabs show evidence of recent sexual activity, within the past seven to eight days. The DNA matches with 99.5% certainty to a man on the international database—a Bruno Hans Hoffman, whose date of birth matches your own.

Hoffman: This is a set-up.

Zeigler: Come on, Bruno, are you really trying to tell us that you weren't having an affair with Sarah? And Violet Black as well?

Hoffman: Violet Black? I've never laid a finger on her, never.

Bauer: Just tell us the truth, Doctor Hoffman. A liaison is hardly a crime. Lying to us, well, that's a different matter.

Marlow: What's the annual salary of a junior doctor, Doctor Hoffman? I'm sure it's at least half of what we're paying you.

Hoffman: (glares)

Bauer: So, I'll ask you again, Doctor: did you have an affair with the prototype, Sarah Schumann? And secondly, did you also have an affair with Violet Black?

Hoffman: If I answer, can I go back to my job, no more questions asked?

Marlow: Of course, Doctor Hoffman.

Hoffman: OK. Then yes. And no.

Bauer: Thank you, Doctor Hoffman. Do you have anything else to add?

Hoffman: It was only once. A moment of weakness. We'd had too much to drink.

Zeigler: Understandable. You are only human, after all.

Marlow: We will excuse you this once. But please understand, your actions have already had a devastating consequence.

Hoffman: Sarah was bound to self-destruct sooner or later, and you know it.

Bauer: Yes, we understand that. But if Violet Black had died, then this debriefing would have necessitated quite a different course of action. You understand that, don't you?

Hoffman: I assume you're referring to her father.

Bauer: No assumptions or references have been made. Doctor Hoffman, you are free to leave. But if we ever find out that you have succumbed to your weakness again, then the consequences will be very serious. Do you understand?

Hoffman: I understand.

Marlow: Thank you, Doctor. We will have a further debriefing tomorrow, and I expect a full disclosure of all of your activities over the past six months.

Hoffman: (grimaces)

Bauer: Goodbye, Doctor Hoffman.

CONCLUDED: 10.17AM
(RECORDING ENDS)

THIRTY

JOHNNO

'Sarah Schumann,' I say. Violet and I are sitting outside the camper van on fold-out deckchairs, watching the sunset colours diffuse into the sky, salmon-pink and mandarin-orange. 'So *she's* the prototype.'

Violet spears a baked bean. 'The first of her kind. Of *our* kind.'

'That makes it sound as if she were created on purpose,' I say, remembering an earlier conversation with Violet: *What if M-fever was an engineered virus, one that was released on the unsuspecting public?* 'And she was German. What do you think Bauer and the ITA have to do with her?'

'Someone's paying the Foundation a lot of money to create people like us, that's my guess. Maybe it's the ITA.' Violet hesitates. 'What I don't get is the reference to my father. What's he got to do with anything?'

'Your dad's a prominent scientist. If word gets out that you were being kept prisoner and experimented on, I guess heads would roll. Unlike me, where no one gives a damn.' I move into the camper van, where I fill my bottle with water. The last cannister is nearly empty, but that's not what's niggling at me.

Why did Sarah think Bruno was having an affair with Violet? Not that I think he was. In fact, I know he wasn't. There's no way Violet could have manufactured the bile-green revulsion in her thought-stream when she relayed *that* part of the debriefing to me.

But now I'm remembering the time Bruno joined us in the swimming pool, and how he and Harper were still horsing around long after the rest of us got out. I'm remembering all the times I'd glimpsed Bruno and Harper talking—down corridors, while shooting hoops outside, over breakfast—before Berlin, anyway. After Violet and I arrived back from our disastrous mission, Bruno and Harper weren't talking at all.

Violet wanders in and sits on the bed. 'It was Harper, wasn't it? The other girl, I mean.'

'I think so.' I touch her lower lip. There's only a small scab there, even though the injury only happened yesterday morning. 'I wonder how Sarah Schumann found out, though.'

Violet's brow wrinkles. 'Ethan and the others got PAs on Christmas Day. Maybe Harper messaged Bruno, and Sarah saw it. Or Sarah read Bruno's mind and thought I was the other woman.'

I nod. 'Perhaps because Bruno flew with us to Berlin.' The memory of the twisted face of Violet's attacker looms before me. The light was dim, but I'll never forget it. Pale skin. Black beanie. A stud in her nose. A bullet hole in her right temple. The hot scent of blood and flesh. The terrible moaning-gurgling as she died.

Violet pulls me down beside her. 'You did what you had to.'

'She was one of us,' I say, confused feelings tangling in my head.

'But she went crazy.'

'*They* probably drove her crazy.' I inhale, remembering how Greta tried to do the same to me. 'Greta was with Mila this afternoon.'

'What were they doing?'

'I guess you'd call it conditioning.' Recalling Greta's cold, clinical manner is making my skin crawl. 'Mila was lying in one of those pods. She was restrained and had electro-dots on her forehead and chest.'

'To record her brain and heart activity?'

'No, the complete opposite. Greta was showing Mila a series of photographs and giving her electric shocks.'

'Photographs of who?' Violet's mouth drops open. 'Wait, like her parents?'

'And other people too. Family and friends, I'm guessing.'

Violet's thought-stream turns grey. 'Do you think that's what they did to us?'

'I *know* that's what they did to us,' I say. 'No wonder you nearly have a heart attack every time you think about your parents.'

'Greta's a monster,' Violet whispers. 'She's no better than Sarah Schumann. No, worse, because Sarah didn't ask to be like that.'

'No...' So many questions, not enough answers. 'What do we do now, Vi?'

She focuses on me, her thought-stream running clear again. 'The voices. I—we—should try and find them again.'

'How are we going to do that?'

She strokes my thigh. 'You know how our thought-streams sometimes merge when we go to sleep?'

'Yeah...' I'm not feeling sleepy though, not when she's touching me like *that*.

'We should do that before we travel next time.'

'We should do *this* before we travel next time,' I tease, trailing kisses from her nose to her belly. When I reach her thighs, she lets out a noise that sounds like a cross between a sigh and a growl. It's not long before we're slotting together, our bodies and thought-streams merging, each indistinguishable from the other.

(*our breath*)

(*our blood*)

And when Violet whispers, 'Now,' we launch, as one, out and beyond, into—

The unknown.

*

If I am an arrow, then Violet is the archer, setting us on our course. It's a much greater *shift* than before, as though the Earth has tilted on its axis, as though we are traversing the outer arms of a spiral that for so long has had us clasped in its centre.

As we approach our destination, I sense an intense concentration of energy, a glow that comes from both within and without. With a jolt, I realise we've arrived, and I concentrate on taking form. Above me tower trees with massive trunks, sparse rays of sunlight spearing through to the forest floor below. The turf beneath my eagle-claws is soft, mossy, damp. Turning, I look straight into the beady eyes of a sparrow.

My sparrow.

Guten Tag, Violet think-says. We touch beaks before facing the clearing visible through the trees. A collective hum is vibrating through me, as if we're close to a gigantic capacitor. A new collective, one we've never been in touch with before.

There's no need for me to ask Violet how she knows we're in Germany. The evidence is on the sign visible through the trees: *Spirale Forschung.*

Spiral Research, I translate, taking in the compact black building with the helicraft landing pad on top. No fence. No need, I'm guessing.

Violet points her beak towards the sky. *Can you hear them?*

How can I not? At least five of them, possibly more. Five others like us.

Do you think they've been deconstructed?

I concentrate, shake my head. *No. Mila was ... I shudder. Reduced to a bundle of reflexes and instinct.*

And conditioning, Violet think-says.

Some would call it torture, I reply. The thought-streams we're picking up on are distinct, intact; nothing like Mila's fragmented mind-mess. Seeing a blur of movement, Violet and I take flight into the branches of nearby trees.

The guards below, who are clad in black trousers and flak jackets, gaze up at us.

'Vögel,' the smaller one says dismissively. The chunkier one hoiks and spits into the dirt before wandering off.

Always an eagle, Violet think-says to me.

You know it, I reply. *Call me boring, I guess.* The yellow sound of her laughter fills me with glassy delight, and for a moment I'm so distracted I don't hear *her* speaking.

Who are you?

I'm still trying to work out how to respond when Violet answers, also in German. *I'm Violet Black, and I'm with Johnno Fletcher. Who are you?*

The owner of the voice hesitates.

It's not a trick, I think-say. *We've got nothing to do with the Foundation.*

No, Violet corrects. *We've got everything to do with the Foundation. We've been virally optimised, kept prisoner for months and now we've escaped. Sound familiar?*

A second voice chimes in. *This is another one of their games, Emma. Don't listen.*

No, Leon, wait, Emma think-says. *Are you students? Are you taking part in the research project too?*

Is that what you call it? I think-ask, wondering if they can detect the bitterness staining my thought-stream. I've got a fix on Emma now, and I can see she's confused by the use of the word prisoner. She doesn't think she's a captive, but why?

They call it the Spiral Project, Leon answers, his hostility fading, but only a little. *I assume you were paid, as we were? But you've been detained for months, you say?*

It takes me a couple of seconds to process his memory—an advertisement placed on the university websites and social media, asking for healthy volunteers for a study on the effects of a new drug on cognition and memory. *Generous reimbursement offered, terms and conditions apply.*

When did you agree to do this? Violet think-asks.

Four weeks ago, Emma says, even as I detect Leon sifting through *my* memories. What the hell, I let him have them, those from the past six months, anyway. *It's taking longer than we thought,* she adds, *but you've got to admit, it's amazing.*

Christ, Leon think-says. *Christ, you've got to be...*

We're not kidding, Violet think-says.

Leon is shaking his virtual head. *How are we supposed to believe you? How do we know this isn't an elaborate trick?*

We're right outside, I say, while thinking that an eagle and a sparrow aren't going to cut it. If we want to convince them, we need to show them something unexpected.

Come outside, Violet think-says, picking up on my idea. *Out of the front door and turn left. Look for two wolves, one white, one black.*

Two wolves? Emma is hovering between excitement and terror.

Are you kidding? Leon think-says. *Why would we want to come out and meet a pair of wolves?*

The question is, why wouldn't *you want to come out and meet a pair of wolves?* Violet counters, before morphing into a white wolf, seemingly effortlessly.

You're getting good at this, I think-say. Here we are again, two wolves, black and white, like pawns on a chess board.

No, Violet says. *We're not pawns. Not anymore.* She looks past me to the couple emerging through the trees. The girl has long, flame-coloured hair hanging to her waist and a puffer jacket zipped to her chin. The guy in the black beanie clutches her shoulders from behind.

'Don't move,' he says, to her or us, I'm not sure.

It's OK, Violet think-says. *We're not going to hurt you.*

We prefer the taste of wallabies, I almost add, but I don't want to freak them out any more than they are already.

'How do we know you're not just a projection?' Leon is surveying the surroundings, as if expecting to find a huge camera somewhere.

Touch us. I sit on my haunches. *If you dare.*

Leon's long face creases into a scowl. He steps forward, his hand extended, and tentatively touches Violet on the back. His expression changes into one of shock, followed by amazement.

How do you ... is that something we're *going to learn to do?* he asks.

Maybe, I think-say, inclining my head when Emma strokes me beneath the chin. A brave move; I could bite her hand off if I chose to. *It depends on whether the virus that infected you is the same as the virus that infected us, I guess.*

Virus? Leon is frowning again. *What virus?*

The one they used in the research trial you're taking part in, I reply.

Oh, Violet think-says. *What did they say they were giving you?*

A medication. Emma tugs on the end of her sleeves. *They said it might give us a mild fever, maybe some hallucinations.*

It sure did, Leon think-says.

I stretch. *But there were some unanticipated side-effects, right?*

Right. Leon is still suspicious, wondering if he's hallucinating again. *They said they need to monitor us for a couple more weeks in case of seizures.*

Sounds familiar. Violet stands and starts winding in and out of the trees. *I'll be interested to see what your doctors say when you ask if you can leave. Maybe you can ask them about Sarah Schumann.*

Sarah who? Emma asks, just as I detect a new smell, cologne and musk and danger-danger-danger. Men. Guns. Shit.

Go, I think-yell to Violet, and we shift.

The deafening gunshot and explosion of pain in my chest are almost simultaneous.

THIRTY-ONE

VIOLET

It's the most painful return yet, my gut twisting into tight knots, my nerves stretched over knife-blades.

'Whoa.' I turn to Johnno. 'That was cl—' The words die in my throat. He's glassy-eyed, his chest heaving, his right shoulder glistening and bloody and raw.

'Oh no. Oh no, oh no.' I don't know what to do. There's so much blood soaking into the bed and his skin is so pale.

'I was too ... slow.' His eyes roll back, whether from pain or blood loss or both, I don't know. My pathetic first-aid knowledge is dribbling back to me, and it's no help. All I can remember is RICE: Rest Ice Compression Elevation, yeah, right. Shaking, I grab my t-shirt off the floor and press it over the wound.

Johnno groans and grips my wrist. 'Stop. Hurts.'

'I have to stop the bleeding.' My voice is trembling, too. *Don't panic.*

Don't panic. What did Johnno do when I was bleeding out?

Called for help. Got me to hospital. Neither of those are an option, not immediately anyway.

But I'm a healer. A healer. I'm not sure if I'm up to this, though.

'Hold this,' I say, before going to fill the water bottle from the almost-empty cannister, our last one. A mistake, because when I return to his side, he's out to it, his arm dangling over the side of the bed. Suppressing a sob, I press the blood-soaked t-shirt over the glistening mess again, triggering a low growl from Johnno.

'You're going to be OK.' I raise the bottle to his lips. 'You'll be so much better by tomorrow.' The words *I promise* almost escape, but I choke them down. I can't make a promise that I don't know if I can keep. Johnno's thought-stream is ragged and pale, and I can feel his heartbeat deep within me, rapid and thready.

'Hurts,' he repeats, which has me leaving his side again to search for pain relief.

In the first aid kit I find a blister pack of Panadol and a bottle containing Voltaren, which I remember using for period pain in the past. I take both to Johnno and force him to raise his head enough to swallow two of each. Too much? Not enough? How am I supposed to know?

I sit beside him, holding the t-shirt over his ruined shoulder. I'm pretty sure I can see exposed bone and muscles. God, I'm not cut out to be a paramedic or a nurse. What if the bullet is still in there?

'Just hold me,' Johnno whispers. 'Please.'

There's nothing else I can do, so I lower myself until I'm lying beside him, my hands wrapped around his shoulder. Listening to his short, sharp breaths. Feeling the knife-edge of his agony deep within my own body. Healing never hurt so much before, but as the minutes slide past, I hear his breathing become more regular, feel his heart begin to slow.

'You're going to be OK,' I tell him as my own head begins to whirl, as the bite of his injury settles deep within me.

'Should have kept the rest of that brandy,' he murmurs.

'Should have,' I murmur back. If only, if only. We weave in and out of sleep, our thoughts-streams foggy and fragmented.

Sarah Schumann, your precious prototype

Johnny Johnny Johnny

She was twenty-one years old

Once we know how to control his memories, his cognitive pathways

A university student majoring in physics

Cause of death was

Little Albert became very distressed

Irreversible brain injury

Touch us. If you dare.

They call it the Spiral Project.

*

It's early morning, chinks of light pushing through the curtains. I prop myself up on my elbow. Johnno is asleep, his chest rising and falling. Gently, I try to peel away the bloody t-shirt, but it's stuck to his wound. He moans and I take my hand away.

'Sorry,' I whisper.

Johnno grunts, opens his eyes. For a moment I'm worried he doesn't recognise me, but then he touches my cheek and says, 'Watch it, Liesl.'

'No, you watch it,' I tease back, my anxiety temporarily abating but returning when I touch his forehead. 'You've got a fever.'

'Just part of the healing,' he says, and I notice how dry his lips are. I wash my hands and fill a water bottle.

'You need to drink all of that,' I tell him.

'Getting bossy now,' he mutters, but his mind is wide-open, and I hear, *Love you, Vi,* and it's all I can do not to start crying.

I nudge his sweat-damp hair off his forehead. 'I love you too, Johnno,' I say softly. 'Now, drink.'

Once he's emptied the water bottle, which doesn't take too much persuasion, I fill a basin with soap and water and soak off the t-shirt.

'How's it looking?' he asks, once I've helped him turn onto his side.

'It's better than it was.' It's true. The hole where the bullet entered is still there but the exit wound doesn't look quite so open, quite so raw. I can't see bone anymore, but I'm pretty sure I can still see muscle. My head whirling, I say, 'I think it's about fifty percent better.'

'Yeah, that's how it feels,' he murmurs. 'One more day, and I'll be good as new, right?'

'I guess so.' The redness around the edges of the wound is worrying me, though. What if it's infected? Can it set in that quickly? Do my healing powers extend to infections?

Johnno touches my thigh. 'Stop worrying, Vi.' I don't know how he can stay so calm. I guess he's got no choice.

'There's hardly any food left.' A can of baked beans and a box of crackers, to be exact.

'You can hunt.'

'But *you* can't,' I point out, tearing off a length of sheet to use as a bandage. 'It's not as if I can bring anything back for you.'

'Can if you're close. I can eat kangaroo.'

'And there's only about a litre of water left,' I say.

Johnno hesitates. 'Well, I should be better by tomorrow. Even by tonight. We can fly to the waterhole.'

'OK,' I say, trying to sound positive, even though I'm starting to think it's all too hard. I'm so sick of struggling, so tired.

He squeezes my thigh. 'Get yourself a drink of water. You need to keep your strength up too.'

I do as he says, then turn on the van for the air con before lying next to him again, my palm on his bandaged wound.

Johnno lets out a breath. 'You're my morphine, you know that?'

'Thought you hated drugs.'

'At the moment,' he says, 'I'll take anything.' That's how I know he's still hurting more than he's letting on. I should have figured that out from the way his heart rate has picked up again, from the way he's blocking me.

There's nothing else to do, though, so I stay next to him, trying to absorb as much pain as I can. Hoping I'm enough. Knowing there are so many ways to die, even if you're young and fit and virally optimised.

*

I wake with a start. Our heart is galloping, and there's a layer of sweat between us, despite the air-conditioned interior of the van. Johnno is mumbling, incomprehensible sounds, his thought-stream all over the place.

(*it burns*)

Johnny Johnny Johnny

I will never forgive you. Never, never.

(*burns*)

'Johnno,' I say, but there's no reply. Crap. No wonder he's dreaming about burning, because that's just what his skin feels like. His body temperature must be thirty-nine degrees at least. I slide off the bed and use a small amount of precious water to soak a dishcloth before draping it over his forehead. When I peel away my sheet bandage, I see that the wound is smaller than before. It's also hot and inflamed. My stomach churns. Why, why can't I heal him properly? Maybe it's something to do with the L25. Maybe the drug has eroded my ability to heal. Johnno was right, I never should have taken it. If I hadn't taken it, then we wouldn't have gone to Germany, wouldn't have taken on something we couldn't handle, and Johnno wouldn't be ... what? I don't even want to think the word. Am I going to lose him as well?

Guilt spearing me, I check the clock on the dashboard: quarter past nine in the morning. Next I check the fuel tank. The hydrogen's a quarter full.

Enough to get us out of here. Enough to get Johnno to a doctor.

'No,' he moans. I'm not sure if he's heard what I'm thinking or if he's just sore. Either way, he's delirious, his eyes glazed and shiny. I kneel beside him and make him take a few sips of water.

'We're going for a drive.' I kiss him on his hot cheek. *I do forgive you, Wolf Black,* I add, switching to think-speak, and Johnno gives me a brief, beautiful smile and passes out.

THIRTY-TWO

JOHNNO

There is a ball of fire inside me, eating into my shoulder and my chest, burning me alive. I am being punished for everything I've done—for being an insolent little brat, for letting my sister die, for sacrificing Ethan to save Violet, for everything, everything.

(Johnny where are you when I find you I'm going to kick your arse

(it burns)

And I can't stand it anymore, so I hurl my dream-flow out, out, out, seeking another, someone who isn't scared and hurting and I *leap—*

*

I'm sitting in a room with octagonal walls, drumming my fingers on the circular table in front of me. I recognise the gold nail polish on those fingers; recognise the long legs, which I've crossed at the knee.

Greta's fingers. Greta's legs. Greta's thought-stream.

And *me,* Johnno Fletcher, squatting within her midbrain. There's no way I could have done this before the L25. *Greta, Greta, what have you done?*

Greta twitches a little before focusing on the person across the table from her.

'What I'm about to tell you is classified information,' she says. 'Do you understand?'

'I understand,' the woman says. She's late twenties at the most, with her hair worn in a high ponytail, an electronic stethoscope hanging around her neck. From Greta, I glean that the woman's name is Alice Wang.

'Good. Because the last person who told us that clearly *didn't* understand, and we had to terminate his position.' Greta sips on her coffee. 'It's probably going to be the end of his career, which is a shame, as he was quite promising.'

Is she referring to Bruno? I wonder if Alice Wang, presumably his replacement, knows that they haven't terminated just his position but probably him as well. I'm thinking of delving into Greta's recent memories to find out if that's true when she adds, 'I'm going to explain this to you from the beginning. It's a complex situation, but scientifically very exciting.'

'Sure.' Alice sits up straighter.

'A few years ago, scientists in Germany found that an altered form of the measles virus led to enhanced cognition in monkeys—an improved ability to solve problems, and in a much shorter period of time. They called the virus M-fever.' Greta pushes a plate across the table. 'Would you like another pastry?'

'No, thank you. So, there was cross-transmission to humans?' Alice asks, and I sense Greta carefully choosing how she's going to tell Alice the rest of the story.

'That's right.' Greta reaches for the coffee plunger and tops up her cup. 'Now, this is where the first problem arose. In most of the monkeys, the M-fever caused only a mild illness. Approximately five percent of them developed encephalitis, but they all recovered. It was those subjects that the scientists were interested in, because they showed not only improved cognition, but also better communication skills in ways the scientists couldn't explain.'

Alice frowns. 'But in humans, M-fever is a serious illness.'

'That's right.'

'So how did the illness spread from monkeys to humans? Did it mutate or something?'

'Not exactly. The scientists were always very careful with infectious precautions, so there was very little risk of accidental exposure.' Greta drinks more coffee. Her brain cells, her neurons, are zipping along faster now, although they're no match for mine. 'The first problem,' she continues, 'occurred in the phase I trial. Do you remember what a phase I trial is?'

'Testing on healthy volunteers,' Alice answers.

'That's right. Although technically that refers to drugs. And we were testing the effects of a virus.'

Alice's eyes widen. 'The volunteers agreed to that?'

'They did.' Greta sculls more coffee. Me, I'm aware of a vague ache in my shoulder. No, I can't return to my body now. I need to listen to what Greta's going to say next. 'There were six volunteers. Four of them were university students, one was a struggling artist, and the sixth was unemployed.'

People who need money, I think. People who have no choice but to sell their bodies. Is that ethical? I'm sure it's not.

'The subjects were offered a generous sum of money for their trouble,' Greta says. 'They were advised that they would need to be monitored for approximately four to six weeks after the infection. And then...' She spreads her hands.

Alice is hanging on her every word. 'They got really sick?'

Greta nods. 'They did. So sick, in fact, that...' she clears her throat, 'it was fatal for five of the subjects.'

'They died?' Alice puts her hand to her mouth. 'When did that happen?'

'About a year ago.'

'And the survivor? What happened to them?'

'Like the others, she became very unwell, with respiratory failure and encephalitis,' Greta says. 'Just like the monkeys. But she survived. And when she got better—you know what I'm going to say, don't you?'

'Her cognition had improved,' Alice says.

'That's right. Our experiments showed faster mental processing speeds almost immediately, something that improved exponentially as the weeks went on. But that wasn't all. The subject was able to access the thoughts, memories and emotions of other people. Some would call it telepathy, although it wasn't a two-way communication, perhaps because she had no one like herself to communicate with.'

For the first time, an expression of disbelief crosses Alice's face.

'I'm not joking,' Greta says, plucking a PA off the table. 'Watch this.'

The screen at the front of the room lights up. If I were in my own body, I'd probably be shaking, adrenaline coursing through me. Because there *she* is, with her delicate features and diamond stud in her nose, her turquoise eyes staring straight into mine. She's wearing her blonde hair in plaits. So pretty. So dangerous.

'This is Sarah,' Greta says. 'A university student, majoring in physics.'

Sarah. Sarah Schumann, the prototype, the girl whose brilliant, virally optimised brain ended up splattered all over a wall in Berlin, because of me.

The camera pans out, and I see that Sarah is sitting in a dentist-style chair, electro-dots attached to her temples.

'Sarah,' the invisible interviewer says. Invisible, but the voice is instantly recognisable: Greta from the past. 'Tell me, what is your first memory?' She's speaking in German, but I don't need to read the English subtitles on the screen.

'Um.' Sarah's mouth twists. 'I remember lying in bed, crying because I'd lost my teddy bear. Except it wasn't a teddy. It was a rabbit that I called Teddy.' Her gaze grows distant. 'My older brother used to tease me about that.'

'Thank you. And, Sarah...' Past-Greta pauses. 'Tell me, what is *my* first memory?'

Sarah's eyes focus again. 'Well,' she says, barely hesitating, 'it's kind of hazy, but you're being held down.

Something sharp is going into your arm.' Her tone softens. 'That must have been horrible.'

'They did what they had to,' Past-Greta says.

'Because you...' Sarah frowns, 'had leukaemia?'

'Yes.' Past-Greta's tone sharpens. 'Are you getting anything else?'

Sarah's face drains of colour. 'Yes, I ... oh my God. Oh my God.'

'What's the matter, Sarah?' Past-Greta asks. I can't see her making a single move to comfort Sarah, who is trembling and crying.

'They died? Everyone else died? Why didn't you tell me? Am I going to die too?'

'Cut,' Past-Greta says softly. The screen goes blank.

'Whoa,' Alice says again. 'She got all that from you?'

'And more,' Greta says. 'We had to be very careful after that. Imagine if someone could hear everything you were thinking, if they could access every memory you'd ever had. Imagine how dangerous that could be.' She's holding something now, the contours of which I can feel in her hand. It's a device that looks like a hearing aid, small and tan-coloured. 'It took us a few months, but the NET scanner allowed us to work out a way to block the subject accessing us by emitting a neutralising frequency.' She passes the device to the young doctor. 'You'll be needing this.'

'So, Sarah's here?' Alice's fingers close around the blocker.

'No,' Greta says. 'As is often the case with the prototype, there were ... issues. Sarah became obsessive, fretful. It seems being able to access the thoughts of others became too much for her.' She's lying, I realise, can sense it in the corkscrew turns of her thought-stream. 'Eventually, it transformed into a full-blown psychosis,' Greta continues—but I'm accessing something different.

Sarah wanted to leave, to return to university, but we had so much more work to do.

'Were you able to treat it?' Alice asks.

'We tried,' Greta says. 'At first, it seemed as though the antipsychotics were working. She developed a good relationship with your predecessor, Doctor Hoffman.'

A relationship we chose to turn a blind eye to, because she settled down for a while.

Greta sighs. 'We had no idea that they were having a full-blown affair until it was too late.'

And once we found out that Bruno was in a sexual relationship with one of our VORTEX members, it was all too easy to plant the seeds for the self-destruction into our problem prototype.

Alice fiddles with her stethoscope. 'What do you mean, too late?'

'She found out that Doctor Hoffman was cheating on her,' Greta says. 'It sent her into a rage. She became suicidal.'

'She killed herself?'

'Yes,' Greta says, and, in her mind, that is the truth, the only truth that matters. 'It was devastating for all of us.'

'But...' Alice says. 'What caused the M-fever epidemic? Like, how did it end up being transmitted to the general public?'

Greta says, 'We'll never know for sure.' She's lying again. I probe for more, trying to grasp her slippery alternative truths, but the pain is returning and I am cold, so cold, and that's it, I'm *shifting*, and *whack—*

*

I'm shaking uncontrollably, my teeth chattering, and the pain has ratcheted to a new level. There are unfamiliar voices, hands, a prick in the crook of my left arm, and someone is saying, *gunshot wound,* and someone else is saying, *antibiotics, stat.* I can still hear Greta even now, can hear her corkscrew truth, which is that they will do anything to ensure the return of Violet Black alive, at all costs, and I'm calling out to Violet but I can't hear her. I can't.

THIRTY-THREE

VIOLET

There are no words for the relief I feel when the helicraft turns up. It's three hours since we reached the main road, two hours since I flagged down a truck and asked for help.

My boyfriend is seriously injured. We need an air ambulance, now.

The helicraft paramedics, two women in green uniforms, take one look at Johnno and ask me to stand aside. I do as they ask, standing in the darkness while they put needles in his veins and an oxygen mask over his mouth and nose. The whole time, I'm trying to comfort him with think-speak. *You're going to be OK now, we'll be OK, I promise.* He's not replying, which is worrying the hell out of me, although he's been slipping in and out of consciousness for several hours. I never envisaged this happening, thought we were invincible, that I had special powers, could heal ... why did I think there'd be no price to pay if I took L25?

'Excuse me, miss.' The younger paramedic's voice startles me. 'Can you tell me when this happened?'

'Um.' I try to think back. 'Yesterday. No, maybe the day before. Is it past midnight yet?'

'Three am,' she says. 'Are you all right?'

'Fine.' I'm not. I sink into the dirt, and she brings me a bottle of water and wraps a blood-pressure cuff around my arm.

'What's your boyfriend's name?' the paramedic asks. The cuff inflates. I drink, cough, drink some more.

'Jonathan,' I say. 'Jonathan Fletcher.'

'Can you tell me his date of birth?'

I shake my head. 'I'm not sure.' I feel stupid for not knowing. 'He's nineteen, twenty this year.'

The paramedic pats my shoulder. 'We're going to fly him to Alice Springs Hospital. I'd recommend you come with us, leave your vehicle here. You don't look in a state to be driving yourself anywhere.' She shines a torch on the blood-pressure machine. 'As confirmed by your low blood pressure, which is eighty-six on sixty. Drink up, we can't have you fainting on us too.'

'Is he going to be all right?'

'I hope so. He's running a fever, hypotensive—that's low blood pressure—and his lungs sound a bit wet.'

'Wet?'

'He's septic,' the paramedic says. 'His blood vessels are leaky, which puts strain on all of his organs.' That makes me feel even worse. I should have got help for him sooner, shouldn't have thought I could ever heal such a huge wound. What was I thinking?

'Ready,' her partner calls out.

'Good.' The paramedic helps me to my feet. 'Just one more question. How did this happen?

I swipe my arm past my lips. 'I was attacked,' I say. 'By two men in a black Jeep. They tried to r-rape me and when Johnno went to help me, they sh-shot him.' A sob escapes. It's not an act. I'm completely overwhelmed, don't know how much more I can take.

'All right, love,' the paramedic says gently. 'You're safe now. You can tell all of this to the police, get them to track those bastards down.' She goes to help load the stretcher into the helicraft. After retrieving a few items from the Fuse Camper, I climb in beside Johnno.

'Johnno,' I whisper, stroking his forehead. There's a large bandage on his shoulder, plastic tubing feeds into an IV in his left arm. 'Johnno, you're going to be OK now.' He's not hot anymore, but his skin is clammy, his breathing rapid. When I reach for his thought-stream, it's running deep and slow, way beyond my reach. No wonder I can't talk to him. *Please, please, be OK.*

The older paramedic passes me a pair of headphones. 'Buckle up,' she says, and once the blades have started turning, 'What's your name, love?'

'Violet,' I say. 'Violet Black.'

*

Things move pretty fast once we reach the Emergency Department, with doctors and nurses coming and going, administering fluids and antibiotics and taking blood samples and scans with a mobile CT machine. We've been there for about half an hour when I'm asked to sit in a waiting room with a small, darkened window and magazines that date back to last century. The only other person there is an old man, who is watching an e-screen and mumbling to himself.

I can't read. I can't watch the e-screen. I just keep reaching for Johnno, over and over, but his thought-stream is no more accessible than before. Eventually I start nodding off, jerking awake whenever I hear a voice or an alarm. Time passes, sometimes slowly and sometimes fast, until the quality of the light in the room changes, and I realise dawn has arrived.

I rub my eyes. The old man has gone. The clock above the door says it is quarter past six. I feel my stomach growling. I hear footsteps, the low murmur of voices.

'Violet?' A woman strolls in, a stethoscope tucked into the front pocket of her scrubs top. 'I'm Lacey Searle, one of the intensive care doctors.'

'Hi.' I sit upright, rubbing my arms.

'You'll be pleased to hear that Jonathan is in a stable condition,' she says, which gives me a really odd feeling, as though she's talking about someone other than the person who saved my life on at least one occasion, and is now in danger of losing his own. 'His blood pressure is much better, although he's still running a fever. He's on the acute list for surgery this morning, so they can tidy up that wound.'

'Can I see him?' I reach for Johnno again—almost an unconscious action by now, as if checking my PA—and for the first time in many hours detect a flicker.

'Of course,' the doctor says, her eyes darting towards the door. 'There are a couple of people who'd like to talk to you first. Police. I hope that's OK.'

'Sure,' I say. Like I have a choice.

She pats me on the thigh and stands up. 'Just ask for directions at the front desk when you've finished.'

'To where?' My brain is sluggish from lack of sleep and food. I need to concentrate, need to figure out how to navigate this next step.

'The intensive care unit,' the doctor says, nodding at the man and woman entering the room, who are wearing blue uniforms. 'See you soon.'

The cops smile at me. I don't smile in return. They ask me if I want a cup of tea or coffee and I say *yes, coffee,* although I think it will take more than a dose of caffeine to help me now. I don't register their names. They already have mine, but we go through the formalities anyway.

'Can you state your full name and date of birth?' the male cop asks. He has chipmunk-round cheeks, a trimmed beard with grey flecks in it.

I stare into the muddy liquid inside my cup. 'Violet Elizabeth Black,' I say, following up with my date of birth. The female cop, who is blonde and freckly, is entering my answers into a mini-Tab. Within seconds, I know, her search will inform her that the Violet Elizabeth Black with that date of birth is deceased.

She doesn't comment on that, though, not yet. She merely passes the mini-Tab to Chipmunk Cheeks before focusing on me. 'Violet, can you tell us exactly what happened to you and your boyfriend—how long ago?'

'Two days ago.' I push limp locks out of my eyes. 'At least, I think it was two days ago. It's all a bit of a blur.' I tell them about the men driving up while Johnno was out running. I tell them about how they hit me and held me down, fingering the scab on my lip. 'And I screamed, and Johnno came back and there was a fight. That was when they shot him.'

'That was when they shot him,' Freckles echoes. 'Two days ago, you say?'

I nod. Chipmunk Cheeks says, 'The doctors tell us that the degree of healing in that wound is more consistent with it having happened over a week ago. How do you explain that?'

'I can't,' I say, which sounds more plausible than *because I got it halfway healed overnight with what I guess you'd call a laying on of hands, except it looks like my healing powers don't extend to infections. Or that the L25 has taken as much as it has given.*

Freckles takes the mini-Tab off her partner and taps the screen. 'Could you please explain to us how you came to be in possession of a Fuse camper van that was reported as stolen six days ago?'

'Well,' I say, 'that's easy. We stole it.'

Their expressions don't change, but I can tell they're surprised. I can tell because I have a fix on both of their thought-streams now. I need to work faster, smarter, than I ever have before.

'We figured we needed it more than them.' I sift through Chipmunk Cheeks' memories, panning for gold.

Freckles narrows her eyes at me. 'Are you aware that there is a warrant out for your arrest?'

'There is no warrant out for the arrest of Violet Black and Jonathan Fletcher,' I say evenly, 'because everyone thinks they are dead. But I guess you've been told we may be using those names as aliases, right?' And there is gold shining right up at me, great big fat nuggets. *Unbelievable.*

And yet, nothing surprises me anymore.

'What names do you have on this warrant?' I continue. 'Let me guess, Liesl Meyer and Wolf Schwarz?'

Chipmunk Cheeks shrugs. 'Looks like you have all the answers already, Ms Meyer.'

'It's Violet,' I correct, turning my attention to Freckles's memory cache. The very thought of what I'm going to ask for next is sending torrents of adrenaline through me. 'I need three things from you.' *Don't shake. Don't show them any emotion.*

I'm going to die, going to die, going to die.

Stop it, stop it.

'Three things from us?' Freckles laughs. 'No, Violet or Liesl or whatever your name is, that's not how it works. I don't think you realise how much trouble you're in. Tell me, who really shot your boyfriend? Had a fight, did you?'

I could ask for a lawyer at this stage, I suppose. I could, but it won't help me. Bending forward, I say, 'No, that *is* how it works.' When Chipmunk goes to open his mouth, I hold up my hand. 'Just listen. Because I know all about *your* dirty little habit, and I could get you chucked in jail faster than you can say child pornography.' I point at Freckles. 'And I know all about your habit too, although at least you're only hurting yourself, I suppose. Not sure I could say the same about your dealer.'

They're both gaping at me now. Gaping and sweating and trying not to look at each other.

'This is what I want,' I say. 'Three things. I'm not asking you to do anything illegal, although it doesn't sound as though that bothers you, anyway.' If I weren't so tired and hungry and nervous, I might be enjoying this. 'The first is, I want you to keep the fact that Johnno and I are here to yourselves. No reporting back to anyone.'

Freckles doesn't react, maybe because she's thinking about how she needs to get rid of her meth stash right now. Whatever, that's her problem.

Chipmunk gives me a steely look, inclines his head slightly. Neither of them is going to fight me on my first demand. I know, because I'm reading their thought-streams, and faster than ever.

'Two, I want a room booked for me in a nearby hotel under the name of Jessica Lemon. Nothing fancy, but something with room service meals would be good.'

Freckles's pale eyes blaze at me. She's hating me right now. Fine, join the club.

'And third, I need one of your PAs and some privacy for a few minutes. I'll need your password.' The shaking has reached my larynx and my teeth.

I'm going to die if I do this.

I'm going to die if I don't do this.

'Are you sure you're up to this?' Chipmunk asks, his voice cold. 'You don't look very well to me, I must say.'

'PA,' I say. 'Now.' It takes all my effort to push the words out. I'm going to end up with a bullet in my head. No, worse, I'm going to be returned to the Foundation and tortured, deconstructed in the most painful way possible.

A PA lands in my lap. 'Passcode is 45568,' Chipmunk says, then stalks out of the room, Freckles close behind him.

It takes several attempts to enter the passcode, several minutes to bring myself to dial the number. My chest is squeezing so hard I worry I'll pass out before anyone picks up the PA. *Pick up, pick up, pick up.*

The PA stops ringing, and a voice says, 'Hello?'

'H-hi,' I stammer, clutching my belly. I'm going to throw up. My bowels have turned to liquid.

He hesitates, then says, 'Who is this?'

'It's Violet,' I say. 'Your daughter.' Then my heart explodes behind my eyes, and everything goes black.

THIRTY-FOUR

JOHNNO

My shoulder is aching. Aching, but in an abstract way, more to remind me that I'm alive rather than make me wish I was dead. I'm surfacing from a black, limitless ocean: a salmon swimming towards a river of consciousness. Fragments of a conversation I once had with Violet float before me.

You changed your name?

After my sister died. I guess I was trying to ... forget. Reinvent myself.

Phoenix rising.

From the ashes, yeah, that's the one. Unless you're a Black Wolf, that is.

'Jonathan, hi.' A face blurs into view. Brown eyes, long eyelashes, a black ponytail. 'Here.' The next thing to appear is a plastic container, just in time for me to puke into it. 'General anaesthetic does that to some people.' The nurse wipes my lips with a wet cloth. I sink into the pillow, exhausted. Blink.

'Do you like to be called Jonathan? Johnny?'

'Johnno,' I croak. Something is squeezing my arm. A blood-pressure cuff. When I touch my neck, I feel plastic tubing and realise it must be a tube running into my vein, like when Violet was in hospital in Berlin.

Hospital. Violet. Berlin. No, I'm not in Berlin, where am I? My heart thuds. The nurse rolls up a fresh flannel and drapes it across my forehead.

'I'm Gina,' she says. 'You're in Alice Springs Hospital. Do you know what day it is?'

I shake my head. If I hadn't lost track of the days before, I certainly have now. *Violet,* I think-say, casting around for her thought-stream, but there is nothing, a blank. Anxiety rises up my throat.

'Violet,' I say. 'Is she OK?' The last thing I can remember is lying in the rear of the camper van, sweating and shaking and hurting.

'Is that your girlfriend?'

'Yeah,' I say, even though *girlfriend* seems a barely adequate description after everything we've been through. Another halfremembered conversation bobs to the surface of my thought-stream.

Felt different when you were a wolf, didn't it?

Most things feel different when you're a wolf.

'I imagine she's catching up on some sleep,' the nurse says. 'I'm sure she'll be along soon. Now, how's your pain on a level of one to ten, if ten is the worst pain ever and zero is nothing?'

'Um, I—five?'

Gina smiles, pats my arm. 'There's no right or wrong answer, but it sounds like you could do with a top-up.' She pushes a button into my hand. 'Just press that if you're sore.'

'OK. Thanks.' I don't squeeze the button. What if the morphine or whatever they're giving me is interfering with my ability to communicate with Violet?

'Would you like a drink of water?'

'Sure.' I let Gina help me sit up, swirl the water around in my mouth before swallowing it. There's a metallic taste in my mouth, grit, a vague ache in my lower jaw—something to do with the anaesthetic? I touch the bandage on my right shoulder.

'They washed out the pus,' Gina says. 'You're going to be just fine.'

'Sure,' I repeat, but I don't believe her. If I were going to be just fine, I'd be able to talk to Violet. If I were going to be just fine, there wouldn't be a pair of men in suits halting at the foot of my bed.

'Is this a good time?' The older one has grey hair, a grey suit, even a grey shirt and tie.

'Just a few minutes,' Gina says, before leaving me with them.

Grey Guy extends his hand. 'My name is Inspector Scott Murphy, and this is my colleague, Detective Constable Harry Wilson.'

'Where is she?' I ask.

Murphy retracts his hand, unshaken. 'I assume you're asking after your girlfriend?'

'Well, yeah, since I don't know anyone else around here.' I can't get a fix on him, his partner either. Maybe it's not the morphine. Maybe my latest illness has stripped me of my virally optimised abilities. *That* thought sends a shiver down my spine.

'She's being looked after,' Murphy says, which only amplifies my concern. 'You'll be seeing her soon enough, don't worry.'

That's when I notice the device in his right ear, an identical match to the one Wilson is wearing. My heart starts hammering. Murphy might be old enough to need a hearing aid, but Wilson doesn't look a day above forty. Gina is at my side in a flash, frowning at the monitor.

'We won't be much longer,' Wilson says politely.

Gina gives him a stony look. 'If his heart keeps racing like that, I'll have to ask you to leave.' I've only known her for a few minutes, but I'm liking her already. Murphy and Wilson, not so much.

'Sure.' Murphy waits for her to drift away before pulling a chair up to the bedside. 'So, Jonathan—may I call you Jonathan? Or is it Wolf?' I stare at him. He says, 'Mr Schwarz, then. Can you tell me who shot you?'

My mind races. Have they questioned Violet about this as well? I'm sure they have, and if so I have no idea what she's already told them, but I'm pretty sure it wasn't *Johnno got shot in a Bavarian forest when in his wolf form.*

'I don't remember,' I say. 'It's all a blur.'

'I'm sure it is.' Murphy drums his fingers on his knee. 'Let me trigger your memory. Nine days ago, you abducted three women from a research facility located four hundred kilometres north of King's Canyon, is that right?'

'I never abducted anyone,' I say.

'Correct me if I'm wrong,' he says, 'but you abducted three women, then dumped the older two women—doctors, I might add—in the middle of nowhere, presumably to die. You then fled with the third woman, Liesl Meyer, in a stolen vehicle.'

I grit my teeth, then wish I hadn't. One of my left lower molars is hurting, and I don't know why. 'Her name is Violet,' I say. 'Violet Black.'

Murphy nods at Wilson, and Wilson starts typing something into the mini-Tab. 'She said you might say that.'

'Because it's the truth.' *Dickhead.*

'Do you want to know what else she told us?' Murphy angles forward, his voice low, conspiratorial. 'She said you forced yourself on her.'

'She—*what?*'

'More than once. Said you'd had your eye on her for some time. Enjoy it, did you?'

My breathing quickens. 'I never did anything she didn't want me to, never.' Apart from kissing her in Berlin, that is. Does that count?

Murphy shrugs. 'I suppose the word *rape* is a bit ambiguous. What is very clear to me, Mr Schwarz, is that eventually she couldn't take it anymore and shot you in self-defence. Have I jogged your memory enough?'

Gina returns, brandishing a kidney dish. 'Gentlemen, I'm going to have to—'

'Soon,' Murphy barks, before turning back to me. 'Does the name Sarah

Schumann mean anything to you?' And when I don't answer, 'How about Mila Hermann?'

My mouth is so dry I can barely force the words out. 'I want to speak to a lawyer.'

'I'm sure you do, Mr Schwarz,' Murphy says, as Wilson snaps a handcuff around my left wrist. 'Because I'm placing you under arrest for two counts of murder, multiple counts of rape, and two counts of grand theft auto. Do you have any questions?'

'Yeah,' I say. 'Can I have a PA?'

'Sure,' Murphy says. 'After we transfer you to a maximum-security facility. Don't worry, they have some of the best doctors in the world.' He bares his teeth at Gina. 'We'll be freeing up a bed for you very shortly, Nurse.'

Gina glances between Wilson, who is attaching the other half of the handcuff to the bedrail, and me. 'He's too unwell to transfer,' she says, but she sounds less sure of herself now, and I can hear what *she's* thinking loud and clear: *I never would have guessed.* My relief at knowing I can still access someone is overshadowed by my terror at what's about to happen to me next. 'Let alone cause any harm to anyone.'

'Psychopaths are very good at seducing their victims before they kill them,' Murphy says smoothly. 'A bit like a black widow spider.'

'Screw you,' I say, trying once more to overcome his blocking device, with no luck.

'Temper, temper,' Murphy murmurs, standing up.

'I do have a question,' I say. 'Is Violet—Liesl—alive?'

Murphy straightens his tie. 'Why, yes,' he says. 'We're sending her home.'

THIRTY-FIVE

VIOLET

Whump whump whump. I can't move. My arms and legs are strapped down, and there is a blindfold over my eyes. When I turn my head, I realise I'm wearing headphones, too.

Whump whump whump. Helicraft. No.

'There, there,' a male voice says. 'Don't fuss. It was only a faint, but at such a convenient time. Inevitable, of course.'

When I try to access his thought-stream, there's nothing, a black hole.

He's blocked. The Foundation. No, no, no.

'Let me introduce myself. Detective Scott Murphy in some circles, although I prefer to be called by my correct title, which is Doctor. A doctor twice over, in fact, since I have a PhD as well as a medical degree.'

'Do you want me to congratulate you?'

'That won't be necessary.' Murphy actually sounds serious. 'I must say, this is all going entirely as predicted. You were always bound to return eventually. It was only a matter of waiting for you to be flushed out.'

'Where are you taking me?' My mouth tastes metallic, like blood and something else.

'Back to home base, where else? There are some people who'd love to reconnect with you.'

There's no point in replying to that, so I don't. I lick my dry lips, run my tongue over my teeth. Something is different. There's a smooth area in my left lower molar that wasn't there before, as if something is stuck there. It's aching a little, too, although that's nothing compared to my head, which feels as though it's about to split open. I can't remember the last time I ate, have no idea what time it is.

'What did they give me?' I ask, anger pulsing through me. 'Some sort of sedative?'

'Ketamine. Very effective. Lethal in overdose, of course, but most things are.'

'Where's Johnno?'

'We're taking care of him, don't worry.' A ring scrapes against my cheek and the blindfold is removed. Murphy is wearing headphones, too, and a grey suit. 'As for you, I'm a little worried about your tendency for ... making things up, should we say?'

'I'm not the one making things up.' My voice is shaking. I don't know if I've ever hated anyone this much before, not even Sarah Schumann. Is this how *they* drove her crazy? 'Your cop colleague is a paedophile, did you know that?'

Smiling, Murphy trails his finger along my thigh. 'Oh, no,' he says. 'I think you've got the wrong end of the stick, Ms Black. You're hardly a child.'

My stomach curdles. They didn't do something to me while I was unconscious, did they? How would I know?

'Thought you were so smart, didn't you?' Murphy is practically purring with delight. 'I don't think you realise quite how long the outermost arm of the spiral is.'

I want to say, *I called my father, and he'll be busting a gut to find me now.* I want to say, *Are you scared of wolves?* But I don't, because I don't want to give Murphy any more information that he could use against me. Also, we're thousands of feet in the air. It's probably not a good time to freak out the pilot by releasing my dream-flow wolf, or snake, or whatever else it will take to overcome El Creepo.

'Landing in five,' another voice says through the headphones. The pilot, I'm guessing, although I can't access him either.

As for Johnno, he's lost to me too. What if I never see him again? What if *we're taking care of him* means permanently, as in killing him?

The helicraft is descending rapidly. I don't need to look out the window to see where we're going.

Game over. No, that's the old Violet speaking, the scared, helpless Violet. I'm not that girl anymore.

The virally optimised Violet knows that the game has only just begun.

THIRTY-SIX

JOHNNO

When I wake, there's another blank space in my brain, just another period of time where I've floated in the subterranean land of unconsciousness. Shiny-white surfaces curve around me, the all-too-familiar interior of a pod that's only slightly wider and longer than my body.

In the periphery of my vision, I see flashing lights. Images flit across the ceiling. Clouds, a bird, a slow-moving plane. I try to move, only to find I'm restrained at my ankles and wrists.

I turn my head, taking in the small room, which smells of disinfectant, and the large metallic boxes attached to the walls, which are the source of the flashing lights.

WEB scan. The Foundation. Of course. Despair thrums through me. I should have known we'd never escape.

Violet, where are you?

Of course, there's no reply. All I can hear is Murphy's hateful accusation: *She said you forced yourself on her.*

Closing my eyes, I force myself to breathe slower, deeper, falling into a memory of swimming in a desert waterhole, the sounds muted and distorted. I remember returning to the surface, Violet sitting on a rock, her wet hair glistening in the sun. I remember how her neck had rested on my arm as I'd lathered her hair with soap, my heart diving deep within my chest. I'd blocked her, then, worried she'd hate me for falling in love with her.

Maybe you should travel as a fish next time, she'd said. And, *You're the best at solving the problems they're always giving us.*

How useful do you think that really was? I'd answered. It all seems pointless now that I'm lying captive and immobilised, helpless, stripped of my ability to communicate.

But ... how do I know that's true?

I inhale. Exhale. Think of how it feels to soar in an updraft, to run on all four legs, my muscles rippling beneath my wolf-flanks, to tumble with my wolf-mate, her hot breath in my nostrils. And I'm—

Gliding above a dark-brown, circular building with spokes radiating off it, a building surrounded by the lush bush I've grown up with—kahikatea and pine and mānuka and punga and moss. And oh, how fresh the air is, and how good it smells, moist and earthy. I hear bellbirds, tūī, the stirring of wind through leaves.

Home. I'm home, but still a prisoner.

At least, my body is a prisoner.

You're the best at solving the problems they're always giving us.

You can figure this out, Johnno, I tell myself, rising above the forest, my wings beating the air. *You're a Phoenix, rising from the ashes. You're Wolf Black, Black Wolf. You can travel anywhere you want. You can take the form of any animal you choose.*

I'm flying over the Waitākere Ranges, my eagle-heart pounding, when there is a blur, a *shift,* and—

I'm lying in my pod, still restrained, the pain in my gut so intense I think I might pass out. It's dark now, but I can hear the low murmur of voices, as if coming from just outside the room.

'Remarkable,' the first voice says. 'I've never seen a NET scan light up like that.'

'Yes, the native virus appears to produce the best results,' another, familiar, voice replies. Marlow, the prick. I'm imagining what my wolf self could do to shut him up when he adds, 'You should see *her* scan. It's off the scale.'

'Nothing like a good epidemic every now and then.' Laughter. 'Do you think they—'

'Oh, I imagine so,' Marlow replies. 'Her initial test is negative, but it's too early to tell.'

One of my lower molars twinges, and I wince. *Not a great time to be needing a dentist,* I think, and I try to throw my dream-flow out again, but my limbs are growing heavy and my mind is beginning to blur and distort.

Something is ... something is...

*

I'm floating as though in a swiftly moving current, with no form, no shape, no sense of direction. Something is pulling me on, drawing me in, its syrupy thought-stream flowing around me.

I don't know who you are, it says. A hum reverberates through me, so intense it is almost painful. Is this another one of their tricks? Have they dosed me with L25, or worse, something more powerful?

I am *shifting,* blink, and I'm in a room with a single bed and a floor-to-ceiling window with a view of a black sand beach. I peer down at the hands of the body I appear to be occupying: smaller than my own, with a trio of freckles in the space between the left thumb and index fingers. Male hands, not old, going by the lack of wrinkles and sunspots.

Who are you? I think-ask, and his body jerks, his hands flying up to the sides of his skull.

I can't read you, he says, a pea-green frustration tinging his thought-stream. *Why can't I read you?*

I don't know, I reply. *I can hear you though.* He's receiving the information I'm choosing to give him, even if he can't sift through my thoughts and memories. He's VORTEX, one of us ... but can I trust him? What choice do I have? *I'm Johnno.*

He stands up and we look out of the window. The waves are coming in sets, forming massive peaks that rise higher and higher until an especially monstrous one crashes on the shore and they start all over again.

You know that view is fake, don't you? I think-say.

Yeah, I know. He hesitates. *So, you're new here?*

Not exactly. Sensing his confusion, I add, *It's a long story. How long have you been here?*

He places his fingers on the glass. *Since last October. I tried to get help for a friend who was trapped here ... and look what happened.*

What was your friend's name?

Ethan, he says. *Do you know him?*

Yeah. I knew him.

He's dead, isn't he?

Yeah. His grief is washing over me, so intense I can hardly bear it. *His heart was weak.*

The guy falls silent. I think-say, *You're Rawiri, right?*

I used to be. Before.

I know all about that, know all about casting off the names that haven't served me well.

So, what do they call you now? I ask.

He turns away from the fake view, and in the mirror above the sink, I see his reflection. He looks so much older than I'd imagined, with his sunken eyes and shaven head. On his right bicep is a tattoo that I recognise straight away—the Rod of Asclepius, a serpent winding around a staff—an exact match of the tattoo Ethan had on his arm.

They *don't call me anything.* He plucks a mug off the desk in the corner and balances it, heavy in his palm. *But in Eternity, I'm Ariel, Keeper of Secrets.*

He hurls the mug at the mirror, shattering the glass into tiny pieces.

'Get out,' he says aloud. 'Get out, get out.' He shakes his fist at the fragmented image, his pinkie and index fingers extended in a gesture I recognise as the sign to ward off the devil, to ward off *me.*

I don't get a chance to argue, because at that moment I'm whipped out of his thought-stream and into my own, spiralling deeper and deeper, a whirlpool with no beginning and no end.

Violet's wrong. I can't solve this problem, not now, not ever.

Q: What happens to a Black Wolf when he falls into the vortex?

A: I don't know I don't know I don't know.

THIRTY-SEVEN

VIOLET

It's been fifteen days since my return to the Spiral Foundation, fifteen days since anyone talked to me, and I'm going crazy.

I've been locked in a windowless room with only a bed, a small basin and a toilet, marking time by the periodic arrival of my meals. One piece of toast for breakfast, a sandwich and an apple for lunch, a bowl of lentils for dinner.

It's not enough. My stomach hurts from the constant hunger, and I haven't washed properly since the day the tattooed man tried to rape me, unless you count my attempts at washing myself with soggy bits of toilet paper. Worst of all, I can't even travel. My dream-flow is paralysed.

I think it's got something to do with my tooth. I don't have a mirror, but I'm pretty sure there's a filling in my left lower molar, although I've never had a filling in my life. My tongue keeps returning to it, over and over. Hard. Metallic. Foreign.

Every morning, the flap on the bottom of my door opens and a tray slides in. I can't pick it up, because it's attached to the rail-like mechanism below, so I have to either sit on the floor in front of it or take the food off and sit on my bed. A time later—thirty minutes? an hour?—the flap opens, and the tray slides out again. Every morning, I peel a strip off a piece of toilet paper and add it to the growing pile beneath my mattress.

Fifteen days. Fifteen strips of toilet paper.

This morning, the fifteenth morning, I wake with a bad taste in my mouth and overwhelming nausea. I make it to the toilet just in time to throw up what little there is in my stomach. When the tray appears, though, I'm still hungry enough to devour the piece of toast, and drink two plastic cups of water.

Clearly they don't trust me with glass. I don't blame them.

As soon as I've finished eating, I feel better. Weird. I pace around my room, six paces between each wall. *The game has only just begun,* I whisper, over and over. Except, it hasn't. I've been in a holding pattern since I arrived. They're keeping me alive for a reason, I know that, but why the solitary confinement?

And yet, something is different this morning. I don't know how I know that. Perhaps whatever they've inserted into my tooth isn't completely blocking my virally optimised brain, or maybe they're using it to drug me, just like with the arm implant. Maybe that's why I felt sick this morning.

I keep pacing, reciting the words that have been circling around my mind ever since I saw them in Ethan's diary four months ago.

Conditioning. Intensification. Bavaria. The prototype.

Eternity. Asclepius. Spiral. Tattoos. Left-handed? Rawiri? Tracking.

I have my own pieces to add to the puzzle, like *Spirale Forschung* and *Bruno and Harper* and *Dad.* What did my father do after I called him? Did he dismiss it as some kind of crank call? But how could he *not* recognise his daughter, the carrier of fifty percent of his genes?

Did you even try to find me, Dad? Or did you go back to your own life, defending your vaccine and your research?

A new, terrifying thought strikes me: what if my father tried to find me and had to be silenced by the Foundation?

And where is Johnno? For all I know, he could be in the room next to me. He could still be in hospital. He could be dead.

No. No, they would want to keep him alive, even in a deconstructed form. That thought makes me want to cry.

And what about Audrey and Harper, Callum and Mila? What about the German students in the Bavarian forest? And Rawiri, what about Rawiri?

Nausea is creeping up on me again. I sit on the bed. Perhaps I won't be up to my three hundred press-ups and three hundred sit-ups today. It's an attempt to retain some muscle strength, a strategy to pass the long, long hours.

'The prototype,' I whisper. 'Bruno and Harper. Rawiri. Eternity.'

That's when I hear it. A knock on the door, a soft greeting.

'Violet.' The door opens. I look up ... and burst into tears.

*

He's not alone. Dash, our previous fitness instructor for martial arts and shooting and all other physical activities, is flanked by two security guards. They're wearing flak jackets, guns with long barrels tucked into their belts. Dash looks the same as always in his black combat trousers and sleeveless black t-shirt. He's not carrying a gun, not that I can see, but I know he could snap my neck in seconds if he chose to.

'Hey,' he says. I wish I could stop crying. What's wrong with me? 'Come on,' he says, looking all awkward, like he wants to hug me but isn't allowed. 'Let's get you out of here.'

I don't even look behind me as we leave the room. There's nothing to leave behind, nothing that is mine, anyway. My nausea forgotten, I let Dash lead me to a lift bank, where he pushes the button labelled G.

We're on One Below, as I suspected. I wonder how many others like me are down here, wonder how many have kept their minds.

Have I kept my mind, or am I halfway to being deconstructed? How am I supposed to know?

Dash squeezes my shoulder. 'You're all right,' he says. I wish he'd stop being so nice to me.

We ascend in the lift, the security guards standing uncomfortably close to me. When the doors open, Dash guides me not to my old room, but towards the infirmary. The guards walk a few paces behind us, their eyes boring into my neck. I wish I had my slingshot; wish I could fling my dream-flow wolf out of my earthly body.

Johnno, I try, for what must be the thousandth time since we were separated. *Phoenix. Wolf.* But I'm talking to myself, it seems.

It's no surprise when Melody walks out of the infirmary, although I'm not used to seeing her with short hair.

'Hello, Violet.' She doesn't look as pissed off as I thought she might, considering it's only been three weeks since Johnno and I dumped her in the desert, along with Greta.

I sniff—my tears seem to have pooled in my nose—and glance at Dash. 'Are you staying?'

He hesitates before shaking his head. 'I'll see you later,' he says. 'I can take you to your room, bring you something to eat.'

At the mention of food, my mouth floods with saliva. It's annoying, as if I'm no better than a dog or—

(*A wolf*)

The image is lightning quick, gone before I can grasp it.

Johnno?

Melody gives Dash a dismissive nod and he turns on his heel. The guards don't leave, though. No, they follow us in. I can't help but remember the last time I was in here with Melody, when I lied to her and told her I had an itch *down there* before taking her hostage with the Javier virus.

God knows where the vial is now. It's probably dead, anyway. At least, I hope it is.

'So, Violet,' Melody says, after directing me to sit on the single bed. 'How are you feeling?'

'Like crap,' I reply. 'Thanks for asking.'

'Hmm.' Melody's nose has wrinkled slightly. I guess I stink. 'Well, you can count yourself lucky that the Foundation considers you valuable enough to leave intact.'

'Like the prototype? Or wait, do I need to have slept with Bruno to achieve that kind of status?' I glance at the guards, who are standing in the corner, their eyes still on me. Guess I'm considered dangerous. I'm not sure if I should be pleased or bothered by that.

Melody doesn't even flinch. 'He's no longer with us,' she says. 'And I wouldn't recommend sleeping with the staff, if I were you. As for having sex with your fellow VORTEX members, well, there's not much I can do about that.'

A hot flush creeps up my neck. 'You don't know anything,' I mumble. How could they know about me and Johnno?

'We'll see.' She slaps a blood-pressure cuff around one of my arms, a tourniquet around the other. 'We need to take some blood tests, get you cleaned up. Are you hungry?'

I want to say no, but I can't. I'm so hungry I feel as though I'm going to throw up again, which doesn't make sense. I try not to jump when Melody inserts a needle in my arm, don't look away as my blood swirls into the vacuum containers she pushes onto the end. She listens to my heart and lungs, then asks me to lie on my back so she can feel my stomach and check my reflexes with an electronic tendon hammer. Lastly, she shines a torch into my eyes and mouth.

'You're looking pretty good,' she tells me. 'I just need one more sample.'

'Yeah, what do you want? An eye? A piece of my brain? I hear Greta's pretty good at virtual lobotomies.'

Melody's lips grow thin. 'You might want to try keeping your mouth shut for once.'

I'm tempted to push her further, to see how much it will take for her to lose her cool. The last thing I want is to end up in solitary confinement again, though, so I do as she says. A sample of my urine, whatever, I should count myself lucky they don't want anything grosser.

'Good,' she says, when I hand her the urine pottle. 'I'll get Dash to take you to your room.' She takes a PA out of the pocket of her jumpsuit and taps on the screen. He's there within a couple of minutes, now wearing a cap, like he's been outside since I last saw him.

The guards still stick to us like glue, but keep a bit more distance this time, maybe ten paces behind us rather than four.

'Look,' Dash murmurs. 'I'm really sorry about—you know.'

I wrap my arms around myself. 'Why are you still here? Is there anyone left to train?'

He glances at me. 'Well, there's you.'

'Me?' I give out a short laugh. 'As if they're going to let me out again. I'm as good as useless anyway.'

A pained expression flits across his weathered face. 'That's not true.'

'Isn't it?' I prod my violated tooth with my finger.

Dash doesn't reply. But when we get to my room, which looks no different from when I left, he says, 'One step at a time, OK?' I could be imagining the slow way he blinks at me after he says that. Could be.

He points at the tray on my desk, which, unlike the tray in my cell this morning, is loaded with food: croissants and yoghurt and fruit, even a smoothie. 'Keep your strength up.' He exits, locking the door behind him.

I fall on the food like a hungry seventeen-year-old. No, like a wolf.

THIRTY-EIGHT

JOHNNO

I'm floating in the in-between, unsure what is a simulation and what is the manufactured product of my virally optimised, sedated brain. I have no idea how long I've been here, have no idea how long I'll continue to be here. All I know is that, now and then, I'm able to escape; to cast my dream-flow beyond my body, beyond the Foundation, beyond the forest in which I'm hidden.

I can't take shape, but I can home in on the unprotected thought-streams of others. An artist painting in her studio. A teenager smoking dope in his bedroom. A politician planning an election campaign.

But none of them is who I am looking for.

I need to find Nicholas Black, Violet's father. I need to find him before it's too late.

THIRTY-NINE

VIOLET

Once I've devoured my second, far more substantial breakfast, I get into the shower. Watching the grime stream off my body—and even after two weeks, much of that is still red dust—I dare to feel a glimmer of hope.

They have kept me alive. Surely if they were going to deconstruct me, they'd have done that by now. But then I remember Johnno, and despair rises again. I can't stand to lose someone else like that, like Ethan. Guilt mingles with my despair when I realise that it would be ten times worse if Johnno died.

Stop it. No one has said he's dead. Yet.

But why would they tell me if he were dead?

Pushing the bad thoughts away, I run the soap over my body, taking pathetic pleasure in being clean at last. Closing my eyes, I imagine Johnno's lips on my skin, his mouth on my throat.

Together, we are infinite. Alone, we are nothing.

But I *am* alone. No Ethan, no Johnno, no Callum or Audrey or Harper.

And yet, the only one who I know for sure is dead is Ethan, if only through the memories of Harper, who was the first to find him after his cardiac arrest. The image is too painful for me to dwell on. I let my mind continue to wander. Quite apart from the VORTEX members, what about the students at the Spirale Forschung?

I can't attempt contact with any of them, though. At least, not while this damned thing is in my tooth.

After shutting off the water, I wrap a towel around myself (so white, so clean), and stare at the mirror. It's been weeks since I've seen my reflection, and it's a bit of a shock. I still haven't got used to my iris tattoo, blue rather than the brown I was born with. My face is thinner, my hair longer. Opening my mouth as wide as I can confirms my suspicions. There's something foreign in one of my molars, something grey and metallic.

'Damn it,' I whisper, before going to get dressed. I'm brushing my hair when there is a knock on my door. I don't even bother telling whoever it is to come in. As expected, the door opens anyway.

Melody eyes me up and down. 'That's an improvement.'

'If I offended you so much, then perhaps you should have let me take a shower sooner.'

'If you hadn't bitten the hand that feeds you, then perhaps we would have,' she retorts. If only she knew that my wolf form could bite her hand clean off.

Except, my wolf form is currently out of action, disabled.

'Greta would like to speak with you,' Melody says. Ice-cold fear ripples down my spine. Is this it? Is Greta going to deconstruct me?

Wordless, I accompany Melody down the corridor until we reach a door I recognise, the door to the Oval Room. It's the same room in which Bauer briefed Johnno and me before our trip to Berlin, the same room where they debriefed me on my return. Melody pauses in front of the retinal scanner, and the door slides open. My stomach clenches as soon as I hear Greta's voice. Just another conditioned response.

For the second part of the experiment, Albert was placed in a room with a white rat.

'Violet. You look well.' Greta rises from her seat and indicates for me to sit opposite her. Melody sits between us, at the head of the table.

'That's a miracle,' I say. 'Since I've been half-starved for the past two weeks.'

'I can't imagine you ate too well while roaming around the desert either,' Greta says. 'Sounds like you and Mr Fletcher had quite an adventure together.' She and Melody exchange a *look.*

Ignoring that, I ask, 'What have you done with them?'

Greta's long lashes flutter behind her green-rimmed glasses. 'I assume you're referring to your fellow VORTEX members?'

'Audrey,' I say. 'Where is she?'

'Audrey didn't fare so well on her mission,' Greta says. 'In fact, one might say she had a nervous breakdown.'

'Like Sarah Schumann?' The words escape before I can check them. Greta's eyes dart towards Melody, back to me.

'Where did you hear that name?'

'She's the one who tried to kill me,' I say, and, when neither of them replies, 'Your precious prototype didn't turn out the way you hoped, so you let her self-destruct. Is that what you've done to Audrey?'

Greta leans forward. 'I don't know where you've got your information from, Ms Black, but you seem to have a twisted version of the truth. Sarah Schumann was psychotic, something that was not apparent when we employed her. As for Audrey, I'm sorry to tell you that she chose to end her own life.'

My chest squeezes hard. 'You're lying.'

Greta's coral-pink lips peel away from her teeth. 'We have video evidence, Ms Black, if you'd like to see it.'

'I don't want to see it,' I say, but it's too late, and the screen on the wall has lit up. Audrey is sitting on a chair, her hair dishevelled, her pupils unnaturally dilated. She's staring at something in her lap, her breathing rapid. I should look away, but I don't, not until she lifts the plastic bag and tugs it over her head. The fit is snug, too snug, and when she inhales I clap my hands over my eyes. I can't block my ears, though, can't help but hear the drumming of her heels on the floor, followed by a sickening thud.

'Cause of death, asphyxiation,' Greta says. 'Such a shame.'

I lower my hands. 'No,' I say. 'The cause of death is the Foundation, just like with all the other people who have died because of you and your insane experiments.'

'I realise you are upset, Violet,' Melody says softly, 'but you are being overly dramatic.'

Struggling to control the tremor in my voice, I say, 'What about Harper? What have you done with her?'

'Harper is recovering well,' Greta says.

I steel myself. 'Recovering from what?'

She points her PA at the screen again. 'Just a tiny procedure.

She's so much happier now.'

I stare, aghast, at the video footage. Harper is strapped blindfolded to a bed, electro-dots stuck to her temples, a plastic ventilation tube snaking out of her mouth. As I watch, her head arches back on her neck, her arms and legs contracting.

'Oh my God,' I say. 'Oh my God, that's—'

'Electrotherapy,' Greta says. 'Don't worry, she was fully anaesthetised. And she's so much happier than she was before.'

'You're monsters.' I'm trembling all over. 'If anyone ever finds out what you're doing, you'll be sent away forever.'

'Electroconvulsive therapy is practised all around the world,' Greta says. 'It's hardly torture. As for you, I see no need to administer such treatment.' She smiles. 'You've really exceeded all expectations, Violet. I don't think you realise how special you are.

If you cooperate with us, you could lead a very happy and fulfilling life.'

Acid rage bubbling in my gut, I say, 'I'm sure the same was said to the Jews when they were sent to Auschwitz.'

Melody tuts. 'You do have a tendency to be dramatic, Violet. You've hardly been tortured. The past fortnight has merely been a cooling-down period, a necessary measure after the stress of your escapade with Jonathan.'

'Yeah?' My voice rises. 'And where is he? What are you doing to him? Because I'm telling you now, if you're giving him electric shocks and whatever else, then there's no way I'm cooperating with anything.'

Greta says, 'I can assure you he is perfectly safe. He's recovering from his injury. You'll see him again, in time. I'm sure he will also be interested in recent developments.' She glances at Melody. 'Do you want to tell her, or shall I?'

Melody clears her throat. 'Your test results were very interesting, Violet. Would you like to know what they showed?'

'Let me guess. I've mutated?' Maybe I shouldn't speak so soon. What if I *have* mutated? What if they found traces of, I don't know, wolf genes in my DNA? Is that even possible?

I'm so caught up in my train of thought that I think I've misheard Melody at first. Because surely she didn't say...

Melody smiles. 'That's right. We'll arrange for an ultrasound, but judging from your blood test, I'd say you're about five weeks along.'

'Five—what?' No. No, it can't be. 'There has to be a mistake. I had an injection.'

'Well,' Melody says, 'I guess it failed.'

I can't read her thought-stream, can't delve into her memories, but I know this from the way she's averted her gaze, from the way her hands are twisting in her lap: she is lying. There were no hormones in that injection. She knew this might happen. Not just that, she *wanted* this to happen.

I leap up. 'I hate you!' I scream. I pluck Greta's glass of water off the table and throw it at the wall, taking great pleasure in the shattering noise. 'I hate you, I hate you!' In a flash, the security guards are in the room, but there's no need for them to restrain me. I can already feel the jab in my gums, sedative dissolving into my bloodstream and up to my brain.

'Really, Violet,' Melody murmurs as I collapse into her arms, 'you'd think you would have learned by now.'

FORTY

JOHNNO

I can't float in my dream-flow state forever, not when someone else is pulling the strings on my puppet-like existence. Units of time later—hours? days? weeks?—I'm jerked into my earthly body, eyes scraping open, breathing against the shards of glass in my lungs. Seems the longer I'm away from my body, the more painful it is to return.

'Good morning, Mr Fletcher.' Marlow straightens the cuffs of his white suit jacket. 'Back in the land of the living, I see.'

I don't speak, partly because my tongue is glued to the roof of my mouth, and partly because I have nothing to say. When I go to sit up, I realise I'm in a bed rather than a pod. The bush view out of the window is depressingly familiar. It's the same room they gave me when I first arrived last August, still reeling from my sister's death.

Marlow passes me a glass of water. 'You'll be pleased to know that you've made a full recovery from your gunshot wound.'

I swallow water, cough, swallow some more.

'Still nothing to say, Jonathan?'

I could tell him it's Johnno. I could, but I don't want him to call me by that name, because the last person who called me that was Violet. *Please, please, be OK.*

'I expect you'll also be pleased to know that Violet is safe and well,' Marlow continues.

'I'm not sure if your definition of *safe and well* is the same as mine.' My voice comes out all croaky. Guess it's been a while. How long is a while? I have no idea.

'Apparently not. You're lucky you're not both dead. The desert is pretty unforgiving like that.' He pulls a chair up to my bed and perches on it. 'Tell me, who shot you?'

I look at him for a moment before saying, 'I don't know who they were. They were holding Violet down.' The memory of Violet's assault is a fist in my chest. It's not such a leap to imagine one of them shooting me.

Marlow gives me an intent look back. 'Did they rape her?' So clinical, as if we're discussing the weather.

I grit my teeth. 'No.'

'Thank God for that,' he says, almost to himself. 'That could have ... well. Anyway.' He focuses back on me. 'You must be wondering, where to from here?'

'Hard to wonder anything when you've been in a coma for days.' Pride stops me from asking exactly how long, but Marlow supplies me with the answer anyway.

'Sixteen days. I hope you'll forgive us for sedating you, but the last thing we wanted was you doing something rash before you'd been restored to full health.'

'So you can deliver me back to Greta?' I ask. 'Like a fattened calf?'

'Now, now, no need to be like that.' He adjusts his tie. 'Anyway, there's been a slight change in directive, shall we say. Tell me, Mr Fletcher, how would you fancy another trip to Germany?'

'To do what?' I ask, wary.

'We need some help to train the next generation of VORTEX members. We think you'd be ideal.'

I narrow my eyes at him. Is this some kind of trick? 'What makes you think I'd be interested in that?' And why would they trust me to do it?

Marlow crosses his legs. 'Our WEB scan shows your cognitive capacity has increased hugely since we last evaluated you. That, along with your experience in the army, would make you a valuable addition to our team.' No doubt catching my incredulous expression, he says, 'It could be a very good career move for you. As we've already discussed previously, the salary would be seven hundred and fifty thousand euro per annum.'

'Before you drugged me, you mean.'

Marlow frowns. 'I don't know what you mean.'

'Cut the crap,' I snap. 'Greta's plan was to experiment on me and deconstruct me, to turn me into some sort of obedient robot. How come that's changed all of a sudden?'

He inclines his head slightly. 'Well, firstly, you and Violet have talents that we don't want to let go to waste. And secondly, I have a piece of information that may affect how you view the terms of your employment, and your future with the Foundation.'

'Such as?' Why do I get the feeling we're playing a game of chess, and that he's just put me in check?

'Tell me,' he repeats (Jesus, I wish he'd stop saying that), 'you and Violet became quite close while you were away, is that right?'

I tense. 'Hard not to be when you're spending every minute together.' I'm reluctant to give him a single piece of information he could use against me.

'Did you use contraception?'

Huh? 'That's none of your business.' But why is he—oh. Oh no. No, no, no.

'Well,' Marlow says, 'perhaps not, but it should have been *your* business. You know what I'm about to say, don't you?'

I do. I do, but I can't quite fathom it, and yet now I know why he's looking so confident, because now he's moved me into checkmate and now I—we—are screwed.

Oh, you bastards. You complete pricks.

'Congratulations, Mr Fletcher,' Marlow says. 'Have you got any questions?'

FORTY-ONE

VIOLET

The following morning starts off much as the last one in the windowless cell did, except I'm delivered a better breakfast after my vomiting episode. Chia-seed pudding with berries on top, a smoothie, a bagel with cream cheese and jam. I'd been considering going on a hunger strike, but I'm starving, and I know I'll feel better after I eat.

Halfway through, I start crying. It's no different from what I did for most of the afternoon and evening. My body hasn't been under my control for some time—apart from our nine days in the desert—but now things are a hundred times worse.

There's a hostage inside me demanding to be fed. A hostage that *they* are going to use to make me do whatever they want. A hostage that, eventually, they will want to do tests and experiments on.

I push away my tray and crawl into bed, tugging the covers up to my chin.

Closing my eyes, I focus on the last image I have of Johnno—lying on a narrow bed in the emergency department while medical staff inserted needles and catheters and tubes into him. His skin was so pale, the tattoo above his eyebrow visible for all to see.

Johnno, I send. *Phoenix. Wolf.* It's useless, of course. Surely *they* can't keep blocking me forever, though? If they do, then how are they going to use me like they did in Berlin?

But maybe it's not me they want. Maybe I'm just the incubator.

No, no, no. I curl up, the balls of my hands pressed into my eyes. It's no good, I'm crying again. Maybe it's the hormones. Or maybe, more likely, it's the realisation that I'm a fly caught in the Foundation's gigantic web.

*

I spend the next hour in bed, drifting in and out of sleep until I hear a knock on my door. The door doesn't open, as I expect. Instead, my visitor says, 'Violet? Can I come in?'

'I can't let you in,' I say, my voice dull, but my heart leaping a little when I realise it's Dash.

'I can unlock it. If that's OK.'

'Sure.' I roll onto my side, my back to the door to hide my puffy eyes, and hear a beep and click.

'Are you going to spend all day in bed?'

'Might as well.'

'Come on, Vi, you can't spend the rest of your life like that.'

'The rest of my life?' I turn to face him, unable to stop my burst of anger. 'What do you know about the rest of my life? For all I know, they'll be slitting my throat as soon as I've—I've—'

'Ssh.' Dash sits beside me and gives me an awkward hug. 'Like I said,' he murmurs, 'you can't spend the rest of your life like that.' And when I go very still, wondering if I'm imagining things, he adds, so softly I almost miss it, 'Not here, OK?' He straightens up. 'Want to come for a swim?'

The last thing I want to do is reveal my body, even though there's nothing to see from the outside yet. But for the first time in days, I dare to think I might get out of here after all.

'Fine,' I snap for the benefit of the camera. 'If it'll stop you nagging me.'

My time in Berlin taught me how to act. It taught me how to hate, too. Most of all, it taught me that nothing is as it seems.

*

The pool is deserted when Dash and I arrive, apart from a pair of budgies strutting around the deckchairs. The sky is as blue as always, the water barely rippling in the slight breeze. After dumping my towel on a deckchair, I sit on the side, dangling my legs in the water. Dash dives in the deep end and begins swimming laps: one, two, three, four. I slide in. The pool is a perfect temperature. If only I could relax enough to enjoy it.

Dash touches the side and stands up. 'Feeling better now?'

'Kind of.'

'Here.' He nudges a flutter board towards me and takes one for himself. 'Let's do some slow kicking, shall we?'

I roll my eyes at him. 'Olympic training, OK.' But I do as he asks.

We're halfway across the pool when Dash says, 'Have you seen Harper yet?'

'I haven't seen her. Or Callum.'

'You'll see them soon enough. Callum and Harper, I mean. But I've got to warn you, they're ... different.'

'I heard.' Panic-grief strafes through my chest, but I try to focus on my breathing, try to look calm for the cameras mounted on the outside of the building. We reach the other end and turn, like synchronised swimmers.

'Look,' Dash says once we're a safe distance away from the poolside, so quietly that I have to strain to hear him, 'you can't stay here.'

'Well, fine, I'd better go pack my bags.' Sarcasm. I can't help it. I'm so sick of it all, so sick of fighting a battle I can't win.

'Listen for a minute, will you? I can help you.'

I hesitate. 'How?'

'Keep kicking,' Dash murmurs. 'Look, they're getting twitchy. They've eliminated Callum and Harper's combativeness, sure, but at the expense of their VORTEX abilities. And as for the phase III experiments with the volunteers, that's been a complete screw-up as far as I can tell. You and Johnno are all they have, and they have no idea how to control you.'

Struggling to process all of that—because if Callum and Harper are useless, then I hate to think what long-term plans the Foundation has for them—I say, 'No, they *do* know how to control us. By using our—' I can't bring myself to say *unborn child.* It still doesn't seem real, and besides, it's probably closer to a tadpole than a child at the moment. 'And they've put something in my tooth, do you know about that?'

'Yeah,' he says, and then neither of us says anything until we've reached the middle of the pool again, when Dash instructs me to float on my back. 'I can help you,' he repeats. 'But you're going to need to do exactly as I say, OK?'

'I don't know why you're doing this,' I say. 'Why should I trust you?' If *they* find out, they'll kill him, or worse.

Dash's laugh sounds hollow. 'Because I can't stand by and watch this anymore,' he says. 'They employed me when no one else would, but if I can't live with myself, then why bother?'

I stand up. 'What do you mean, when no one else would?'

Dash shakes his head. 'The less you know about that, the better. It's risky, but if we get this right, you could be back in New Zealand by the end of the week. Are you in?'

I don't even hesitate this time. 'Yes. I'm in.'

'Good.' He raises his voice. 'All right, let's give it a rest for now. I'll see you later for a VirtReal sim, OK? Maybe around three?'

'Three o'clock.' Abandoning the flutter board, I swim to the end of the pool and get out.

Don't get excited. Don't get excited.

Too late.

FORTY-TWO

JOHNNO

It's April Fool's Day, and I'm still reeling from yesterday's news. If only it were a joke. When I'd asked if I'd get to see Violet soon, if I could, God forbid, return to Australia, Marlow had merely said, *In time. She's not due until December.*

I'm playing by their rules for now, as in literally. I'm solving mathematical and physics equations, or trying to. Seems I'm not much good at sending and receiving information from other sources at the moment. Funny, that.

'All right,' Marlow says after an hour of me doing badly, 'I think we need to make some adjustments.' His brow is furrowed, one half of his shirt tail hanging out of the front of his trousers.

I lean back in my chair, one of the swivel ones Tilly and I used to spin each other around on. 'What sort of adjustments?'

Marlow regards me coolly. 'It's about time you had a dental check-up, don't you think?'

*

A couple of hours later, I lie on a bed in the infirmary while a dentist pokes and prods inside my mouth.

'I need to do a bit of work on one of your teeth,' he says. 'Looks like someone's done a pretty rough job of this filling here.'

'Yeah, well, it's been annoying the hell out of me,' I tell him, once he's taken his fingers out of my mouth.

'I'm sure,' the dentist murmurs, before stuffing cotton wool in my left cheek and numbing my gum with an injection. A couple of minutes later, there is an intense tugging in my lower jaw, and then it's out, a small cylindrical object gripped between his pliers. Almost immediately, I'm aware of a low-level hum, the sound-vibration I've become accustomed to in the months since I got M-fever.

I'm not getting much from the dentist though, not yet.

'Can I keep it?' I ask, figuring it might come in useful, but he ignores me and goes on to fill my tooth with something that tastes kind of chalky. A *real* filling, I'm guessing. I'm getting something from his thought-stream now, brief flashes, like the sun emerging from behind the clouds. He's under the impression that I'm a wanted criminal, and wants to get out of here as soon as possible. He's thinking of the security guards standing outside the door. He's thinking of the danger money he'll be getting in return for extracting the *monitor* from my tooth.

He doesn't have a clue.

'Right,' he says, after getting me to rinse and spit in a basin. 'All done.'

'Thanks.' I sit up, swinging my legs over the side of the bed. 'How are my teeth?'

'Perfect, apart from that one.' He doesn't even rinse his instruments, just chucks them into a bag and slings it over his shoulder. Once he has left, the security guards come to escort me to my room. When Marlow arrives half an hour later, saying it's time to re-run the tests, I tell him I've got a crook gut.

'I've been to the loo, like, ten times.' I clutch my stomach. 'Guess it must have been something I ate.'

'Maybe,' Marlow says, unimpressed. 'I'll get someone to come and check on you later.'

'OK.' I leap up and hurry into the bathroom, slamming the door behind me. Marlow doesn't stay to listen.

Which is good, because I have work to do.

*

Once I've stayed on the loo for an acceptable period of time, I press the button beside the window until it is tinted black, as if it's night rather than two in the afternoon. Lying on the bed, I close my eyes.

Violet, I think-whisper over and over, but there's no trace of her thought-stream, not even a shimmer. Either she's comatose or she's blocked, just as I was before the dentist removed my tooth implant. At least I know she's not dead now. No, she's far too valuable. I wonder how valuable the offspring of a couple of VORTEX members is, what kind of price that would fetch on the black market.

Offspring. That. Our child. Temporarily overwhelmed, I lose focus, at least until a voice jerks me into alertness.

I told you to leave me alone. It's Rawiri or Ariel or whatever his name is.

I wasn't trying to bug you. I don't leave him though, not yet. *You can hear me now, though ... right?*

I can hear you. Rawiri's irritated. Somehow I've disrupted his thought-stream right when he was in the middle of programming.

Are you making a new game? I think-ask.

Rawiri hesitates. *It's not new, exactly. It's the next version of Eternity.*

Trying to find more of us?

His reply is swift, vehement. *No.*

Then what? I don't really have to ask. I'm streaming him loud and clear. *Oh. Wow. Do you really think that'll work?* Eternity II is nothing like Eternity I. The new version features a plague of a pox virus, an organisation of unscrupulous healers, a group of adolescents with telepathic abilities. *What do they call that, VirtReal imitates life? Life imitates VirtReal?*

Get out. Rawiri isn't very good at blocking, maybe because he's never had to do it before. That's when I realise he's never been in close proximity to anyone else like us, not in all these months.

That must be really lonely, I think-say, expecting to get chucked out of his head at any second.

Piss off, Rawiri says, but his thought-stream is wavering, softening.

Hey, I think-say. *Have you ever travelled?*

Have I ... what?

Like this. I show him my memories as an eagle, a wolf, a sparrow. Rawiri's heart speeds up, and I sense something else, a yellow-orange glow. Curiosity. Disbelief. Hope. I can feel the thrum of his dream-flow, too, shapeless and molasses-thick.

I've hovered above the building before, he replies. *But I've never ... I don't know if that's possible.*

Watch. I concentrate my dream-flow until it is super-dense, super-coiled, before flinging it out.

And oh, I am Black Wolf again, at last, at last. I'm padding between the trees, the forest floor moist beneath my paws. I hear tūī, bellbirds, the whisper of wind in leaves. I smell moss, dirt, and faintly, my own wolf-scent.

Pricking my ears up, I inhale, taking in the scent of an *other.* Swivelling my head, I stare straight into the other's amber eyes.

Holy shit, I think-say.

Took the words right out of my mouth, the Rawiri-lion replies. If I knew better, I'd almost think he were smiling.

FORTY-THREE

VIOLET

It's lunchtime, a couple of hours after my swim with Dash, before I see anyone else from VORTEX. Harper and Callum are sitting opposite each other at one of the long tables that used to accommodate the rest of the collective. I can almost see them now. Ethan, with his blue-black hair and his Rod of Asclepius tattoo, a snake winding around a staff. Audrey, with her gentle smile and way with words. Johnno, who was always trying his hardest not to look at me, back when he was Phoenix and I was oblivious to how he felt about me.

I blink, and the ghost-images dissolve. Harper looks up and smiles. It's nothing like her old smile, which was sparkly and sassy. This is more like the automatic smile your parents teach you to deliver to shopkeepers and aunties who give you presents you don't like.

'Hi, Harper.' I sit next to her. 'How are you?'

'I'm fine,' Harper says, an automatic answer to accompany her automatic smile. 'I'm sorry, have we met?'

I frown. 'It's me. Violet.' Do I look so different? Apart from the black regrowth in my hair and the scar on my arm where Johnno cut the implant out, I don't think I've changed all that much.

'Violet, OK. Hi.' Harper gives me another empty smile.

A grey sense of despair weighing on me, I turn my attention to her companion. 'Hey, Callum.'

Callum, who is shovelling food into his mouth like it's merely a chore he has to complete, glances up. 'Hi.' It's clear he doesn't recognise me, either. That's not the only thing that's different. His nose is crooked, as if it has been broken since I last saw him.

Did you put up a fight, Callum? But it was no good, was it? They broke you anyway.

I don't feel hungry anymore, but my stomach is empty and the nausea is creeping up on me again. So I force myself to eat, just like Callum, until my plate is empty. There is no conversation, none of the usual banter. When I stand up to leave, no one says goodbye.

Dash is right. Johnno and I are the only ones left. The others are either dead, or might as well be.

I wait until I get to my room before letting the tears escape.

*

I haven't been in my room long, maybe twenty minutes, when Melody comes to collect me for my first ultrasound. If it weren't for my earlier conversation with Dash, I'd be resisting every step of the way. But I'll play along, be good Violet for now. I need to have at least some of my privileges restored. There are no security guards today, and since I went swimming with Dash my door has been left unlocked.

'How are you feeling?' Melody asks once we reach the infirmary. She's wearing tiny diamantes in her eyebrows, some new fashion trend, no doubt.

'I'm OK,' I say, cautious but polite.

'Good.' She passes me a hospital-style gown and draws the

curtains. 'Put this on. I'll be with you soon.'

I slip the gown on, wincing as my arms brush my tender breasts. I'm sure they're getting bigger, too. Does that happen this early on?

Melody pushes a machine on wheels through a gap in the curtains. 'I'll need you to remove your underwear,' she says, after instructing me to lie down.

'What?' I scowl at her. 'Why?'

She slides a pair of gloves over her hands. 'At this early stage, the only way we can see the foetus is with a transvaginal ultrasound.'

I stare at the ultrasound probe. 'You're going to put that—no.'

She touches my arm, and I flinch. 'Relax,' she says. As if. 'It won't hurt. I promise.'

I hesitate, but do as she says, knowing that if I refuse she will sedate me anyway. I can't afford to be groggy.

It's risky, but if we get this right, you could be back in New Zealand by the end of the week.

When she inserts the probe, I close my eyes, trying to control my breathing. It's cold and slightly uncomfortable, but

Melody is right, it doesn't hurt. A minute or so later, she says, 'There it is. Do you want to see?'

I stare at the image on the ultrasound screen. Melody points. 'This is your uterus. And this,' she points to a blob at one end of the oval-shaped cavity, 'is the foetal pole.'

She could be lying. For all I know, that could be nothing, a wrinkle in the lining of my uterus. And yet, I'm not imagining the nausea or my sore boobs. Denial can only get you so far.

'In a week or so, we'll able to see a heartbeat.' Melody takes the probe out.

I yank the sheet over me and sit up. 'Don't think I'm letting you do that to me every week.'

'I'm sure that won't be necessary.' Her tone is lacquer-smooth. 'We can check the foetal DNA in a few weeks, too.'

My heart speeds up. 'How?' Will they be sticking needles in my stomach, or worse, in the same place she just put that probe? No way am I letting them do that.

No, I won't, because I'm not planning to be here.

'Relax.' Melody chucks her gloves in the bin and crosses to the basin. 'All we'll need is a sample of your blood. It's very clever. We can sequence the foetus' whole genome that way.'

I scoop my clothes off the end of the bed. 'What if I don't want that?' What if my baby—I still can't get used to those two words—doesn't want that? What if *they* find something terrible, such as a gene predicting early death? And, perhaps even more terrifying, what if the L25 I took a few days ago has led to some sort of horrible birth defect, like blindness or brain damage? But I don't voice any of that. Instead, I say, 'What about my DNA? Have you tested that?'

Melody smiles. Of course. Stupid question.

Trying to control my growing fury, I say, 'And did you find what you expected?'

She perches on a stool. 'The DNA tests on you and the rest of the VORTEX group seemed normal at first, nothing out of the ordinary. But our recent, repeat tests on your DNA gave us some very unusual results. Unheard of, in fact.'

'Unusual how?' I tug my clothes on and smooth my hair.

She hesitates. 'Have you ever heard of telomeres?' When I shake my head, she says, 'They're regions at the end of the chromosomes that protect them from damage and deterioration. The telomeres naturally shorten as we age, and it's thought that many age-related diseases are due to their shortening. For a long time, scientists have been interested in finding out if we can slow aging, or even stop it, by halting the shortening of telomeres. No one has ever been able to do that, of course.' She looks up. 'Not to date, anyway. But when we tested your telomere length a few days ago, we found that it was no different from when you first arrived. The same is true for Harper, Callum and Jonathan.'

'So we're not getting any older?' I prod my filled tooth with my tongue. It's buzzing ever-so-slightly, and I can't work out why.

Melody's eyebrows glitter at me, the diamantes reflecting the overhead lights. 'Chronologically you are, of course. But biologically ... well, it's still too early to tell whether you're...' She laughs. 'Immortal. That sounds crazy, doesn't it?'

'Yeah. Really crazy.' My brain races ahead. People are always paying for things that they think will make them look younger. Stem cell regeneration, fat dissolution, skin plumping. My mother had told me more than once that some people would do anything, pay any amount, to stay young.

Anything.

My mind is coming up with questions faster than I can process them. Like, what if the baby has inherited the telomere thing from me and Johnno? Does that mean it will never get any older after it's born? Or does that only happen once it's fully grown? From the way Melody is looking at me, I know she wants to answer all of those questions and more.

'Have you finished?' I ask, injecting as much ice into my tone as I can muster. It's either that, or start screaming at her.

'Certainly.' Melody stands up and opens the door. 'Take care of yourself, Violet. You have two people to think about now. And, potentially, so many more people than that.'

I want to tell her she's disgusting. I want to tell her I'd rather be dead than be the next prototype, or worse, give birth to the ultimate prototype. Instead, I say nothing and take the long way to my room, via the outside of the building.

*

My room is an oasis, the air con set to just the right temperature, clean sheets on my bed. I flop onto my stomach—guess I won't be able to do that for much longer—and push my pillow aside so I can lie with my head in my arms.

That's when I see a black spiral notebook with a pen clipped onto the front cover. Someone has left it under my pillow, but who? My heart thudding, I open it up. The front page has every letter of the alphabet listed, each with a symbol beside it: A = &, B = #, and so on. At the very bottom, someone has written in letters so tiny I have to squint to read them: *tear this out and keep it somewhere safe.*

Someone. Dash—has to be. I tear it out, slowly, casually, and gaze at the next page. The only text I can recognise is the numbers, 1, 2, 3. Each number has a line of code written beside it. Looking between the page I've just torn out and the code, I manage to decipher the first line. *(1). Meet me at 5am tomorrow in library. Lights will be off.* Frowning, I begin deciphering the rest of the instructions. Number two is terrifying but vital. There will be pain. There will be blood. It'll be no worse than what I've already experienced, but if we get this part wrong, I'll have ruined my only chance to get away. Numbers three, four, five and six outline the rest of the plan, which will only work if no one betrays me along the way—including Dash.

Number seven says: *If you have any questions write them in code and leave the piece of paper inside the Nietzsche book in the library by 9pm. I'll leave your answer in the same place.*

Questions. I think for a moment, chewing on the end of the pen. Then I turn to a fresh page and slowly, painstakingly, translate a short sentence into Dash's code.

It's not a question. No, this is a request: *I need you to get a message to my father.*

I tear out the page, fold it into tiny squares and push it into my bra.

Time to visit the library.

FORTY-FOUR

JOHNNO

Rawiri can't get enough of being a lion. It's just gone midnight, and he's still prowling through the bush. I stick close behind him, my wolf-gut satiated from the possum I tore apart soon after leaving my earthly body in bed.

This is awesome, he think-says. *Why would you want to stick around in your boring body?*

Because they *could do anything to it while I'm gone,* I reply.

They already have, Rawiri says darkly. He crouches, his tail swinging from side to side. Seconds later he pounces, and I hear a crunch, followed by moist smacking sounds.

Mouse? I ask.

Mmm.

You're disgusting.

You can talk, Possum Breath, Rawiri retorts. If I were in my human form, I'd be laughing.

Well, I say, *it's all fun and games until someone shoots you.*

True. He sits on his haunches, licks a paw. *What are you going to do, Wolf?*

What do you mean?

About your pregnant girlfriend. The one who used to be Ethan's girlfriend.

None of your business, I retort, feeling like he's just whacked me around the snout.

Sorry.

It wasn't like that, in case you were wondering. No one cheated on anyone.

I said sorry. But what are you going to do? You know what'll happen, don't you?

I don't want to think about it, I say, but I'm getting his images now, babies and needles and stop, stop, stop.

They'll experiment on it, he says, as if I haven't got the point already. *They'll claim it for themselves, clone it and sell it to the highest—*

He yowls when I tackle him, sending him flying. We tussle for a minute or so, nipping at each other before declaring a wordless truce. The last thing we need is to wake up with bite wounds all over our earthly bodies.

If you've got any brilliant ideas, I'm all ears, I think-say, panting.

Rawiri's eyes are twin orbs. *You can rip people's throats out. How do you need anything more brilliant than that?*

It's not that simple. My wolf self can do that, but I have to leave my body behind. There's no way I can manage that. Not by myself, anyway.

What if you don't have to do it by yourself? Rawiri stretches slowly, languidly, as though we're discussing the best way to gut a fish rather than our escape. *You forget, I spend all day plotting.*

Yeah, with expendable characters.

Please yourself. I sense him withdrawing, ready to return to his body. I'd let him, if it weren't for the images he showed me before. Jesus, like things weren't complicated enough.

Wait, I think-say. *Tell me your plan.*

FORTY-FIVE

VIOLET

I'm lying awake in bed, going through the instructions I decoded a few hours earlier with a growing sense of doubt. Impossibility. Inevitability.

This isn't going to work. The plan relies on too many people. They're going to track me down and lock me up for the rest of my life, deconstruct me and take the baby away. The baby that isn't even a baby yet, just a blob of dividing cells. The baby I don't feel any emotional attachment to, and yet ... and yet ... I can't let *them* experiment on an innocent child.

Around one am, I feel another buzz in my tooth, much like what I'd been experiencing off and on throughout yesterday. Is the Foundation checking in on me? Is the implant releasing a drug I don't know about? If so, it's nothing mind-altering. I'm alert, jittery, terrified.

I'm not sure how much sleep I get, maybe three hours at the most. At four-thirty, I wake for the last time. The last time in this room, and hopefully, the Foundation.

I dress quickly. Black leggings, a t-shirt, white trainers with orange soles. Spirals on everything, damn it.

My tooth buzzes again. It won't be doing that for much longer. My gut shrivels in anticipation. Nausea is creeping up on me again, so I gobble a bread roll I brought back from dinner last night and feel better. Sort of.

Oh God, oh God, oh God.

At five to five, I pee, wash my hands and face, brush my teeth. Four minutes later, I'm moving down the corridor, towards the library.

This can't work.

This has to work.

It's dark inside the library. Leaving the lights off, I make my way towards the rear of the room, where I used to sit with the others, reading books at impossible speeds. Dash is at my elbow in seconds, his liniment scent strangely terrifying.

Terrifying, because I know what he is about to do to me.

'Are you sure you don't want anything to take the edge off?' Dash murmurs. I know what he means. A sedative or morphine, even alcohol, like when Johnno and I sliced each other's arms open.

'No.' I sink into a chair. I need to be alert, can't afford to have my senses blunted for this final attempt. Also, I'm vaguely terrified of taking any more drugs after the L25, especially now it's not just me they could be affecting. The new fear threatens to choke me again—*the baby, oh God, I can't believe this is happening to me*—but I shove it away. I can't think about that now. If we don't get this right, we could all be dead.

Light shines into my eyes, and I see Dash's face, backlit by the LED lamp strapped to his forehead. He's gripping a set of bungy cords. 'I need to tie you to the chair,' he says.

I brace myself. 'OK.' A cord around each ankle, the same around my wrists. For my head, he slides a beanie over my scalp and tapes my forehead to the back of the chair. Finally, he inserts a thin wedge of wood between my teeth on the right side of my mouth, so I can't bite him.

I'm shaking all over. I can't move, can't stop what's about to happen now.

Dash picks up pliers and a wad of gauze. 'I'll be as quick as I can.'

It's not quick.

*

I must have blacked out, because the next thing I'm aware of is the carpet next to my cheek. My mouth tastes like blood, and my lower jaw is throbbing.

'You did well,' Dash whispers, helping me sit up. 'But you must let me give you something for the pain. I can't have you fainting on me again.'

I take the water bottle he gives me, along with a couple of tiny pills. 'What are they?'

'Codeine. They won't knock you out, don't worry.'

'OK.' I swallow them down. *Did I scream? Please tell me I didn't scream.* If I did, then I guess no one heard me, or they'd surely have been here by now.

Dash rises to his feet. 'We've got to go.'

'Where's the tooth?'

'I've got it. I left it in your room—OK?'

I nod. My room, yes, good idea. No one will be too concerned if they think I'm in there, having a sleep-in. I rub the side of my face. The pain is less intense now, and there is something else. A hum, a pulsation. Not from the region of my tooth socket, but deep within me.

Johnno, I think, but before I can reach for him, Dash is hurrying me out of a side door and into the crisp morning air. His SUV is only a few steps away. I climb into the boot, relieved to see the back seats are folded down for more room, and pull the army blanket over me. The boot door slams, followed by the driver's door.

Less than a minute later, the SUV stops, and a voice says, 'Where're you off to so early, mate?'

'A run, where else? Thought I could do with a change of scenery.' I'm guessing Dash is pointing, although of course I can't see a thing.

'You're crazy, man,' the guard replies. Dash laughs. The SUV starts moving again. No shouts, no gunshots. Too easy.

FORTY-SIX

JOHNNO

The second of April starts off much the same as the day before. I wake up, eat my breakfast, go to the gym. Solve Marlow's stupid maths and physics problems in fifteen minutes.

'Wow,' he says. I've never heard him say *wow* before, so I guess I did well. Beyond expectations, in fact.

'Might have to find something harder.' I rub a scratch on my neck, glad no one can tell it's from a lion's claw. Rawiri hasn't learned his own strength yet.

'I'm sure you'll find plenty to challenge you in Germany.'

Germany. Shit. I'd forgotten about that. 'When am I leaving?' I ask.

'Tomorrow,' Marlow says, ever so casually.

My jaw drops. 'What? I'm not ready.'

'You're more than ready, Mr Fletcher, as you've just demonstrated.' Marlow drums his fingers on the table between us. 'Although I'm also very interested to see how you could apply your mastery of quantum mechanics to questions related to time theory.'

'In what way?'

Marlow gives me a contemplative look. 'Such as, why does time flow in one direction, something Einstein called "time's arrow"? Is there only a single possible past? Is there a point in space where time flows backwards, and if so, how could we utilise that? There are several unanswered problems you could turn your mind to.'

'Nobel Prize, here we come,' I say, not even bothering to hide my sarcasm. Marlow doesn't reply, just raises an eyebrow at me. I grind my teeth. 'Look. About this Germany thing.'

He holds up a finger. 'I wasn't *asking* if you wanted to go tomorrow, Mr Fletcher, I was *telling* you. Got it?'

Rage ignites behind my eyes, but I push it away, give him the answer he wants. 'Got it. Can I go now?' *Great, I need to talk to Rawiri* now.

'Your transport will arrive at five am tomorrow,' he says as I exit the room. Prick.

I don't know much about time's arrow, not yet, but I know it's getting very short. I hurry to my room, shut the door and fix on my target.

Tonight? Even Rawiri sounds rattled.

Yeah, I reply. *Or you'll be doing this on your own. Which, as you know, will be virtually impossible.*

OK, he think-says. *I guess we've got no choice. But we need to wait until most of them are asleep.*

Midnight?

Perfect. Rawiri's thought-stream fades away.

I rotate my shoulder, which is a little stiff but remarkably unscathed, considering it was blown apart only a few weeks ago. What to do now, except wait?

That's when I remember Violet's father. Surely I can find him now that my virally optimised abilities aren't blunted by the stupid tooth implant. Then, when—if—Rawiri and I escape, we can head straight to the person who might be able to help us. Violet had told me her father's research lab is located on the North Shore, not too far from the hospital. It's a Monday, so chances are that's where he'll be.

I lie down and close my eyes. *Nicholas Black,* I think. *Nicholas Black.* I fling my dream-flow out, and as I do, more questions spring into my expanding brain.

Does one's dream-flow travel forwards, or does it follow the curve of spacetime? Does it obey the second law of thermodynamics?

More importantly, is Nicholas Black the answer to all our problems?

I should have known the last question was as unsolvable as the others.

FORTY-SEVEN

VIOLET

The early morning sun is spilling into the SUV, and the temperature is rising, even though it can't be more than twelve degrees outside. It's an hour since Dash parked about five hundred metres off the road, an hour since he left me to go for a run, and I'm starting to worry that we have already failed at the third step.

(3). I'll park the car and go for a run, which is something I'd normally do, so if anyone tracks me they'll think nothing of it. A man calling himself Ace will pick you up and take you to the airport. Don't go if he gives you any other name. There will be a gun in the bag I've packed for you. Use it if you have to, but you must leave it behind.

I tighten my fingers around the grip of the gun. The old Violet could never have shot anyone, maybe not even to save her own life. The new Violet wouldn't hesitate.

And there it is, the distant sound of a car engine. I take a deep breath, release the gun's safety catch. *Please be Ace. Please be Ace.*

The car draws closer, closer ... and whips past. I let out my breath. What if Ace never comes? I can't stay in the boot all day. Dash never told me how long his run was going to be, but he took a day bag loaded with food and water. He could be hours.

I'm so caught up in my looping thoughts that I don't notice the engine noise getting louder again until it's very close, the tyres kicking up stones and gravel as it slows. It's the same noise as before, low and throaty. I guess they must have turned around.

The car stops, and I hear music blaring, followed by a door slamming. I breathe in, out.

The boot opens. I blink at the man in front of me: tall and dark-skinned, with several teeth missing. As if in sympathy, the throbbing in my jaw intensifies again.

'Hi, Violet,' he says. 'I'm Ace.'

*

The drive is long, five hours in a station wagon that stinks of cigarette smoke. The smell is so intense I'm worried I'm going to throw up. The whole way, Ace plays music at full blast, a horrible mixture of rap and heavy rock. I lie in the back with a blanket over me, as per Dash's instructions. Every now and then, I drink from the water bottle in the bag Dash packed for me, or nibble on some of the snacks: a muesli bar, an apple, crackers.

When I access Ace's thought-stream, I find that he doesn't really know anything about me. As far as he's concerned, he's doing a favour for a friend, one that will earn him some much-needed cash. He thinks he's helping me flee from a violent relationship.

I guess in some ways he's right.

I can tell we're getting closer to civilisation when I start hearing the swish of other cars passing. Do *they* know I've escaped yet? How could they not? For all I know, scum like Chipmunk Cheeks or Detective Scott whatever-his-name-is could be driving past at this very second.

Curling into a ball, I draw the blanket over my head.

Johnno, I think-whisper. *Johnno, are you there?* And *there* it is, a whoosh, so swift, so unexpected, it takes all the breath out of my lungs.

Violet, Johnno think-says. *Violet, where are you? Are you OK?* We lose words for a while after that, communicating in eddies and swirls and (*oh God*) I feel his heart thundering behind my ribs and his breath in my collapsing lungs (*are you*) and I fan my fingers over my leaking eyes and show him how I'm coming home, at last, at last. When the words finally come, Johnno says, *If you need help, I can help just like last time, don't even hesitate* and the memories rush in. A camper van. Thick, unmoving air. Two men, holding me down. Black Wolf leaping through the door.

No, I think-say. *I mean, yes. Of course.*

When Johnno shows me what he's going to do, he and Rawiri, my terror returns.

Wait for me, I beg. *Just wait for me to get to my dad and we'll get you out. You don't have to risk your life like that.*

We can't wait, he replies, *there's not even time,* and I think he might be blocking me but at that moment the car comes to a halt. I raise my head. We're in a car park. In the distance, I see a control tower, an airplane with a kangaroo emblem on the tail.

The boot flies open and Ace gives me a gappy smile.

'Here.' He helps me out, lights a cigarette. 'Need anything else?' I smell jet fuel, hear the roar of a plane taking off. Johnno's heart is still behind my ribs, one heartbeat for every two of mine.

'No,' I lie, my head swimming, my legs wobbling, my jaw aching. 'Thank you.' I pick up my bag, the one Dash packed for me, and start walking towards the terminal.

*

Once inside, I check the departures board and see the direct flight to Auckland leaves at four pm.

(4). Go to counter two. Do not go to any other counter.

Someone bumps into me, and I jump. *Oh no, oh no.*

'Sorry.' The backpacker, a wiry guy with a scraggly beard, gives me an apologetic grin.

'S'OK,' I mumble, trying to focus. I can see counter two now, but there's no one there. What am I meant to do? When I look at the departure board again, I see that check-in for the flight doesn't open until two pm, which is still ten minutes away. I hurry towards the nearest bathroom and lock myself in the toilet. After emptying my bulging bladder, I wash my hands and splash water over my face, then fill my empty water bottle.

Johnno's blue-tinged concern swirls through my consciousness. *Are you all right, Vi?*

I smile, sag against the wall. *I'm all right. Are you?*

As good as I can be. Are you through security yet?

No. Soon, I hope.

Do you really think it'll work?

I stop smiling. *I don't know. Dash seemed to think it would.* The alternative is too dreadful to contemplate.

Sorry. I'm just ... I wish I could help.

I'll be OK. I tilt my head back. *I'm sorry too. For ... you know.* I picture the cells dividing inside me: cells that have half my DNA, half Johnno's.

It's not your fault. You didn't know there was nothing in the injection Melody gave you.

Nothing useful, anyway.

It's not the worst thing that could happen. Johnno's thought-stream softens and I'm getting his images again, his remembered sensations. A white roof. Sultry air. A pair of bodies winding around each other, like DNA, twisting and turning.

I don't regret what we did, I reply, knowing that if that was all the time we were ever going to have together, then I'll take the consequences.

Me neither. Johnno's thought-stream shifts. *Got to go. Be careful, Vi.*

No, you be careful, I counter, but he's gone. Bracing myself, I exit the bathroom and glance towards counter two. There's a woman in uniform there now, her dark hair tied up in a bun. No one else is waiting, so I stroll right up, my pulse thundering in my ears.

'Hello.' She smiles, revealing a perfect set of teeth, and unconsciously, I run my tongue over my newly empty socket. 'Where are you flying to today?'

'Auckland. At four.'

She starts typing. 'Great. Name?'

'Sarah,' I say. 'Sarah Schumann.'

FORTY-EIGHT

JOHNNO

BRIEFING
COMMENCED: 5.30PM
PRESENT: JONATHAN FLETCHER
(VORTEX
MEMBER), DR NOEL MARLOW
(NEUROLOGIST),
ALICE WANG (JUNIOR DOCTOR), MR
HANS
BAUER (CHIEF OF INTELLIGENCE,
INTERNATIONAL TERRORIST AGENCY,
ITA).

Bauer: Welcome, Mr Fletcher. It's been a few months since we last met, I believe.

Marlow: Fifth of January, according to our records.

Bauer: The Berlin debriefing, yes, of course. You've had quite an eventful time since then.

Fletcher: That's a euphemism, if ever I heard one.

Bauer: Excuse me?

Marlow: Just ignore him. Carry on, Mr Bauer.

Bauer: Certainly. Mr Fletcher, I understand you have now fully recovered from your gunshot wound. In addition to that, Doctor Marlow tells me you have made several cognitive leaps since we last met.

Fletcher: If you mean that I'm smarter than I was before, then I'll take your word for it.

Marlow: We are very excited about the next phase. We're confident that Mr Fletcher will be able to use his new abilities to educate the Bavarian cohort. For various reasons, we were unable to progress as we would have liked with the collective consciousness experiments with the New Zealand cohort.

Fletcher: Because you killed half of them off, you mean.

Marlow: Mr Fletcher, please, I would ask that you keep those sorts of comments to yourself.

Fletcher: Certainly.

Bauer: I must admit, I'm somewhat concerned about Mr Fletcher's level of antipathy.

Marlow: Mr Fletcher, would you like to comment on that?

Fletcher: My brain is having trouble processing your commands, which seem to defy logic. Just saying.

Marlow (muttering): For Christ's sake.

Bauer: Mr Fletcher, what is your level of commitment to this experiment? Please bear in mind that if you refuse to participate, we will have to find alternatives for your abilities.

Fletcher (smiling): Hey, just messing with you. Call it a negotiating strategy. I'd like to discuss my salary.

Marlow: Your salary? I thought that had already been addressed.

Bauer: We can discuss your salary. What is it you want, Mr Fletcher?

Fletcher: I'm thinking seven hundred and fifty thousand euro a year is pretty cheap for what you're about to get from me, which probably amounts to a series of major scientific breakthroughs.

Marlow: We're open to negotiation, Mr Fletcher, within reason. Let's raise it to one million per year.

Fletcher: I was thinking more along the lines of one and a half million.

Bauer: That sounds reasonable.

Fletcher: And I want the first half as an advance into my bank account. You know, the one I had under Wolf Schwarz when I was in Berlin.

Marlow: Whatever for?

Fletcher: Call it security.

Bauer: We can deposit a hundred thousand into your bank account, Mr Fletcher, as an advance for services rendered. How does that sound?

Fletcher: I guess we can compromise, as long as it goes in tonight.

Marlow: What's the hurry, Mr Fletcher? Wanting to make a purchase?

Fletcher: I'm nineteen, I have no patience. I want it before the mission begins.

Bauer: We will deposit it before midnight, Mr Fletcher. And from tomorrow onwards, we shall be reverting back to your Berlin identity.

Fletcher (smiling): Great. I always thought I made a good Wolf.

Marlow (clears throat): Doctor Alice Wang will be travelling with you. Have you met?

Fletcher: No, not yet. Hi, Alice. How much are they paying you?

Wang: I'm not sure I should be—

Marlow: Significantly less than you, Mr Fletcher, or should I say, Mr Schwarz.

Fletcher: Pleased to meet you, Alice.

Marlow: Your transport will arrive to pick you up at five am tomorrow, as I said. We're going to leave you with Doctor Wang now, so she can conduct a final medical examination.

Fletcher: I'm not sure I like the word final.

Marlow: Oh, don't worry, Mr Fletcher. I'm sure Doctor Wang has a very fine bedside manner.

Wang (flushing): Maybe he'd prefer a male doctor.

Marlow: I'm sure he wouldn't. I'm sure you'll be very professional, Doctor Wang. You're both adults, after all.

Bauer (standing): Thank you for your time, Mr Fletcher. I'll see you on the other side.

Fletcher: On the other side, yes.
CONCLUDED: 5.43PM
(*RECORDING ENDS*)

FORTY-NINE

VIOLET

'Sarah Schumann.' The woman, whose badge reads *Iris Hanson,* holds my gaze for a moment before angling a screen towards me. 'Look into this, please.' It's the retinal scan for my e-passport, just like when I travelled to and from Berlin, except I was travelling under another name—Liesl Meyer. I stare at the screen, my mind racing.

Dash, please tell me you've sorted this out, or I'm going to get arrested, and we'll all be screwed.

'Thank you, Sarah.' Iris's slender fingers fly over her keyboard. 'Have you got anything to check in?'

'Um, no.' Is that weird? Before I can worry too much about that, Iris says, 'You can proceed through security now, Sarah. The flight will commence boarding at six twenty.'

I have no idea what just happened, how Dash managed to change my identity to that of a dead person, but I'm not exactly going to argue.

Scooping up my bag, I say 'Thanks' and take off towards the scanners. There are only about ten people in the line, including the backpacker who bumped into me before.

'Flying home?' he asks.

'Y-no. Just on holiday,' I say, remembering my German accent.

'Oh, I see. Have you been to New Zealand before?'

I shake my head. 'No. But I hear it is very beautiful.'

'Well, let me know if you want someone to show you around.' He gives me a tray, then takes one for himself and starts emptying the contents of his pockets into it.

'I will,' I mumble, not really in the mood for being chatted up. The backpacker saunters into the X-ray, stopping to hold his hands up. I go in next, raising my arms while wondering how to shake him off. The machine doesn't beep, but I've barely stepped out before a female security officer moves into my field of view.

'Can you step aside please, ma'am?'

'It didn't beep,' I protest, temporarily forgetting my German accent.

'Just routine,' she says, running a rod over my bag and clothes, then inserting it into a machine. No trace of drugs, thank God, which seems like a miracle after several hours in Ace's dodgy station wagon. After a cursory pat down, she waves me on. My heart slows again. *Just routine. Just routine.*

'Can I buy you a drink?' Oh, great. It's him, the backpacker.

'That would be nice,' I say, 'but I can't drink, since I'm pregnant and all.' Damn it, I've forgotten my German accent again.

The backpacker shuffles his feet. 'Right. Sorry, I mean, congratulations.'

'Yeah,' I say, my brain working overtime, 'and I've had a very bad day, because someone stole my wallet and I couldn't even afford to buy lunch.'

'Oh no.' His eyes widen. 'Well, let me buy you some. Can't have a pregnant woman starving, can we?'

'I'm sure they will feed me on the plane,' I say, hoping that's not too much of a rebuff. Despite Dash's snacks, I'm so hungry, I could eat a wallaby.

'That'll be hours away. Come on, I could do with some company.' He holds out his hand. 'I'm Ben, by the way.'

Thank God, thank God. Shaking his hand, I smile back. 'I'm Sarah. And thank you, that is very kind of you.'

*

'So, how come a pregnant woman is travelling by herself?' Ben asks, once we're seated opposite each other at a table that's still scattered with crumbs from the last customer.

'I'm not.' I cram a loaded corn chip into my mouth, chew and swallow. 'Well, right now I am but my boyfriend is waiting for me in New Zealand. We're just doing our own thing for a week.'

'Cool, cool.' Ben sips on his beer, swipes foam off his beard. 'Like I said, you're going to love New Zealand. I've been travelling for six months, so I'm looking forward to getting home.'

'I bet,' I mumble around another mouthful of food. Not wanting to seem rude, I add, 'So, what was your favourite destination?'

'Hmm. That's a really hard question. But I'd say my top three places were...' Then he's off, talking with minimal interjections from me. It's good timing, because at that moment I sense Johnno's thought-stream tangling with mine.

You all right, Vi?

I'm good, I answer. *I got through security and passport control, no questions asked.*

Dash must have some contacts in high places.

I'd say so. And now I'm having lunch with a friendly backpacker.

Yeah? Where's she from?

He, I correct, watching Ben gulp on his beer, *is a Kiwi, like us.*

Right. Johnno's block is fast, but not fast enough.

Come on, you're not getting all jealous on me, are you?

Only if he's chatting you up, he teases back. At least, I think he's teasing, but he's still kind of blocking me.

He stopped with that once I told him I was in the family way, I retort, before briefly tuning into Ben, who's telling me all about the Dead Sea.

'Wow,' I say, 'that sounds awesome,' and to Johnno, *He offered to buy me lunch. I was hungry. Starving, actually.* The enormity of the situation hits me again, whack, and my vision blurs.

Hey, OK, I was only kidding.

I turn my head so Ben can't see my tears.

'Are you all right?' Ben asks.

Nodding, I murmur, 'I'll be right back,' and take off towards the toilets.

Vi, I didn't mean to make you cry, Johnno think-says. *I just miss you and I'm really scared one of us isn't going to—*The block goes up again, a brick wall to slam my emotions against.

Isn't going to make it? I hurtle into a cubicle and lock myself in. *Don't you dare give up on me, Johnno. I'm pregnant with our baby and you can't leave me now.*

Johnno think-says, *I'm sorry. All I want is for all of this to be over so we can hang out like a normal boyfriend and girlfriend.*

I sniff. *Imagine that.*

I am, he replies. *Actually, scrap that. I quite like our wolf times together.*

Me too, I think-say, a smile breaking through the tears. How can I smile at a time like this? How can I not? What if these are the last words we ever say to each other?

These are not my last words, Vi, he replies. *So I won't tell you I love you.*

I won't tell you I love you either. I take a deep breath, flush the toilet. *I'd better go.*

Tell me when you've boarded the plane, OK?

I will.

I love you, Liesl.

I love you too, Wolf.

FIFTY

JOHNNO

It's 11.30pm, four and a half hours since Violet told me she boarded her plane. I haven't heard from her since, but I can tell from the slow waveform of her thought-stream that she's asleep.

What happens once you get to Auckland? I'd asked her. *Dash said someone would come to get me,* she'd answered. *Someone called June.*

I have no idea who June is, or what her relationship to Dash is, but Dash has got Violet this far, I guess. In an hour and a half, give or take, her plane will land.

As for me, I'm getting twitchy. It's half an hour until Rawiri and I activate the plan, one that could go wrong in a heartbeat. I touch the scar on my shoulder, remembering the last time that happened.

They won't know what hit them, Rawiri had said. *Literally.*

I hope he's right. I'd wanted to practise my new form tonight, but we've run out of time.

Why does time only flow in one direction? Is there only a single possible past?

I don't know about the past, but the future, my future, is nearly here.

As if sensing my pondering, Rawiri chooses that moment to dive into my thought-stream. *Are you ready?*

I sit up. *Yeah, of course.*

I turn my bedside lamp on and slide out of bed, touch the window. It's double-glazed, of course. I pick up the physics textbook I took from the library today and wrap it in a blanket before leaving it on the end of my bed. *Force is equal to mass times acceleration, Doctor Marlow, remember?*

An average male lion weighs close to two hundred kilograms.

*

At midnight, as the second of April segues into the third, I lie on my bed, thinking of supercoils and infinite density, of time's arrow and the convergence of past and present and the future, and concentrating my dream-flow until it is almost unbearable, a black hole ready to suck me in unless I spit it out. And finally, there it is, a *shift,* a blur, and I am standing inside the fence near the rear of the building, the rain-soaked turf beneath my paws. I smell Rawiri before I see him, his musky scent flowing into my nostrils. So far, so good.

I can smell them, Rawiri think-says. *Can you?*

Yeah, they stink worse than you. Cheap aftershave and cigarettes mixed with sweat. I can hear them too, the shush of their boots through grass, the low murmur of voices.

You're pretty rank yourself, mate. Rawiri starts slinking around the perimeter, his tail hanging low. I set off in the opposite direction, testing out my feline sinews and joints. *Force equals mass times acceleration. Force equals mass times acceleration—*

Shut up, will you? Rawiri interjects. *I can hardly hear them.*

Sorry. I focus, fixing on the closest thought-stream before delving into the guard's short-term memory to find the location of his keys, along with the automatic opener for the gate. I'll have to be quick.

My bowels are turning to liquid. I stop to empty them, glad I'm not in my human form.

I'll take the chunky guy, Rawiri think-says.

They're both chunky. They're in my sights now, two burly men in flak jackets, machine guns hanging from their hips. If they empty one of those into us, we'll be shredded. What happens if we die? Do we go back into our human forms, or will there be lion guts and fur all over the place?

Have some confidence, Fletcher, Rawiri says. *I'll take the one lighting the cigarette, OK? You take the guy with the beanie.*

OK. Sure. I continue to creep forward, stopping once I'm within pouncing distance. So close. So far.

'Did you hear that?'

I freeze. The voice belongs to Cigarette Guy. His partner, who's wearing an All Blacks beanie, says, 'All I can hear is your arse. What the hell have you been eating?'

'Missus cooked baked beans for dinner,' Cigarette Guy says, and farts. For some reason, they find that completely hysterical and that's good because, at that moment, Rawiri think-says, *now,* and I leap—

And I bring Beanie Guy down, hard, his head striking the ground so he doesn't even have a chance to scream before blood spurts all over me and I drag him into the bushes, oh God, I just killed him—

And Rawiri says, *GO,* and I *shift,* whoa, and I'm on my bed, razor blades in my gut, but I can't stop. Not now.

I can still taste his blood, but there's no time to contemplate what I just did, so I pick up the textbook in the blanket and swing it at the window, once, twice. The shattering of glass is loud, too loud. I crawl through the hole I've made, barely registering the shards of glass cutting my arms and legs. When I run into the bushes, I can't find the guard at first, and I'm not sure whether to be disturbed or relieved—maybe he isn't dead after all—but then I trip over him (oh God), and he's not moving and his neck and chest are wet. Fumbling in his trouser pockets for his keys, my hands sticky with his blood, I hear an alarm. The broken window must have set it off, why didn't we think of that?

I wrestle the keys out at last and run for the Jeep parked near the gates, think-calling, *Rawiri,* as the tail-lights flash, unlocked, and when he doesn't answer, I say, *Ariel,* and that's when he says, *Go, Johnno, you have to go RIGHT NOW,* though I can't leave him behind, but someone is running towards me, and I fling open the door and jump in and press the ignition button, slam my foot down on the accelerator, and I'm driving full tilt at the gate, the gate opener attached to the rear-vision mirror flashing, *please open,* and it does, it does.

And I career through, skidding sideways for a second before time's arrow kicks in, and I'm flying forward, but Rawiri is nowhere to be seen.

And he think-shouts, *Go, Johnno, it's your last chance,* and then he's gone, like a candle has been extinguished.

And I'm driving and crying, so distracted I nearly veer off the road, and then I hear Violet, sweet Violet, and she's saying, *Johnno, are you OK? Please tell me you're OK.*

Yes, I say. *Yes, but I just killed two men, and one of them was Ethan's best friend.*

FIFTY-ONE

VIOLET

I wake gasping, as if I'd been swimming underwater and had forgotten how far I was from the surface, my breath coming in short bursts, my heart galloping, and for a minute I could have sworn I was a—

(lion?)

'Is everything OK?' The flight attendant hovers beside me, a tiny crease between her jewelled eyebrows.

'I'm fine,' I say, curling into my seat, which isn't easy, since I'm on the aisle with a very large man beside me. 'Just a bad dream.'

'Must have been pretty vivid.' She holds out a steaming jug. 'Would you like a cup of tea?'

'Um, yes. Thanks.' I push the cup towards her, seeking out Johnno. My hand jerks—crap—and the flight attendant slaps a wad of paper towels on top of my tray.

'Are you sure you're—'

'I don't want a cup of tea,' I snap. She tuts and pushes her trolley down the aisle, her thoughts clearly audible: *Entitled brat, I can't wait to finish this shift and it's not even half over.* I'm too wound up to care, because I can still feel Johnno's heart racing, his panic clouding my thought-stream. *Johnno,* I say, *are you OK? Please tell me you're OK.*

Yes, he answers, his panic dimming a little, but only a little. *Yes, but I just killed two men, and one of them was Ethan's best friend.*

Rawiri? Oh no, oh no.

Rawiri, yes. We were meant to get out together— after we— God, Vi, we did what we had to but I killed a security guard.

Before he killed you, I interject, a shiver rippling through me.

Yeah, and then we went back for our bodies, and that's when I lost him.

Wait, I say. *Wait, how do you know he's dead?*

Because I can't hear him anymore. And he's got to be. They'll have shot him by now, I'm sure of it.

Johnno, I say. *Johnno, wait, you don't know that.* And it dawns on me that I can help them, even from thirty thousand feet in the air. Yes. Yes, I can.

No. His words are whiplash-quick. *No, you mustn't.*

Keep driving, I tell him. *Get help. I'll be with you soon.*

Violet, no, he repeats, but it's too late.

I'm already there.

FIFTY-TWO

JOHNNO

Driving away from the Foundation is the hardest thing I've ever done when every nerve, every atom in my body is drawn towards *her,* Violet, my white wolf. She's in my vicinity now, her magnetic pull almost unbearable.

Be careful, I plead, barely pausing for a Give Way sign. *Please, please, be careful.* Violet doesn't answer but I'm channelling the reverberation of her dream-flow, even as her earthly body remains in the plane, thirty-two thousand feet above the Pacific Ocean. In forty minutes, maybe less, the plane will land. If Violet hasn't returned to her body, she'll be dragged off to hospital for sure.

No, I can't let that happen.

Something darts in front of the car and I touch my foot to the brake, then accelerate again. A possum or a rabbit, maybe a cat. I wonder what form Violet has taken. A wolf? A panther? A bird?

Violet, I try again. No reply. Where am I driving to, anyway? Rawiri's plan to go straight to his parents' house is no good when I don't know where that is. Even if I did, turning up by myself all covered in blood just seems like a really good way of getting the emergency services called.

Glancing at the GPS on the dash, I see that it's 12.27am, and that I'm close to Titirangi. With shaking fingers, I tap in the only destination I can think of: Auckland Airport; travel time twenty-nine minutes.

Take the next left, an automated voice announces, before reminding me that I'm twenty kilometres over the speed limit.

'Screw your speed limit,' I yell. 'Screw you, Marlow and Bauer and Melody and Greta.' And then, because Violet's not listening, 'And screw you too, Nicholas Black.'

The speedo needle inches up to one hundred kilometres per hour.

FIFTY-THREE

VIOLET

I'm flying. Over the tree tops, the drizzly air clinging to my feathers, the scents of moist soil and pine and rain-soaked bitumen swirling through my nostrils. I can feel Johnno, so close, his panic sparking through my veins (*please, please, be careful*). But it's not Johnno who needs my help, not at this moment. No, I'm seeking *him,* Rawiri, the Keeper of Secrets.

The hub-and-spoke building seems smaller than before, but the fence is higher, the barbed wire a new addition. I perch on the roof, taking in the activity below. Alarms. Shouts. People running. In the distance, a siren.

I'm listening to something else, though, something within: his thought-stream running so deep I can barely make it out.

Rawiri, I think-say. *Rawiri, is that you?*

Who is ... are you ... A faint glow, yes, he's there. He's there and he can hear me, for now.

I'm Violet, I confirm. *Where are you?*

I don't ... Rawiri fades out. Either he's sedated or badly injured or both. But I've got a fix now, a link so strong that no one will be able to break it unless one of us dies.

I'm not going to let that happen.

I *shift,* and I am crouching behind his eyes, and oh, his skull feels as though it's about to cleave open, his vision blurry. We are lying on the floor in a small room, squinting at the woman standing over us. She has long black hair, dark eyes and a gun.

A gun. I do a quick inventory of Rawiri's body. Apart from his head, which is pounding, nothing else is sore. It's cool, and drizzle is blowing in through the broken window.

'Don't move,' the woman says. 'Or I'll do it again.'

Wait, I tell Rawiri before making the next *shift,* and almost simultaneously, I *leap* and bring her down with a sickening thud, my mouth on her throat. She smells like soap and toothpaste, and suddenly, urine, and she is lying very still, not making a sound, because that's what you do when a panther has you by the throat.

Rawiri appears behind me, staggering slightly, and says, 'I've got this.' He presses the gun to her temple. 'Don't say a word,' he says. 'Or I'll give you double what you gave me.' *Stun gun,* he tells me in think-speak. The siren is getting closer.

Stun her as soon as I release her, I say, *and then get out. Just one thing...*

Yeah? Rawiri asks. I smell blood—his, I think. The woman whimpers again. I sink my teeth into her throat, not hard enough to break skin, but enough to leave marks. She shuts up.

I'm going to create a distraction, I think-say. *And you're going to run, because the gates are about to open for that ambulance. OK?*

Rawiri hesitates.

Go, I think-say, and I release the woman, hear a simultaneous groan. I jump through the shattered window,

Rawiri right behind me, and as I *shift* I see him dart along the fence line, just as the gates swing open and an ambulance drives in. The area in front of the Foundation is crawling with people, mostly men carrying guns, but no one is looking at Rawiri because when I spread my massive wings and launch myself into the air, all eyes are upon me, the first Andean condor ever to be sighted on these shores.

By the time the first gunshot cracks the night air, Rawiri has disappeared, and by the time the second gunshot arrives, my breath is gone.

FIFTY-FOUR

JOHNNO

I'm on the motorway, trying not to speed because the last thing I need is to get pulled over by some undercover cop or clocked by a traffic drone, and the whole time I'm checking the GPS. Ten minutes to go. Nine minutes, eight minutes, seven. I hurtle over the Māngere Bridge, sea on both sides of me. It's been a long time since I saw this much water at once.

It's raining properly now, sheeting down the windscreen, and one of the wipers is screeching so badly I feel like ripping it off. It's five to one in the morning, but as I draw closer to the airport, the traffic builds until I'm sitting at the traffic lights surrounded by identical Zubers, like a bad dream.

When the lights go green, I'm off, zipping in and out of lanes, flying around a roundabout and into the international airport. I zoom up to the front doors and jump out. There's a plane coming in to land, its tail just visible above the terminal. Maybe it's Violet's and maybe it isn't. I'm running, and no one is looking at me because it's normal to run at airports, but I have the sense to duck into a bathroom as soon as I get inside. There I wash my hands, rusty water swirling down the plughole, and feel ill all over again.

I just killed two men. I just killed two men.

The door swings open and an elderly man walks in wheeling an enormous suitcase. I duck around him and make straight for the nearest arrivals screen to check out the list of incoming flights. Sydney, Melbourne, Singapore, Alice Springs.

Alice Springs. Scheduled 1.05am. Estimated 1.07am. The time on the top of the screen says 1.06. I blink. The screen changes, and I can barely breathe, because it says *landed* beside *Alice Springs.* I start moving forward, trying to get as close as I can to the automatic doors between customs and the main body of the terminal. The doors keep opening and closing, ejecting bleary-eyed travellers in ones and twos and threes.

'Excuse me,' someone says. Ignoring him, I keep walking. 'Excuse me,' he repeats, more loudly this time, and I turn, irritated, and say, 'What?'

'You dropped these.' The man holds up a set of keys.

'Thanks,' I say, taking a closer look at him. He looks familiar, but why?

He frowns, his eyes roving over me. 'Do I know you?' He's wearing blue leather trousers, a black t-shirt, a Bluetooth earpiece. With a jolt I realise I know exactly who he is, because I've accessed his thought-stream before, because he shares a quarter of my unborn child's DNA.

'Not exactly,' I say, as my past, present and future simultaneously converge, 'but you may have gone to my funeral.' I stick out my hand. 'Johnno Fletcher. I've recently returned from the dead, just like your daughter.'

FIFTY-FIVE

VIOLET

I can't breathe. I can't breathe, I can't breathe. There's something over my mouth and nose, and I struggle against it for a moment before sucking in a huge lungful of plastic-scented air.

'There you go, deep breaths,' someone says. Two faces peer down at me. One is the overweight man sitting next to me, the other the flight attendant.

'How are you feeling?' the flight attendant asks, while thinking, *For God's sake, is this shift never going to end?*

I lift the oxygen mask off. 'Fine.' Guns. Rawiri. Did he really get away?

'I thought you'd stopped breathing for a moment there,' the man says.

'I was just having a deep sleep.' I sit upright, embarrassed to see that while the seats in front of me are empty, all of the passengers behind us are waiting. 'Have we landed?'

'Take your time,' the flight attendant says. 'Is someone picking you up?'

'Yes.' I stand up, relieved to see that there's no sign of damage to my earthly body. I could have sworn one of those bullets whistled right past me. 'Thank you so much for helping me.'

The man shuffles out behind me, panting with the effort of squeezing between the seats, and takes my bag out of the overhead locker. 'You take care now.'

'I will. Thanks.'

Ducking my head, I walk swiftly down the aisle, my heart racing. The Foundation staff must be looking for me by now. For all I know, the airport could be crawling with them, ready to haul me off to their New Zealand base.

Violet.

Startled, I stop moving, and the man bumps into me.

'Sorry,' he says. 'Are you sure you're all right?'

'Fine. Sorry,' I mumble, resuming walking. *Johnno, where are you?* I think-ask.

I'm in the terminal, he think-says, *waiting for you.* Orange-yellow relief floods through me, so intense I start shaking all over. I continue through premium economy, with its extra-large seats and e-screens, and turn left, where a male flight attendant is standing sentry at the door. For a moment I think he's about to pull me aside, but all he says is, 'Thank you.'

'Thank you,' I reply, resisting the urge to start running. I continue on, through the electronic gates, barely registering the fact that my retinal scan has just let me through as Sarah Schumann with no alarms, down the travellator and straight through the baggage area.

I'm nearly there, I think-say, and Johnno replies, *I know.* Next I get stuck in a line for customs, and I tell them I have *nothing to declare,* which isn't true, because I have all sorts of things to declare, like *I've been a prisoner for months* and *I just rescued my dead boyfriend's best friend by turning into a panther.* Then I am rushing through the automatic doors, and there he is, Johnno, with his stubbly chin and tattooed eyebrow, his arms covered in cuts and scratches and I stop dead, because now I can see who is standing next to him.

I should be happy, but I'm trembling all over, my heart pounding, and I can't breathe, again, again. Through the adrenaline haze, I see Johnno indicate to my dad to *stand back,* and then Johnno jogs towards me, but he's not the only one, because there is a blonde woman hurrying towards me from the opposite direction.

In the split second before my vision cuts out completely, I think, *Oh my God, it's Ethan's mum,* but before I can work out why she's here, I'm gone.

*

When I wake, I'm lying in a bed with soft white sheets. On the ceiling is a poster of a dragon standing on top of a mountain, its wings outspread, and that's how I know I'm not in hospital, not in the Foundation.

That, and the lips against my cheek, the voice in my ear. 'It's all right. You're safe. We're safe.'

I turn my head. Johnno is perched next to me. He's dressed in unfamiliar clothes, metallic blue trousers and a white V-neck t-shirt.

'Dad,' I remember, panic rising again.

Johnno lays cool fingers on my forehead. 'Stop. He's not going to hurt you.'

'The conditioning,' I say. *After several such pairings of the rat and the noise, Albert was shown only the rat and became very distressed, reacting by crying and crawling away.*

Am I going to be like Little Albert forever?

Johnno nods. 'Exactly. June says she knows someone who might be able to help you with that.' He passes me a bottle of water. I prop myself up on my elbow, drinking deeply.

'June,' I say. 'That's Ethan's mum, right?'

'Right.' Johnno sets the bottle on the bedside table. 'Lucky she's a nurse,' he adds, when I touch one of the adhesive dressings on his arms. 'Cut myself to shreds when I was crawling through the window.' He leans forward to kiss me again and I pull him closer, breathing in his scent: soap and toothpaste, and faintly, lion. But maybe I'm imagining that.

'What time is it?' I ask.

'Eight.'

'In the morning?'

'No, the evening.' Obviously catching the confused expression on my face, Johnno laughs. It's been a long time since I heard that, and it makes me happy and sad at the same time. 'June gave you a sedative because you were freaking out, and since then you've slept for ages. I guess you were pretty tired. And...' He hesitates.

'And I'm pregnant,' I whisper, overwhelmed again.

Sighing, Johnno climbs in beside me and folds me into his arms. 'We can talk about that tomorrow.'

I gulp, nod. 'Are we at June's house?'

'Yeah. She said we can stay here for as long as we want, until everything is sorted out.'

'That could be a really long time.'

'Yeah. Maybe.' I get the sense there's something he's not telling me, but then he kisses me, and it feels so good to be pressed up against him, and we move against each other until he gives out a soft groan. 'Watch it, Liesl.'

'No, you watch it, Wolf,' I murmur back.

Smiling, he layers his fingers over my belly, nudges his nose against mine. 'Do you think it can hear us?'

'I don't know if it even has ears yet,' I say, and sense the glow of his smile. *Don't make me attached to this baby,* I think, *this baby that isn't even a baby yet,* but when he bends to kiss my navel, I don't stop him.

'Is the door locked?' I whisper, once he has removed the few clothes I'm wearing, namely underwear and a t-shirt with a love heart on the front.

'No one's going to come in,' he says, taking off *his* clothes in record time. I don't have the willpower to argue, let alone resist. And a short time later, when I lose my breath, it's for all the right reasons.

*

Afterwards, we cuddle and doze and cuddle and eventually, we talk.

'My dad,' I say. 'What did he do when I fainted?'

'Well, he was really worried, of course. But after I explained about the conditioning, he knew he had no choice but to leave you with June. He said he'd visit when you're ready—your mum, too.'

'Mum.' The panicky feelings aren't any better when I think about her. Is June right? Can I really be unconditioned, or whatever it's called? What if I'm terrified of my own flesh and blood for the rest of my life? 'But Johnno ... I don't know why ... I don't know how...'

'*They* haven't tracked us down yet?' He hesitates. 'Yeah. Well. I guess you've got someone looking out for you.'

'Dash.'

'No.' He rolls onto his back. 'Look, the only reason we're still free is because of your dad.'

'Right. Well, good,' I say. 'I mean, he's got friends in high places, I guess, and—'

'No. That's not it. I mean, yes, he's got friends, but not in the way you'd think. I accessed him. Before we escaped.'

'You *accessed* him? You didn't tell me that.'

'I didn't have time.'

'No,' I say, starting to get an inkling of what is tumbling through Johnno's thought-stream. 'No, that's not possible.'

Johnno turns to face me again. 'Vi, your dad's going to do everything he can to keep you safe. He'd be a monster if he didn't. But the only reason I'm still here is because of you.' He pauses. 'Your father knows all about the Foundation. He knows all about them, because if it weren't for him the Foundation wouldn't exist at all.'

Johnno is showing me a memory. Not *his* memory, but my father's, a memory from last September, not long after I saw my parents for the last time.

FIFTY-SIX

DEBRIEFING
COMMENCED: 11.00AM
PRESENT: DR NICHOLAS BLACK (CHIEF SCIENTIFIC OFFICER, SPIRAL
 FOUNDATION),
DR NOEL MARLOW (NEUROLOGIST), DR
 GRETA
ZIEGLER (NEUROPSYCHOLOGIST).

Zeigler: First of all, Doctor Black, we'd like to start by acknowledging your loss. We appreciate how difficult this must be for you.

Black (head lowered): Thank you.

Marlow: We tried everything we could, but the heart muscle was just too weak.

Black: Can I see her?

Zeigler: I wish you could, Doctor Black, but the infectious risk ... you understand.

Black: Yes. Yes, I understand. Was she ... virally optimised?

Marlow: No, there was no evidence of that. It's unfortunate that she had the cardiac arrest before we could release her back into your care, although in view of the infectious risk perhaps that was a blessing.

Black: And the others?

Marlow: We have five other subjects under our care, all with varying strengths.

Black: Are there any like—

Zeigler: None like the prototype, no. We have some other ideas we'd like to explore with regards to that, but, in the meantime, we'd like to move on to phase II, using the attenuated virus. How far along is your laboratory in this regard?

Black: We're in the final stages of testing. There have been no deaths in our animal models with the attenuated virus, so it seems far safer than with the native virus.

Marlow: And the cognition and memory testing?

Black: They're very promising. But we'll need human subjects to confirm that's true.

Zeigler: Of course. We're aiming for February. How are you placed for travel to Germany at that time?

Black (coughs): I can clear my schedule for that. I don't have any lectures planned at that time of year, anyway.

Marlow: Perfect. We will make all the necessary arrangements. Do you have any other questions?

Black (hesitates): Did she ... suffer?

Zeigler: No, Doctor Black. It was very quick. Again, I'm sorry. You will keep this confidential, won't you? There could be misunderstandings if the true source of the M-fever epidemic were known. It could mean the end of our research. And as for you...

Black: I understand. Of course.

Marlow: Thank you, Doctor Black. We will make all the necessary arrangements. In the meantime, we'll arrange transfer of funds to your research facility.

Black: Thank you.

CONCLUDED: 11.15AM
(RECORDING ENDS)

EPILOGUE

I am running through the bush, the soil moist and soft beneath my trainers. Through the trees, I see the volcanic cone of Rangitoto. I see the grey-blue waters of the Pacific Ocean. I see the country I thought I'd never return to as a free man.

And now I'm living a paradox, free but not free.

Descending towards the beach, I wonder if today will be the day Rawiri emerges from the bush, if today will be the day we know that Violet didn't risk her life for nothing. Four days since we escaped, and we haven't heard a word.

Glimpsing a flash of red between the pines, I tense and then relax as a female jogger wearing a red cap comes into view.

'Morning,' she says, running past.

'Morning,' I say, and then I'm on the sand, the sun exploding over the horizon. In my head, another voice echoes: *Morning, Wolf.*

Morning, Liesl. I cross the road and pause outside a sprawling two-storey house with large balconies and a four-car garage. The wrought-iron gates swing open and I jog up the cobblestone driveway, past the Mercedes Fuse SUV and up to the front door.

I don't even have to gaze into the retinal scanner before the door swings open.

'Morning.' Nicholas Black is wearing a grey tracksuit, a blue t-shirt, no smile.

'Morning,' I say, kicking off my shoes before continuing up the stairs and down the hallway to Violet's room. She's still in bed, the curtains drawn. I bend to kiss her, inhaling the apple-scent of her hair.

She blinks up at me. 'Good run?'

'Good run.' We gaze at each other for a moment, our thought-streams swirling together, two wolves in a lion's den. Then Violet takes my hand, and says, 'I think I'll be able to have breakfast with Mum and Dad today. That's good, isn't it?'

'That's good,' I say, my eyes straying to the bottle of pills on her bedside table—the pills that stop her from having a panic attack every time she goes anywhere near her parents. The sessions with the psychologist seem to be helping, too, although it's early days yet.

'We're safe now,' Violet says. I sigh and stretch out beside her, sweaty clothes and all, because I don't believe that for a minute, and neither does she.

Let's fly, I think-say, holding her tight and closing my eyes.

Let's fly, Violet replies, and soon enough we're soaring above the house, above the corrugated surface of the sea, and in that instant we're free, released from the inevitability of time's arrow, our past and present and future spiralling into a kaleidoscope second.

Welcome back, Violet Black.

Yeah. Right.

ACKNOWLEDGEMENTS

Thanks to my family and friends: in particular, Grant, Lachie and Maisie, and Nod Ghosh, who has tirelessly critiqued every chapter. Also thank you to Rose Carlyle for giving me the inspiration I needed to write this book (and the next!) and Helen Moore for the tooth idea (yes, that one!). As always, I am grateful to the wonderful team at Penguin Random House: in particular, Harriet Allan, Cat Taylor and Stuart Lipshaw; as well as my editor Sarah Quigley and my agent Nadine Rubin-Nathan.

BOOK 3 IN THE BLACK SPIRAL TRILOGY

BLACK SPIRAL

EILEEN MERRIMAN

NEXT IN THE BLACK SPIRAL TRILOGY

BLACK SPIRAL

PART I: COMPLICITY

ONE

VIOLET

I am lying on the banks of a New Zealand lake, the sand autumn-cool beneath my fur, the stars blazing into my eyes. Beside me, my mate stretches, his muscles flowing beneath his skin.

Another swim? Johnno think-asks, his yellow irises shining at me.

Maybe. I roll onto my back. He nuzzles my neck before licking me, his tongue rasping against my exposed belly: the same tongue that stripped the skin from the possum he caught before our swim. Behind us rise giant sand dunes, still and silent. In the distance, the faint beat of the ocean.

Beat. Heartbeat. One, two, three. I only just became aware of the third today, just another complication in an impossible situation.

I haven't been out here for ages, Johnno think-says, as we snuggle against each other again. His body is heavy, warm, reassuringly solid.

Me neither, I answer. I've only been here a few times, probably because Bethells Beach is an hour's drive from my house.

My house. It doesn't feel like my home anymore, not when I have a crippling panic attack every time I get anywhere near my father. The pills and therapy can only do so much to reverse a fear that is not entirely irrational, because nothing can erase the knowledge that my father is the reason I nearly died, not once but twice.

According to government records, I am already officially dead.

My dreamlike state disturbed, I stand up and move towards the lake. Johnno doesn't ask why I've changed my mind. He doesn't have to, because our thought-streams are merging together, even as our earthly bodies lie slumbering in a house on the North Shore of Auckland.

I slip into the lake, the inky black waters closing over my head. As I begin to paddle, I'm aware of three hearts beating. Mine. Johnno's. And the being we created in the middle of the desert five weeks ago; the being I can hardly begin to think of as a baby.

Denial is a powerful state of mind.

*

Fact: Panthers are actually leopards, jaguars or cougars who have a rare mutation called melanism, which hides their normal spots.

Fact: The gestation period of panthers is three to four months. No one knows the gestation period of a virally optimised telepath who can travel as a panther, least of all me.

Fact: Panthers are less fertile than their coloured counterparts, and more unpredictable and aggressive.

I am more fertile than I'd like, as aggressive as I need to be. And I think anyone who works for the Spiral Foundation would tell you that I am anything but predictable.

Welcome back, Violet Black.

PRAISE FOR EILEEN MERRIMAN

Pieces of You

'the kind of book you want to read in one sitting because it is so breathtakingly good ... It feels utterly real. It does not smudge the tough stuff. It is kaleidoscopic in both emotion and everyday detail ... Eileen writes with such a flair for dialogue, for family circumstances, for teenage struggles and joys. This is the kind of book that will stay at the front of my mind all week and longer—I recommend it highly.'—Paula Green, *Poetry Shelf*

'...could well become one of the biggest local YA books of the year. It's intelligent, literate ... pertinent, witty when it needs to be, thought-provoking and relatable.'—Dionne Christian, *NZ Herald*

'Merriman's acute observation and awareness of teen mentality comes to the fore. It all feels very real and fresh.'
—Denis Wright, *The Sapling*

Catch Me When You Fall

'My best pick for 2018 for young adults, the standout for me ... it's kind of heart-wrenching and really real and quirky and a great teen read for girls and boys.'—James Russell, *Radio NZ*

This book ... is interested in life and death struggles, and the way that these struggles interact with the more everyday agonies and ecstasies of coming-of-age ... The story is well-paced and absorbing ... effective in its depiction of the desperation inspired by love and fear of loss.—Angelina Sbroma, *NZ Books*

'When it comes to the medical details, the story pays impressive attention ... the story doesn't only focus on Alex and her physical sickness but also on Jamie and his far subtler mental illness ... well written and cleverly expressed.'—Madeleine Fountain, *NZ Doctor*

Invisibly Breathing

'...more than just a book to be read, but gripping literature which both celebrates love and also exposes society's harmful behaviour towards love that is not considered "conventional". **Rating 5/5 stars**'—Faga Tuigamala, *Tearaway*

'dialogue is crisp and convincing and their characters are well drawn ... a gripping account of two young men on the brink of manhood, uncertain and deeply involved emotionally, facing the reactions of their family and friends ... It is a moving story, well told.'—Trevor Agnew, *Magpies*

'It's a clever book. Ingenious chapter headings, smart sentences, inventive glides of plot and relationships. It's very contemporary, veined with phones and txts and Twitter and *Grand Theft Auto V*. There's a stadium-sized cast of kids, and Merriman gets their blitheness, erratic fuses, invulnerability-cum-fragility spot-on ... her book is bloody good.'—David Hill, *NZ Books*

A Trio of Sophies

'I absolutely endorse this in a Young Adult Section, or High School Library. It could just save a life—and no I'm not being dramatic. It was a book that fifteen-year-old me needed to read, and that twenty-seven-year-old me is glad to have ... Absolutely worth the five stars. And the late bedtime.'—Krystal B, *Goodreads*

'Fast-paced and unpredictable, *A Trio of Sophies* will keep readers on their toes and caught up until the last page. And if it's your first Merriman book, it certainly won't be your last.'—Sarah Pollok, *Weekend Herald*

'This is a page turner make no bones about that ... Much to enjoy in this novel. Best New Zealand YA novel of the year so far. Don't miss it, you will kick yourself if you do. The ending will make you think.'—Bob Docherty, B obsbooksnz.wordpress.com

For more information about our titles
visit www.penguin.co.nz